Praise for

Invisible Monsters Remix and *Invisible Monsters*

“Unlike the original novel, the chapters now bounce around in time and place as Palahniuk originally intended, yet the story remains strong and easy to follow. And with characters such as the pill-popping drama queen Brandy Alexander and a veiled, disfigured ex–fashion model, this remix is still a thrilling experience not to be missed.” —Vivienne Finche, *Sacramento News & Review*

“Chuck Palahniuk’s *Invisible Monsters Remix* isn’t your standard re-release. . . . A shuffling of the plot line with completely new chapters . . . creates a completely new reading experience—just as Palahniuk originally intended it.” —Danielle Strom, *Portland Monthly* magazine

“*Invisible Monsters* is back with a vengeance. . . . Remixed with new material and design, *Invisible Monsters Remix* reads like a road memoir of pills, betrayal and plastic surgery. Fans of the previous version will delight over new chapters and spiffy additional images while newcomers will find a book restored to the author’s original vision.” —INFORUM

“A harrowing, perverse, laugh-aloud funny rocket ride. . . . Gutsy, terse and cunning, *Invisible Monsters* may emerge as Palahniuk’s strongest book.” [illegible] *Times*

"The novel adroitly satirizes our culture's obsession with perfection." —Amanda Zurita, *Seattle Metropolitan*

"A must read for fans of the author or the original version of the book. Fans of speculative fiction or the grotesque will also enjoy the ride." —Pete Petruski, *Library Journal*

"One of the freshest, most intriguing voices. . . . He rearranges Vonnegut's sly humor, DeLillo's mordant social analysis, and Pynchon's antic surrealism (or is it R. Crumb's?) into a gleaming puzzle palace all his own." —*Newsday*

"Palahniuk's language is urgent and tense, touched with psychopathic brilliance, his images dead-on accurate. . . . [He] is an author who makes full use of the alchemical powers of fiction to synthesize a universe that mirrors our own fiction as a way of illuminating the world without obliterating its complexity."

—*LA Weekly*

"Subtly moving, this singular writer reminds us that real life is often just as tragic, absurd and fabulously perverse as a Palahniuk novel. . . . Palahniuk shuffles the chapters and adds context to one of his earliest novels about fashion models and the ugly and unreal nature of what a sick society considers beautiful."

—Cherie Ann Parker, *Shelf Awareness*

"Readers who missed out on *Invisible Monsters* the first time around have a wild ride in store." —Marc Covert, OregonLive.com

"A great companion piece to the original, especially for those who've worn away the binding on their paperback."
—Joshua Chaplinsky, *Lit Reactor*

"Does the novel hold up? Yes, and it's even better this way. New readers and rereaders alike are in for a wild ride." —Keir Graff, *Booklist*

"Chuck Palahniuk's stories don't unfold. They hurtle headlong, changing lanes in threes and banging off the guard rails of modern fiction. This time he has really done it. Incredibly, *Invisible Monsters* makes the author's jarring first novel, *Fight Club*, seem like a leisurely buggy ride." —*San Francisco Chronicle*

"Mr. Palahniuk is a supremely talented satirist and a very funny writer." —John Greenya, *Washington Times*

Invisible Monsters Remix

ALSO BY CHUCK PALAHNIUK

Fight Club

Survivor

Choke

Lullaby

Fugitives and Refugees

Diary

Stranger Than Fiction

Haunted

Rant

Snuff

Pygmy

Tell-All

Damned

Doomed

Beautiful You

Make Something Up

Bait

Legacy

Adjustment Day

CHUCK PALAHNIUK

Invisible Monsters Remix

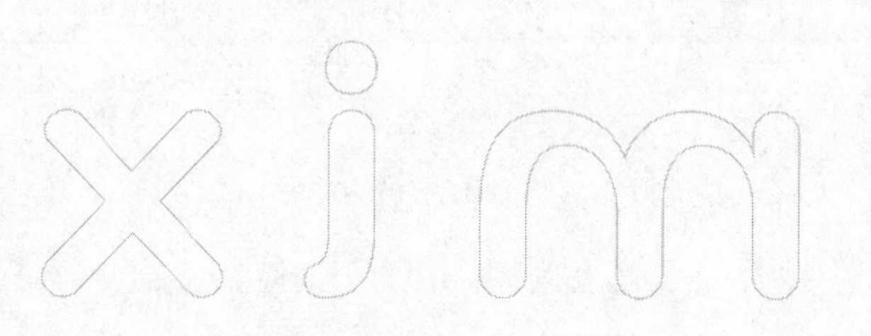

W. W. Norton & Company | New York • London

Previous edition published under the title *Invisible Monsters*

Printed in the United States of America
First published as a Norton paperback 2013

For information about special discounts for bulk purchases, please contact W. W. Norton Special Sales at specialsales@wwnorton.com or 800-233-4830

Manufacturing by LSC Harrisonburg
Book design by Chris Welch
Production manager: Devon Zahn

Library of Congress Cataloging-in-Publication Data

Palahniuk, Chuck.
Invisible monsters remix / Chuck Palahniuk.
p. cm.
ISBN 978-0-393-08352-1 (hardcover)
1. Fashion—Fiction. I. Title.
PS3566.A4554I583 2012
813'.54—dc23
2012008083

ISBN 978-0-393-34511-7 pbk.

W. W. Norton & Company, Inc., 500 Fifth Avenue, New York, N.Y. 10110
www.wwnorton.com

W. W. Norton & Company Ltd., 15 Carlisle Street, London W1D 3BS

6 7 8 9 0

The Wish Book: A Reintroduction to *Invisible Monsters*

This is how old I am: I loved the Sears catalogue. It kills me that I now need to explain what that was. It was an inventory of everything you ever dreamed of owning. Imagine the entire Internet printed on paper and bound along one edge—a stack of glossy paper as thick as a telephone book. Please don't ask me to explain what a telephone book was. By now you imagine I'm wearing a bowler hat and a celluloid collar, driving my horseless carriage, lickety-split, to a torrid three-way with Laura Ingalls Wilder and Abraham Lincoln.

As opposed to you, you who'll always stay so young and hip.

Be that as it may. This modern world isn't all it's cracked up to be.

Nowadays, whatever purchase you moon over, whatever person you lust after, most likely it's presented on a smooth glass or plastic screen. On a laptop or a television. And no matter what the technology, you'll catch sight of your own reflection. In that electric mirror, there hovers your faint image. You'll be superimposed over every email. Or, lurking in the glassy surface of online porn, there you are. Fewer people shut down their computers anymore, and who can blame them? The moment that monitor goes black, you're looking at yourself, not smiling, not anything. Here's your worst-ever passport photo enlarged to life size. Swimming behind the eBook words of Jane Austen, that slack, dead-eyed zombie face, that's yours. That's you.

The Sears catalogue was better. The paper reflected nothing. You could lose yourself in the Sears catalogue. The one published for the Christmas season they called the "Wish Book," and seldom has a name been more accurate because it held hundreds of pages of toys and food and clothes, tools, and you-name-it. You could never remember it all, and every time you opened that book you found something you'd never seen before. Every time you cracked those pages you fell in love. Children and young people are always looking for an anchor, a tether, some attachment to ground them in the impossible world. The objects in the Sears catalogue baited you into adulthood. You couldn't wait to find a job, any job, and start buying stuff. The vastness of stuff was unknowable. It was the world.

That's how I originally structured this book: to be a little unknowable. Reader friends complained about how the dwindling number of pages, those physical sheets of paper you held between the thumb and index finger of your right hand, suggested when the plot of a novel was reaching its climax. At the time I had no washing machine. We're talking 1991. I took my dirty clothes to a Laundromat called City Laundry every Tuesday after work. The place was cluttered with old magazines, old *Vogue* magazines brought in by the owner, Gretchen. They were the only reading material, and I tried reading them. The pages were seldom numbered. The pages were chockablock with artsy photos and quotes, enlarged and lifted out of context. In articles, the feature copy started near the front of the magazine but quickly "jumped" to pages near the back. Trying to read a story was like trying to navigate through a Las Vegas casino. It was designed to entice and seduce you. It was designed to trap you. I got lost. I loved it. I told myself, *Why can't a novel do this?*

So that's how I originally wrote this book. The story would not unspool as a continuous linear series of "and then, and then, and then's . . ." At the end of the first chapter, the reader would be directed to jump to, for example, Chapter Thirty. At the end of Chapter Thirty, she'd be told to jump to Chapter Sixteen. Following the plot would mean paging forward and backward, and you'd never know where the story might end. It might all come to a head at the physical center of the book. Better yet, as you hunted for the next chapter, you'd glimpse marvelous, ridiculous scenes, and you'd wonder, "How will the story ever get *there*?"

Most of the book I wrote while watching music videos on MTV. Yes, that's how old I am. Back then MTV still played videos. Now, no doubt, you picture me wearing high-button shoes and rolling a hoop down a dirt road in—I don't know—ancient Thebes?

Nobody ever had so much fun writing a book. I'd be couch surfing with Alexander Graham Bell and Dolley Madison, watching

Echo & the Bunnymen videos. Abraham Lincoln would order a pizza, and Bell would offer everyone hits of MDA. That's how far back this happened, we didn't call Ecstasy "E." We didn't even call it "X." Louisa May Alcott would be rolling us a fatty.

I'd shake my head no. I'd whine, "Guys, I can't get *high*. I need to write my *novel*."

And Harriet Beecher Stowe would say, "Dude, why can't you do *both*?"

You young people, you who think you invented fun and drugs and good times, fuck you.

That was my original plan for *Invisible Monsters*. Even after the reader reached the words "The End" she'd still sense she hadn't read it all. The book would still hold some lingering secrets. You could open it again and find something—as with the Sears catalogue or *Vogue* magazine or anyone you love—something that you'd never seen before. Think D. H. Lawrence's "Odour of Chrysanthemums" but scored with music by Bronski Beat. That's how I originally wrote this book. It was packed with jumps. Hidden secrets. Buried treasure. I gave the original manuscript to a friend, Monica Drake, the author of *Clown Girl*. She read it the way she had read every other book, from beginning to end . . . page one, page two, page three . . . and then, and then, and then . . . She told me that jumping was too difficult. "Readers," Monica warned me, "most readers, aren't going to want to work that hard." They'd get lost. Back then, neither Monica nor I had been published. We didn't want to make trouble. We just wanted for people to love us.

So I hammered the story into a nice, smooth, straight line. I threw out the magic. A wonderful publisher bought the rights. It was launched in 1999 as a paperback. It's only ever been a paperback. End of story.

Still, Harriet's words kept echoing in my head: "Why can't you do both?"

Twelve years later, the publisher W. W. Norton suggested producing a hardcover version of the book, and I saw my chance. The Brandy Alexander Witness Reincarnation Program. I told myself: Here we go again. *Where you're supposed to be is some big West Hills wedding reception in a big manor house with flower arrangements and stuffed mushrooms all over the house . . .*

You might mark every page with a little X, like leaving a trail of bread crumbs, to make sure you read them all. Or don't. Me, personally? I hope you get lost. I mean, really, would that be so bad?

Now, Please, Jump to Chapter Forty-one

Invisible Monsters Remix

Chapter 1

Don't expect this to be the kind of story that goes: and then, and then, and then.

What happens here will have more of that fashion magazine feel, a *Vogue* or a *Glamour* magazine chaos with page numbers on every second or fifth or third page. Perfume cards falling out, and full-page naked women coming out of nowhere to sell you makeup.

Don't look for a contents page, buried magazine-style twenty pages back from the front. Don't expect to find anything right off. There isn't a real pattern to anything, either. Stories will start and then, three paragraphs later:

Jump to page whatever.

Then, jump back.

This will be ten thousand fashion separates that mix and match to create maybe five tasteful outfits. A million trendy accessories, scarves and belts, shoes and hats and gloves, and no real clothes to wear them with.

And you really, really need to get used to that feeling, here, on the freeway, at work, in your marriage. This is the world we live in. Just go with the prompts.

Jump back twenty years to the white house where I grew up with my father shooting Super 8 movies of my brother and me running around the yard.

Jump to present time with my folks sitting on lawn chairs at night, and watching these same Super 8 movies projected on the white side of the same white house, twenty years later. The house the same, the yard the same, the windows projected in the movies lined up just perfect with the real windows, the movie grass aligned with the real grass, and my movie-projected brother and me being toddlers and running around wild for the camera.

Jump to my big brother being all miserable and dead from the big plague of AIDS.

Jump to me being grown up and fallen in love with a police detective and moved away to become a famous supermodel.

Just remember, the same as a spectacular *Vogue* magazine, remember that no matter how close you follow the jumps:

Continued on page whatever.

No matter how careful you are, there's going to be the sense you missed something, the collapsed feeling under your skin that you didn't experience it all. There's that fallen-heart feeling that you rushed right through the moments where you should've been paying attention.

Well, get used to that feeling. That's how your whole life will feel someday.

This is all practice. None of this matters. We're just warming up.

Jump to here and now, Brandy Alexander bleeding to death on the floor with me kneeling beside her, telling this story before here come the paramedics.

Jump backward just a few days to the living room of a rich house in Vancouver, British Columbia. The room is lined with the rococo hard candy of carved mahogany paneling with marble baseboards and marble flooring and a very sort-of curlicue carved marble fireplace. In rich houses where old rich people live, everything is just what you'd think.

The rubrum lilies in the enameled vases are real, not silk. The cream-colored drapes are silk, not polished cotton. Mahogany is not pine stained to look like mahogany. No pressed-glass chandeliers posing as cut crystal. The leather is not vinyl.

All around us are these cliques of Louis-the-Fourteenth chair-sofa-chair.

In front of us is yet another innocent real estate agent, and Brandy's hand goes out: her wrist thick with bones and veins, the mountain range of her knuckles, her wilted fingers, her rings in their haze of marquise-cut green and red, her porcelain nails painted sparkle-pink, she says, "Charmed, I'm sure."

If you have to start with any one detail, it has to be Brandy's hands. Beaded with rings to make them look even bigger, Brandy's hands are enormous. Beaded with rings, as if they could be more obvious, hands are the one part about Brandy Alexander the surgeons couldn't change.

So Brandy doesn't even try and hide her hands.

We've been in too many of this kind of house for me to count, and the realtor we meet is always smiling. This one is wearing the standard uniform, the navy blue suit with the red, white, and blue scarf around the neck. The blue heels are on her feet and the blue bag is hanging at the crook of her elbow.

The realty woman looks from Brandy Alexander's big hand to Signore Alfa Romeo standing at Brandy's side, and the power-blue eyes of Alfa attach themselves; those blue eyes you never see close or look away, inside those eyes is the baby or the bouquet of flowers, beautiful or vulnerable, that make a beautiful man someone safe to love.

Alfa's just the latest in a year-long road trip of men obsessed with Brandy, and any smart woman knows a beautiful man is her best fashion accessory. The same way you'd product-model a new car or a toaster, Brandy's hand draws a sight line through the air from her smile and big boobs to Alfa. "May I introduce," Brandy says, "Signore Alfa Romeo, professional male consort to the Princess Brandy Alexander."

The same way, Brandy's hand swings from her batting eyelashes and rich hair in an invisible sight line to me.

All the realty woman is going to see are my veils, muslin and cut-work velvet, brown and red, tulle threaded with silver, layers of so much you'd think there's nobody inside. There's nothing about me to look at so most people don't. It's a look that says:

Thank you for not sharing.

"May I introduce," Brandy says, "Miss Kay MacIsaac, personal secretary to the Princess Brandy Alexander."

The realty woman in her blue suit with its brass Chanel buttons and the scarf tied around her neck to hide all her loose skin, she smiles at Alfa.

When nobody will look at you, you can stare a hole in them. Picking out all the little details you'd never stare long enough to get if she'd ever just return your gaze, this, this is your revenge. Through my veils, the realtor's glowing red and gold, blurred at her edges.

"Miss MacIsaac," Brandy says, her big hand still open toward me, "Miss MacIsaac is mute and cannot speak."

The realty woman with her lipstick on her teeth and her powder and concealer layered in the crepe under her eyes, her prêt-à-porter teeth and machine-washable wig, she smiles at Brandy Alexander.

"And this . . ." Brandy's big ring-beaded hand curls up to touch Brandy's torpedo breasts.

"This . . ." Brandy's hand curls up to touch pearls at her throat.

"This . . ." The enormous hand lifts to touch the billowing piles of auburn hair.

"And this . . ." The hand touches thick moist lips.

"This," Brandy says, "is the Princess Brandy Alexander."

The realty woman drops to one knee in something between a curtsy and what you'd do before an altar. Genuflecting. "This is such an honor," she says. "I'm so sure this is the house for you. You just have to love this house."

Icicle bitch she can be, Brandy just nods and turns back toward the front hall where we came in.

"Her Highness and Miss MacIsaac," Alfa says, "they would like to tour the house by themselves, while you and I discuss the details." Alfa's little hands flutter up to explain, ". . . the transfer of funds . . . the exchange of lira for Canadian dollars."

"Loonies," the realty woman says.

Brandy and me and Alfa are all flash-frozen. Maybe this woman has seen through us. Maybe after the months we've been on the road and the dozens of big houses we've hit, maybe somebody has finally figured out our scam.

"Loonies," the woman says. Again, she genuflects. "We call our dollars 'Loonies,'" she says and jabs a hand in her blue purse. "I'll show you. There's a picture of a bird on them," she says. "It's a loon."

Brandy and me, we turn icicle again and start walking away, back to the front hall. Back through the cliques of chair-sofa-chair, past the carved marble. Our reflections smear, dim, and squirm behind a lifetime of cigar smoke on the mahogany paneling. Back to the front hallway, I follow the Princess Brandy Alexander while Alfa's voice fills the realtor's blue-suited attention with questions about the angle of the morning sun into the dining room and whether the provincial government will allow a personal heliport behind the swimming pool.

Going toward the stairs is the exquisite back of Princess Brandy, a silver fox jacket draped over Brandy's shoulders and yards of a silk brocade scarf tied around her billowing pile of Brandy Alexander auburn hair. The queen supreme's voice and the shadow of L'Air du Temps are the invisible train behind everything that is the world of Brandy Alexander.

The billowing auburn hair piled up inside her brocade silk scarf reminds me of a bran muffin. A big cherry cupcake. This is some strawberry auburn mushroom cloud rising over a Pacific atoll.

Those princess feet are caught in two sort-of-gold lamé leghold traps with little gold straps and gold chains. These are the trapped-on, stilted, spike-heeled feet of gold that mount the first of about three hundred steps from the front hall to the second floor. Then she mounts the next step, and the next, until all of her is far enough above me to risk looking back. Only then will she turn the whole strawberry cupcake of her head. Those big torpedo, Brandy Alexander breasts silhouetted, the wordless beauty of that professional mouth in full face.

"The owner of this house," Brandy says, "is very old and supplementing her hormones and still lives here."

The carpet is so thick under my feet I could be climbing loose dirt. One step after another, loose and sliding and unstable. We,

Brandy and Alfa and me, we've been speaking English as a second language so long that we've forgotten it is our first.

I have no native tongue.

We're eye level with the dirty stones of a dark chandelier. On the other side of the handrail, the hallway's gray marble floor looks as if we've climbed a stairway through the clouds. Step after step. Far away, Alfa's demanding talk goes on about wine cellars, about kennels for the Russian wolfhounds. Alfa's constant demand for the realty woman's attention is as faint as a radio call-in show bouncing back from outer space.

". . . the Princess Brandy Alexander," Alfa's warm, dark words float up, "she is probable to remove her clothes and scream like the wild horses in even the crowded restaurants . . ."

The queen supreme's voice and the shadow of L'Air du Temps says, "Next house," her Plumbago lips say, "Alfa will be the mute."

". . . your breasts," Alfa is telling the realty woman, "you have two of the breasts of a young woman . . ."

Not one native tongue is left among us.

Jump to us being upstairs.

Jump to now anything being possible.

After the realtor is trapped by the blue eyes of Signore Alfa Romeo, jump to when the real scamming starts. The master bedroom will always be down the hallway in the direction of the best view. This master bathroom is paneled in pink mirror, every wall, even the ceiling. Princess Brandy and I are everywhere, reflected on every surface. You can see Brandy sitting on the pink counter at one side of the vanity sink, me sitting at the other side of the sink.

One of us is sitting on each side of all the sinks in all the mirrors. There are just too many Brandy Alexanders to count, and they're all being the boss of me. They all open their white calfskin clutch bags, and hundreds of those big ring-beaded Brandy Alexander hands take out new copies of the *Physicians' Desk Reference* with its red cover, big as a Bible.

All her hundreds of Burning Blueberry eye shadow eyes look at me from all over the room.

"You know the drill," all her hundreds of Plumbago mouths command. Those big hands start pulling open drawers and cabinet doors. "Remember where you got everything, and put it back exactly where you found it," the mouths say. "We'll do the drugs first, then the makeup. Now start hunting."

I take out the first bottle. It's Valium, and I hold the bottle so all the hundred Brandys can read the label.

"Take what we can get away with," Brandy says, "then get on to the next bottle."

I shake a few of the little blue pills into my purse pocket with the other Valiums. The next bottle I find is Darvon.

"Honey, those are heaven in your mouth." All the Brandys look up to peer at the bottle I'm holding. "Does it look safe to take too many?"

The expiration date on the label is only a month away, and the bottle is still almost full. I figure we can take about half.

"Here." A big ring-beaded hand comes at me from every direction. One hundred big hands come at me, palms up. "Give Brandy a couple. The princess is having lower back pain again."

I shake ten capsules out, and a hundred hands toss a thousand tranquilizers onto the red carpet tongues of those Plumbago mouths. A suicide load of Darvon slides down into the dark interior of the continents that make up a world of Brandy Alexander.

Inside the next bottle are the little purple ovals of 2.5-milligram–sized Premarin.

That's short for Pregnant Mare Urine. That's short for thousands of miserable horses in North Dakota and central Canada, forced to stand in cramped dark stalls with a catheter stuck on them to catch every drop of urine and only getting let outside to get fucked again. What's funny is that describes pretty much any good long stay in a hospital, but that's only been my experience.

"Don't look at me that way," Brandy says. "My not taking those pills won't bring any baby horses back from the dead."

In the next bottle are round, peach-colored little scored tablets of one-hundred-milligram Aldactone. Our homeowner must be a junkie for female hormones.

Painkillers and estrogen are pretty much Brandy's only two food groups, and she says, "Gimme, gimme, gimme." She snacks on some little pink-coated Estinyls. She pops a few of the turquoise-blue Estrace tablets. She's using some vaginal Premarin as a hand cream when she says, "Miss Kay?" She says, "I can't seem to make a fist, sweetness. Do you think maybe you can wrap things up without me while I lie down?"

The hundreds of me cloned in the pink bathroom mirrors, we check out the makeup while the princess goes off to catnap in the cabbage rose and old canopy bed glory of the master bedroom. I find Darvocets and Percodans and Compazines, Nembutals and Percocets. Oral estrogens. Antiandrogens. Progestons. Transdermal estrogen patches. I find none of Brandy's colors, no Rusty Rose blusher. No Burning Blueberry eye shadow. I find a vibrator with the dead batteries swollen and leaking acid inside.

It's an old woman who owns this house, I figure. Ignored and aging and drugged-out old women, older and more invisible to the world every minute, they must not wear a lot of makeup. Not go out to fun hot spots. Not boogie to a party froth. My breath smells hot and sour inside my veils, inside the damp layers of silk and mesh and cotton georgette I lift for the first time all day; and in the mirrors, I look at the pink reflection of what's left of my face.

Mirror, mirror on the wall, who's the fairest one of all?

The evil queen was stupid to play Snow White's game. There's an age where a woman has to move on to another kind of power. Money, for example. Or a gun.

I'm living the life I love, I tell myself, and loving the life I live.

I tell myself: I deserved this.

This is exactly what I wanted.

Now, Please, Jump to Chapter Forty

Chapter 2

Jump to the Canadian border.

Jump to the three of us in a rented Lincoln Town Car, waiting to drive south from Vancouver, British Columbia, into the United States, waiting, with Signore Romeo in the driver's seat, waiting with Brandy next to him in the front, waiting, with me alone in the back.

"The police have microphones," Brandy tells us.

The plan is if we make it through the border, we'll drive south to Seattle, where there are nightclubs and dance clubs where go-go boys and go-go girls will line up to buy the pockets of my purse clean. We have to be quiet because the police, they have microphones on both sides of the border, United States and Canadian. This way they can listen in on people waiting to cross. We could have Cuban cigars. Fresh fruit. Diamonds. Diseases. Drugs, Brandy says. Brandy, she tells us to shut up a mile before the border, and we wait in line, quiet.

Brandy unwinds the yards and yards of brocade scarf around her head. Brandy, she shakes her hair down her back and ties the scarf over her shoulders to hide her torpedo cleavage. Brandy switches to simple gold earrings. She takes off her pearls and puts on a little chain with a gold cross. This is a moment before the border guard.

"Your nationalities?" the border-guard guy sitting inside his little window, behind his computer terminal with his clipboard and his blue suit, behind his mirrored sunglasses, and behind his gold badge says.

"Sir," Brandy says, and her new voice is as bland and drawled out as grits without salt or butter. She says, "Sir, we are citizens of the United States of America, what used to be called the greatest country on earth until the homosexuals and child pornographers—"

"Your names?" says the border guy.

Brandy leans across Alfa to look up at the border guy. "My husband," she says, "is an innocent man."

"Your name, please," he says, no doubt looking up our license plate, finding it's a rental car, rented in Billings, Montana, three weeks ago, maybe even finding the truth about who we really are. Maybe finding bulletin after bulletin from all over western Canada about three nutcases stealing drugs at big houses up for sale. Maybe all this is spooling onto his computer screen, maybe none of it. You never know.

"I am married," Brandy is almost yelling to get his attention. "I am the wife of the Reverend Scooter Alexander," she says, still half laid across Alfa's lap.

"And this," she says and draws the invisible line from her smile to Alfa, "this is my son-in-law, Seth Thomas." Her big hand flies toward me in the backseat. "This," she says, "is my daughter, Bubba-Joan."

Some days, I hate it when Brandy changes our lives without warning. Sometimes, twice in one day, you have to live up to a new identity. A new name. New relationships. Handicaps. It's hard to remember who I started this road trip being.

No doubt this is the kind of stress the constantly mutating AIDS virus must feel.

"Sir?" the border guy says to Seth, formerly Alfa Romeo, formerly Chase Manhattan, formerly Nash Rambler, formerly Wells Fargo, formerly Eberhard Faber. The guard says, "Sir, are you bringing any purchases back with you into the United States?"

My pointed little toe of my shoe reaches under the front seat and gooses my new husband. The details of everything have us surrounded. The mudflats left by low tide are just over there, with little waves arriving one after another. The flower beds on our other side are planted to spell out words you can only read from a long ways off. Up close, it's just so many red and yellow wax begonias.

"Don't tell me you've never watched our Christian Healing Network?" Brandy says. She fiddles with the little gold cross at her throat. "If you just watched one show, you'd know that God in his wisdom has made my son-in-law a mute, and he cannot speak."

The border guy keyboards some quick strokes. This could be

CRIME he's typed. Or *DRUGS*. Or *SHOOT*. It could be *SMUGGLERS*. Or *ARREST*.

"Not a word," Brandy whispers next to Seth's ear, "You talk and in Seattle, I'll change you into Harvey Wallbanger."

The border guy says, "To admit you to the United States, I'm going to have to see your passports, please."

Brandy licks her lips wet and shining, her eyes moist and bright. Her brocade scarf slips low to reveal her cleavage as she looks up at the border guy and says, "Would you excuse us a moment?"

Brandy sits back in her own seat, and Seth's window hums all the way up.

Brandy's big torpedoes inhale big and then exhale. "Don't anybody panic," she says, and pops her lipstick open. She makes a kiss in the rearview mirror and pokes the lipstick around the edge of her big Plumbago mouth, trembling so much that her one big hand has to hold her lipstick hand steady.

"I can get us back into the States," she says, "but I'm going to need a condom and a breath mint."

Around her lipstick she says, "Bubba-Joan, be a sweetheart and hand me up one of those Estraderms, will you?"

Seth gives her the mint and a condom.

She says, "Let's guess how long it takes him to find a week's supply of girl juice soaking into his ass."

She pops the lipstick shut and says, "Blot me, please."

I hand her up a tissue and an estrogen patch.

Now, Please, Jump to Chapter Thirty-nine

Chapter 3

No, this isn't a typographical mistake.

It's that *Kiss of the Spider Woman* way we have of remembering ourselves instead of the truth. Where were you when JFK was shot? When the World Trade Towers came down? Such momentous events, these, but what you recall is the sweet-fat, milk-orange taste of the Creamsicle you were eating and the irksome drips that ran down the wooden stick to gum up your fingers. The phone rang, and your sister asked, "Are you watching this on television?" You didn't even know what she meant by this. Your mouth still full of Creamsicle, you asked, "Watching what?" And the next thing you knew, Princess Diana would be dead forever.

The way the stylist holds a little mirror so you can look at yourself reflected in the bigger mirror and see to how nice she trimmed the back of your hair, that's how to read this. Hold it up to a mirror and peek in from around the edges. Spy on yourself. Reverse the reversed type to make it readable. A reflection of a reflection equals the truth. See? Two wrongs can make a right!

Witness how Brandy Alexander recounts the story of her favorite movie: Sissy Spacek is naked, taking a shower in a high school locker room, blurred by the veil of warm water. We're lulled by flute music. She drops the bar of soap, and our eyes follow it to the tiled floor, where we discover—blood. Sissy stands in a puddle of red! Alerted by something—a warm feeling? a strange smell? *oh, the frustrating limitations of film*—Sissy looks down at her hand to find her palm cupping blood. Blood trickles down her bare legs. At that point her female peers have noticed, and like a pack of hyenas they advance on her, heckling poor Sissy and pelting her with free feminine napkins. Brandy's favorite part is when Sissy leaps from the shower, naked, like a blood-drenched panther disturbed at the scene of a fresh kill. Her fingernail talons dripping with blood, she claws at Nancy Allen, ripping at her slender throat. Sissy drives her powerful fists into the faces of P. J. Soles and Amy Irving. Her bare, bloody limbs are everywhere, kicking and punching, until the locker room is painted with everyone's blood. She clobbers Betty Buckley so hard that teeth fly. The senior prom gets canceled because nobody can dance because Sissy Spacek broke all their legs. Merely because she wanted to.

Later, Sissy is naked and taking a bath in a claw-foot tub. For most of that movie, her dirty pillows are out. That's what makes a summer classic: tits and blood. She climbs out of the tub, clearly irked, and stabs Piper Laurie to death with a potato peeler. That whole movie is just tits and blood and Nancy Allen's full-frontal vagina stepping over a locker room bench with—welcome back to 1976—a surprisingly big bush of dark hair! Sometimes, the way Brandy tells it, zombies attack and Sissy rips off their undead heads. At the end she doesn't go to hell. Who's to say Brandy gets anything wrong? In her mind, the crowd goes wild. As Sissy Spacek climbs into a top-down 1966 Thunderbird convertible with Susan Sarandon, and the pair of them jump the Grand Canyon to a life of peaceful lesbian freedom in sunny Mexico, Brandy cries every time. Boo-hoo-hoo. Criminy, it never fails. Every freak'n time.

Now, Please, jump to Chapter Sixteen

Chapter 4

On the planet Brandy Alexander, the universe is run by a fairly elaborate system of gods and she-gods. Some evil. Some are ultimate goodness. Marilyn Monroe, for example. Then there's Nancy Reagan and Wallis Warfield Simpson. Some of the gods and she-gods are dead. Some are alive. A lot are plastic surgeons.

The system changes. Gods and she-gods come and go and leapfrog each other for a change of status.

Abraham Lincoln is in his heaven to make our car a floating bubble of new-car–smelling air: driving as smooth as advertising copy. These days, Brandy says Marlene Dietrich is in charge of the weather. Now is the autumn of our ennui. We're carried down Interstate 5 under gray skies, inside the blue casket interior of a rented Lincoln Town Car. Seth is driving. This is how we always sit, with Brandy up front and me in the back. Three hours of scenic beauty between Vancouver, British Columbia, and Seattle is what we're driving through. Asphalt and internal combustion carry us and the Lincoln Town Car south.

Traveling this way, you might as well be watching the world on television. The electric windows are hummed all the way up so the planet Brandy Alexander has an atmosphere of warm, still, silent blue. It's an even seventy degrees Fahrenheit, with the whole outside world of trees and rocks scrolling by in miniature behind curved glass. Live by satellite. We're the little world of Brandy Alexander rocketing past it all.

Driving, driving, Seth says, "Did you ever think about life as a metaphor for television?"

Our rule is that when Seth's driving, no radio. What happens is a Dionne Warwick song comes on, and Seth starts to cry so hard, crying those big Estinyl tears, shaking with those big Provera sobs. If Dionne Warwick comes on singing a Burt Bacharach song, we just have to pull over or it's sure we'll get car-wrecked.

The tears, the way his dumpling face has lost the chiseled shadows that used to pool under his brow and cheekbones, the way Seth's hand will sneak up and tweak his nipple through his shirt and his mouth will drop open and his eyes roll backward, it's the hormones. The conjugated estrogens, the Premarin, the estradiol, the ethinyl estradiol, they've all found their way into Seth's diet cola. Of course, there's the danger of liver damage at his current daily overdose levels. There could already be liver damage or cancer or blood clots, thrombosis if you're a doctor, but I'm willing to take that chance. Sure, it's all just for fun. Watching for his breasts to develop. Seeing his macho babe-magnet swagger go to fat and him taking naps in the afternoon. All that's great, but his being dead would let me move on to explore other interests.

Driving, driving, Seth says, "Don't you think that somehow television makes us God?"

This introspection is new. His beard growth is lightened up. It must be the antiandrogens choking back his testosterone. The water retention, he can ignore. The moodiness. A tear slips out of one eye in the rearview mirror and rolls down his face.

"Am I the only one who cares about these issues?" he says. "Am I the only one here in this car who feels anything real?"

Brandy's reading a paperback book. Most times, Brandy is reading some plastic surgeon's glossy hard-sell brochure about vaginas complete with color pictures showing the picture-perfect way a urethra should be aligned to ensure a downward stream of urine. Other pictures show how a top-quality clitoris should be hooded. These are five-figure, ten- and twenty-thousand-dollar vaginas, better than the real thing, and most days Brandy will pass the pictures around.

Jump to three weeks before, when we were in a big house in Spokane, Washington. We were in a South Hill granite chateau with Spokane spread out under the bathroom windows. I was shaking Percodans out of their brown bottle and into my purse pocket for Percodans. Brandy Alexander, she was digging around under the bathroom sink for a clean emery board when she found this paperback book.

Now all the other gods and she-gods have been eclipsed by some new deity.

Jump back to Seth looking at my breasts in the rearview mirror. "Television really does make us God," he says.

Give me tolerance.

Flash.

Give me understanding.

Flash.

Even after all these weeks on the road with me, Seth's glorious vulnerable blue eyes still won't meet my eyes. His new wistful introspection, he can ignore. The way the orals have already side-effected his eyes, steepened the corneal curve so he can't wear his contact lenses without them popping out. This has to be the conjugated estrogens in his orange juice every morning. He can ignore all that.

This has to be the Androcur in his iced tea at lunch, but he'll never figure it out. He'll never catch me.

Brandy Alexander, her nylon stocking feet up on the dashboard, the queen supreme's still reading her paperback.

"When you watch daytime dramas," Seth tells me, "you can look in on anybody. There's a different life on every channel, and almost every hour the lives change. It's the same as those live video Web sites. You can watch the whole world without it knowing."

For three weeks, Brandy's been reading that book.

"Television lets you spy on even the sexy parts of everybody's life," Seth says. "Doesn't it make sense?"

Maybe, but only if you're on five hundred milligrams of micronized progesterone every day.

A few minutes of scenery go by behind glass. Just some towering mountains, old dead volcanoes, mostly the kind of stuff you find outside. Those timeless natural nature themes. Raw materials at their rawest. Unrefined. Unimproved rivers. Poorly maintained mountains. Filth. Plants growing in dirt. Weather.

"And if you believe that we really have free will, then you know that God can't really control us," Seth says. Seth's hands are off the steering wheel and flutter around to make his point. "And since God can't control us," he says, "all God does is watch and change channels when He gets bored."

Somewhere in heaven, you're live on a video Web site for God to surf.

Brandycam.

Brandy with her empty leg-hold trap shoes on the floor, Brandy licks an index finger and slow turns a page.

Ancient aboriginal petroglyphs and junk are just whizzing past.

"My point," Seths says, "is that maybe TV makes you God." Seth says, "And it could be that all we are is God's television."

Standing on the gravel shoulder are some moose or whatnot just trudging along on all four feet.

"Or Santa Claus," says Brandy from behind her book. "Santa Claus sees everything."

"Santa Claus is just a story," says Seth. "He's just the opening band to God. There is no Santa Claus."

Jump to drug hunting three weeks ago in Spokane, Washington, when Brandy Alexander flopped down in the master bedroom and started reading. I took thirty-two Nembutals. Thirty-two Nembutals went in my purse. I don't eat the merchandise. Brandy was still reading. I tried all the lipsticks on the back of my hand, and Brandy was still propped on a zillion eyelet lace pillows in the center of a king-sized waterbed. Still reading.

I put some expired estradiol and a half stick of Plumbago in my bag. The realtor called up the stairs, was everything all right?

Jump to us on Interstate 5 where a billboard goes by:

Clean Food and Family Prices Coming Up at the Karver Stage Stop Café

Jump to no Burning Blueberry, no Rusty Rose or Aubergine Dreams in Spokane.

He didn't want to rush us, the realtor called up the stairs, but was there anything we needed to know? Did we have any questions about anything?

I stuck my head in the master bedroom, and the waterbed's white duvet held a reading Brandy Alexander that was dead for as much as she was breathing.

Oh, clipped lilac satin of the beaded rice pearl hemline.

Oh, layered amber cashmere trimmed in faceted topaz marabou.

Oh, slithering underwired free-range mink bolero.

We had to go.

Brandy clutched her paperback open against her straight-up torpedo boob job. The Rusty Rose face pillowed in auburn hair and eyelet lace pillow shams, the aubergine eyes had the dilated look of a Thorazine overdose.

First thing I want to know is what drug she's taken.

The paperback cover showed a pretty blond babe. Thin as a spaghetti strap. With a pretty, thin little smile. The babe's hair was a satellite photo of Hurricane Blonde just off the west coast of her face. The face was a Greek she-god with great lash, big eyeliner eyes the same as Betty and Veronica and all the other Archie gals had at Riverdale High. White pearls are wrapped up her arms and around her neck. What could be diamonds sparkle here and there.

The paperback cover said *Miss Rona*.

Brandy Alexander, her leg-hold trap shoes were getting dirt all over the waterbed's white duvet, and Brandy said, "I've found out who the real God is."

The realtor was ten seconds away.

Jump to all the wonders of nature blurring past us, rabbits, squirrels, plunging waterfalls. That's the worst of it. Gophers digging subterranean dens underground. Birds nesting in nests.

"The Princess B.A. is God," Seth tells me in the rearview mirror.

Jump to where the Spokane realtor yelled up the stairs. The people who owned the granite chateau were coming up the driveway.

Brandy Alexander, her eyes dilated, barely breathing in a Spokane waterbed, said, "Rona Barrett. Rona Barrett is my new Supreme Being."

Jump to Brandy in the Lincoln Town Car saying, "Rona Barrett is God."

All around us, erosion and insects are just chewing up the world, never mind people and pollution. Everything biodegrades with or without you pushing. I check my purse for enough spironolactone for Seth's afternoon snack. Another billboard goes by:

Tasty Phase Magic Bran—Put Something Good in Your Mouth

"In her autobiography," Brandy Alexander testifies, "in *Miss Rona*, published by Bantam Books by arrangement with the Nash Publishing Corporation on Sunset Boulevard in Los Angeles, California . . ." Brandy takes a deep breath of new-car-smelling air, ". . . copyright 1974, Miss Rona tells us how she started life as a fat little Jewish girl from Queens with a big nose and a mysterious muscle disease."

Brandy says, "This little fat brunette re-creates herself as a top celebrity superstar blonde whom a top sex symbol then begs to let him stick his penis in her just one inch."

There isn't one native tongue left among us.

Another billboard:

Next Sundae, Scream for Tooter's Ice Milk!

"What that woman has gone through," says Brandy. "Right here on page one hundred and twenty-five, she almost drowns in her own blood! Rona's just had her nose job. She's only making fifty bucks a story, but this woman saves enough for a thousand-dollar nose job! It's her first miracle. So, Rona's in the hospital, post–nose job, with her head wrapped up like a mummy, when a friend comes in and says how Hollywood says she's a lesbian. Miss Rona, a lesbian! Of course this isn't true. The woman is a she-god, so she screams and screams and screams until an artery in her throat just bursts."

"Hallelujah," Seth says, all teared up again.

"And here"—Brandy licks the pad of a big index finger and flips ahead a few pages—"on page two hundred and twenty-two, Rona is once more rejected by her sleazy boyfriend of eleven years. She's been coughing for weeks so she takes a handful of pills and is found semicomatose and dying. Even the ambulance—"

"Praise God," Seth says.

Various native plants are growing just wherever they want.

"Seth, sweetness," Brandy says. "Don't step on my lines." Her

Plumbago lips say, "Even the ambulance driver thought our Miss Rona would be DOA."

Clouds composed of water vapor are up in the, you know, sky.

Brandy says, "*Now*, Seth."

And Seth says, "Hallelujah!"

The wild daisies and Indian paintbrush whizzing past are just the genitals of a different life-form.

And Seth says, "So what are you saying?"

"In the book *Miss Rona*, copyright 1974," Brandy says, "Rona Barrett—who got her enormous breasts when she was nine years old and wanted to cut them off with scissors—she tells us in the prologue of her book that she's like this animal, cut open with all its vital organs glistening and quivering, you know, like the liver and the large intestine. Such visuals, everything sort of dripping and pulsating. Anyway, she could wait for someone to sew her back up, but she knows no one will. She has to take a needle and thread and sew herself up."

"Gross," says Seth.

"Miss Rona says nothing is gross," Brandy says. "Miss Rona says the only way to find true happiness is to risk being completely cut open."

Flocks of self-absorbed little native birds seem obsessed with finding food and picking it up with their mouths.

Brandy pulls the rearview mirror around until she finds me reflected and says, "Bubba-Joan, sweetness?"

It's obvious the native birds have to build their own do-it-yourself nests using materials they source locally. The little sticks and leaves are just sort of heaped together.

"Bubba-Joan," Brandy Alexander says. "Why don't you open up to us with a story?"

Seth says, "Remember the time in Missoula when the princess got so ripped she ate Nebalino suppositories wrapped in gold foil because she thought they were Almond Roca? Talk about your semiconscious DOAs."

Pine trees are producing pine cones. Squirrels and mammals of all sexes spend all day trying to get laid. Or giving birth live. Or eating their young.

Brandy says, "Seth, sweetness?"

"Yes, Mother."

What only looks like bulimia is how bald eagles feed their young.

Brandy says, "Why is it you have to seduce every living thing you come across?"

Another billboard:

Nubby's Is the BBQ Gotta-Stop for Savory,
Flavory Chicken Wings

Another billboard:

Dairy Bite—The Chewing Gum Flavored
with the Low-Fat Goodness of Real Cheese

Seth giggles. Seth blushes and twists some of his hair around a finger. He says, "You make me sound so sexually compulsive."

Mercy. Next to him, I feel so butch.

"Oh, baby," Brandy says, "you don't remember half of who you've been with." She says, "Well, I only wish I could forget it."

To my breasts in the rearview mirror, Seth says, "The only reason why we ask other people how their weekend was is so we can tell them about our own weekend."

I figure, a few more days of increased micronized progesterone, and Seth should pop out his own nice rack of hooters. Side effects I need to watch for include nausea, vomiting, jaundice, migraine, abdominal cramps, and dizziness. You try to remember the exact toxicity levels, but why bother.

A sign goes by saying: Seattle 130 miles.

"Come on, let's see those glistening, quivering innards, Bubba-Joan," Brandy Alexander, God and mother of us all, commands. "Tell us a gross personal story."

She says, "Rip yourself open. Sew yourself shut," and she hands a prescription pad and an Aubergine Dreams eyebrow pencil to me in the backseat.

Now, Please, Jump to Chapter Thirty-eight

Chapter 5

Don't look for me to ever tell my folks about the accident. You know, a whole long-distance telephone crying jag about the bullet and the emergency room. That's not anywhere we're going. I told my folks, as soon as I could write them a letter, that I was going on a catalogue shoot in Cancún, Mexico, for Espre.

Six months of fun, sand, and me trying to suck the lime wedges out of long-necked bottles of Mexican beer. Guys just love watching babes do that. Go figure. Guys.

She loves clothes from Espre, my mom writes back. She writes how, since I'll be in the Espre catalogue, could I maybe get her a discount on her Christmas order.

Sorry, Mom. Sorry, God.

She writes back: *Well, be pretty for us. Love and kisses.*

Most times, it's just a lot easier not to let the world know what's wrong. My folks, they call me Bump. I was the bump inside my Mom's stomach for nine months; they've called me Bump from since before I was born. They live a two-hour drive from me, but I never visit. What I mean is they don't need to know every little hair about me.

In one letter my mom writes:

At least with your brother, we know whether he's dead or alive.

My dead brother, the King of Fag Town. The voted best at everything. The basketball king until he was sixteen and his test for strep throat came back as gonorrhea, I only know I hated him.

It's not that we don't love you, my mom writes in one letter, *it's just that we don't show it.*

Besides, hysteria is only possible with an audience. You know what you need to do to keep alive. Folks will just screw you up with their reactions about how what happened is so horrible. First the emergency room folks letting you go ahead of them. Then the Franciscan nun screaming. Then the police with their hospital sheet.

Jump to how life was when you were a baby and you could only eat baby food. You'd stagger over to the coffee table. You're up on your feet and you have to keep waddling along on those Vienna sausage legs or fall down. Then you get to the coffee table and bounce your big soft baby head on the sharp corner.

You're down, and man, oh, man, it hurts. Still it isn't anything tragic until Mom and Dad run over.

Oh, you poor, brave thing.

Only then do you cry.

Jump to Brandy and me and Seth going to the top of the Space Needle thing in Seattle, Washington. This is our first stop after the Canadian border except us stopping so I could run buy Seth a coffee—cream, sugar, and Climara—and a Coca-Cola—extra Estrace, no ice. It's eleven, and the Space Needle closes at midnight, and Seth says there are two types of people in the world.

The Princess Alexander wanted to find a nice hotel first, someplace with valet parking and tile bathrooms. We might have time for a nap before she has to go out and sell medications.

"If you were on a game show," Seth says about his two types of people. Seth has already pulled off the freeway and we're driving between dark warehouses, turning toward every glimpse we get of the Space Needle. "So you're the winner of this game show," Seth says, "and you get a choice between a five-piece living room set from Broyhill, suggested retail price three thousand dollars . . . or . . . a ten-day trip to the Old World charm of Europe."

Most people, Seth says, would take the living room set.

"It's just that people want something to show for their effort," Seth says. "Like the pharaohs and their pyramids. Given the choice, very few people would choose the trip even if they already had a nice living room set."

No one's parked on the streets around Seattle Center, people are all home watching television, or being television if you believe in God.

"I have to show you where the future ended," says Seth. "I want us to be the people who choose the trip."

According to Seth, the future ended in 1962 at the Seattle World's Fair. This was everything we should've inherited: the whole man-on-the-moon-within-this-decade, asbestos-is-our-miracle-friend, nuclear-powered and fossil-fueled world of the Space Age where you could go up to visit the Jetsons' flying saucer apartment building and then ride the monorail downtown for fun pillbox hat fashions at the Bon Marché.

All his hope and science and research and glamour left here in ruins:

The Space Needle.

The Science Center with its lacy domes and hanging light globes.

The monorail streaking along covered in brushed aluminum.

This is how our lives were supposed to turn out.

Go there. Take the trip, Seth says. It will break your heart because the Jetsons with their robot maid, Rosie, and their flying-saucer cars and toaster beds that spit you out in the morning, it's like the Jetsons have sublet the Space Needle to the Flintstones.

"You know," says Seth, "Fred and Wilma. The garbage disposal that's really a pig that lives under the sink. All their furniture made out of bones and rocks and tiger-skin lampshades. Wilma vacuums with a baby elephant and fluffs the rocks. They named their baby 'Pebbles.'"

Here was our future of cheese-food and aerosol propellants,

Styrofoam and Club Med on the moon, roast beef served in a toothpaste tube.

"Tang," says Seth, "you know, breakfast with the astronauts. And now people come here wearing sandals they made themselves out of leather. They name their kids Zilpah and Zebulun out of the Old Testament. Lentils are a big deal."

Seth sniffs and drags a hand across the tears in his eyes. It's the Estrace is all. He must be getting premenstrual.

"The folks who go to the Space Needle now," Seth says, "they have lentils soaking at home and they're walking around the ruins of the future the way barbarians did when they found Grecian ruins and told themselves that God must've built them."

Seth parks us under one big steel leg of the Space Needle's three legs. We get out and look up at the legs going up to the Space Needle, the low restaurant, the high restaurant that revolves, then the observation deck at the top. Then the stars.

Jump to the sad moment when we buy our tickets and get on the big glass elevator that slides up the middle of the Space Needle. We're in this glass and brass go-go cage dance party to the stars. Going up, I want to hear hypoallergenic "Telestar" music, untouched by human hands. Anything computer-generated and played on a Moog synthesizer. I want to dance the frug on a TWA commuter flight go-go dance party to the moon where cool dudes and chicks do the Mashed Potato under zero gravity and eat delicious snack pills.

I want this.

I tell Brandy Alexander this, and she goes right up to the brass and glass windows and does the frug even though going up, the G forces make this like dancing the frug on Mars where you weigh eight hundred pounds.

The sad part is when the guy in a poly-blend uniform who runs the elevator misses the whole point of the future. The whole fun, fun, fun of the moment is wasted on him, and this guy looks at us as if we're those puppies you see behind glass in suburban mall pet stores. Like we're those puppies with yellow ooze on their eyes and buttholes, and you know they'll never have another solid bowel movement but they're still for sale for six hundred dollars apiece. Those puppies are so sad that even the overweight girls with bad beauty college perms will tap on the glass for hours and say, "I loves you, little one. Mommy loves you, tiny one."

The future is just wasted on some people.

Jump to the observation deck at the top of the Space Needle, where you can't see the steel legs so it's as if you're hovering over Seattle on a flying saucer with a lot of souvenirs for sale. Still, most of this isn't souvenirs of the future. It's the ecology T-shirts and batiks and tie-dyed all-natural cotton fiber stuff you can't wash with anything else because it's never really color-fast. Tapes of whales singing while they do sex. More stuff I hate.

Brandy goes off in search of relics and artifacts from the future. Acrylic. Plexiglas. Aluminum. Styrofoam. Radium.

Seth goes to the railing and leans out over the suicide nets and spits. The spit falls back down into the twenty-first century. The wind blows my hair out over the darkness and Seattle and my hands are clutched white on the steel railing where about a million hands before me have clutched the paint off.

Inside his clothes, instead of the plates of hard muscle that used to drive me crazy, now the fat pushes his shirt out over the top of his belt. It's the Premarin. His sexy five o'clock shadow is fading from the Provera. Even his fingers swell around his old letterman's ring.

The photographer in my head says:

Give me peace.

Flash.

Give me release.

Flash.

Seth hauls his water-retaining self up to sit on the railing. His kiltie tassel loafers swing above the nets. His tie blows straight out above the nothing and darkness.

"I'm not afraid," he says. He straightens one leg and lets a kiltie tassel loafer dangle from his toes.

I clutch the veils tight around my neck so people who don't know me will think like my parents that I'm still happy.

Seth says, "The last time I'll ever be scared was the night you caught me trying to kill you," and Seth looks out over the lights of Seattle and smiles.

I'd smile, too, you know, if I had any lips.

In the future, in the wind, in the dark on the observation deck at the top of the Space Needle, Brandy Alexander, that brand-name queen supreme that she is, Brandy comes out to Seth and I with souvenirs of the future. These are postcards. Brandy Alexander gives us each a stack of postcards so faded and dog-eared and picked over and ignored that they've survived in the back of a revolving wire rack for years. Here are pictures of the future with clean, sun-bleached skies behind an opening-day Space Needle. Here's the monorail full of smiling babes in Jackie O pink mohair suits with three huge cloth-covered buttons down the front. Children in striped T-shirts and blond astronaut crew cuts run through a Science Center where all the fountains still work.

"Tell the world what scares you most," says Brandy. She gives us each an Aubergine Dreams eyebrow pencil and says, "Save the world with some advice from the future."

Seth writes on the back of a card and hands the card to Brandy for her to read.

"*On game shows*," Brandy reads, "*some people will take the trip to France, but most people will take the washer-dryer pair.*"

Brandy puts a big Plumbago kiss on the little square for the stamp and lets the wind lift the card and sail it off toward the towers of downtown Seattle.

Seth hands her another, and Brandy reads:

"*Game shows are designed to make us feel better about the random, useless facts that are all we have left of our education.*"

A kiss, and the card's on its way toward Lake Washington.

From Seth:

"*When did the future switch from being a promise to being a threat?*"

A kiss, and it's off on the wind toward Ballard.

"Only when we eat up this planet will God give us another. We'll be remembered more for what we destroy than what we create."

Interstate 5 snakes by in the distance. From high atop the Space Needle, the southbound lanes are red chase lights, and the northbound lanes are white chase lights. I take a card and write:

I love Seth Thomas so much I have to destroy him. I overcompensate by worshipping the queen supreme. Seth will never love me. No one will ever love me ever again.

Brandy is waiting to take the card and read it out loud. Brandy's waiting to read my worst fears to the world, but I don't give her the card. I kiss it myself with the lips I don't have and let the wind take it out of my hand. The card flies up, up, up to the stars and then falls down to land in the suicide net.

While I watch my future trapped in the suicide net, Brandy reads another card from Seth.

"We are all self-composting."

I write on another card from the future, and Brandy reads it.

"When we don't know who to hate, we hate ourselves."

An updraft lifts my worst fears from the suicide net and sails them away.

Seth writes and Brandy reads.

"You have to keep recycling yourself."

I write and Brandy reads.

"Nothing of me is original. I am the combined effort of everybody I've ever known."

I write and Brandy reads.

"The one you love and the one who loves you are never, ever the same person."

Jump to us going down fast in a TWA return trip home from the moon, Brandy and Seth and me dancing our dance party frug in the zero-gravity brass and glass go-go cage elevator. Brandy makes a big ring-beaded fist and tells the poly-blend service droid who tries to stop us to chill out unless he wants to die on reentry.

Back on earth in the twenty-first century, our rented Lincoln with its blue casket interior is waiting to take us to a nice hotel. On the windshield is a ticket, but when Brandy storms over to tear it up, the ticket is a postcard from the future.

Maybe my worst fears.

For Brandy to read out loud to Seth. *I love Seth so much I have to destroy him . . .*

Even if I overcompensate, nobody will ever want me. Not Seth. Not my folks. You can't kiss someone who has no lips. Oh, love me, love me, love me, love me, love me, love me, love me, love me. I'll be anybody you want me to be.

Brandy Alexander, her big hand lifts the postcard. The queen supreme reads it to herself, silent, and slips the postcard into her handbag. Princess Princess, she says, "At this rate, we'll never get to the future."

Now, Please, Jump to Chapter Thirty-seven

Chapter 6

Jump to Brandy Alexander tucking me into a Seattle bed. This is the night of the Space Needle, the night the future doesn't happen. Brandy, she's wearing yards and yards of black tulle wrapped around her legs, twisted up and around her hourglass waist. A black veil crosses her torpedo breasts and loops up and over the top of her auburn hair. All this sparkle that bends over beside my bed could be the trial-sized mock-up for the original summer night sky.

Little rhinestones, not the plastic ones pooped out by a factory in Calcutta but the Austrian crystal ones cut by elves in the Black Forest, these little star-shaped rhinestones are set all over the black tulle. The queen supreme's face is the moon in the night sky that bends over and kisses me good night. My hotel room is dark, and the television at the foot of my bed is turned on so the handmade stars twinkle in all the colors the television is trying to show us.

Seth's right, the television does make me God. I can look in on anybody and every hour the lives change. Here in the real world, that's not always the case.

"I will always love you," the queen of the night sky says, and I know which postcard she's found.

The hotel sheets feel the same as the hospital sheets. This is thousands of miles since we met, and the big fingers of Brandy are still smoothing the blankets under where my chin used to be. My face is the last thing the go-go boys and girls want to meet when they go into a dark alley looking to buy drugs.

Brandy says, "We'll be back as soon as we sell out."

Seth is silhouetted in the open doorway to the hall. How he looks from my bed is the terrific outline of a superhero against the neon green and gray and pink tropical leaves of the hallway wallpaper. His coat, the long black leather coat Seth wears, is fitted tight until the waist and then flares from there down so in outline you think it's a cape.

And maybe when he kisses Brandy Alexander's royal butt he's not just pretending. Maybe it's the two of them in love when I'm not around. This wouldn't be the first time I've lost him.

The face surrounded in black veil that leans over me is a surprise of color. The skin is a lot of pink around a Plumbago mouth, and the eyes are too aubergine. Even these colors are too garish right now, too saturated, too intense. Lurid. You think of cartoon characters. Fashion dolls have pink skin like this, like plastic bandages. Flesh tone. Too-aubergine eyes, cheekbones too defined by Rusty Rose blusher. Nothing is left to your imagination.

Maybe this is what guys want. I just want Brandy Alexander to leave.

I want Seth's belt around my neck. I want Seth's fingers in my mouth and his hands pulling my knees apart and then his wet fingers prying me open.

"If you want something to read," Brandy says, "that Miss Rona Barrett book is in my room. I can run get it."

I want to be rubbed so raw by the stubble around Seth's mouth that it will hurt when I pee.

Seth says, "Are you coming?"

A ring-beaded hand tosses the television remote control onto the bed.

"Come on, Princess Princess," Seth says. "The night's not getting any younger."

And I want Seth dead. Worse than dead, I want him fat and bloated with water and insecure and emotional. If Seth doesn't want me, I want to not want him.

"If the police or anything happens," the moon tells me, "the money is all in my makeup case."

The one I love is already gone out to warm up the car. The one who will love me forever says, "Sleep tight," and closes the door behind her.

Jump to once a long time ago, Manus, my fiancé who dumped me, Manus Kelley, the police detective, he told me that your folks are like God because you want to know they're out there and you want them to approve of your life, still you only call them when you're in crisis and need something.

Jump back to me in bed in Seattle, alone with the TV remote control I hit a button on and make the television mute.

On television are three or four people in chairs sitting on a low stage in front of a television audience. This is on television like an infomercial, but as the camera zooms in on each person for a close-up, a little caption appears across the person's chest. Each caption on each close-up is a first name followed by three or four words like a last name, the sort of literal who-they-really-are last names that Indians give to each other, but instead of Heather Runs with Bison . . . Trisha Hunts by Moonlight, these names are:

Cristy Drank Human Blood
Roger Lived with Dead Mother
Brenda Ate Her Baby

I change channels.
I change channels.
I change channels and here are another three people:

Gwen Works as Hooker
Neville Was Raped in Prison
Brent Slept with His Father

People are all over the world telling their one dramatic story and how their life has turned into getting over this one event. Now their lives are more about the past than their future. I hit a button and give Gwen Works as Hooker her voice back for a little sound bite of prostitute talk.

Gwen shapes her story with her hands as she talks. She leans forward out of her chair. Her eyes are watching something up and to the right, just off camera. I know it's the monitor. Gwen's watching herself tell her story.

Gwen balls her fingers until only the left index finger is out, and she slowly twists her hand to show both sides of her fingernail as she talks.

" . . . to protect themselves, most girls on the street break off a little bit of razor blade and glue it under their fingernail. Girls paint the razor nail so it looks like a regular fingernail." Here, Gwen sees something in the monitor. She frowns and tosses her red hair back off what look like pearl earrings.

"When they go to jail," Gwen tells herself in the monitor, "or when they're not attractive anymore, some girls use the razor nails to slash their wrists."

I make Gwen Works as Hooker mute again.

I change channels.

I change channels.

I change channels.

Sixteen channels away, a beautiful young woman in a sequined dress is smiling and dropping animal wastes into a Num Num Snack Factory.

Evie and me, we did this infomercial. It's one of those television commercials you think is a real program except it's just a thirty-minute pitch. The television camera cuts to another girl in a sequined dress, this one is wading through an audience of snowbirds and Midwest tourists. The girl offers a golden anniversary couple in matching Hawaiian shirts a selection of canapés from a silver tray, but the couple and everybody else in their double knits and camera necklaces, they're staring up and to the right at something off camera.

You know it's the monitor.

It's eerie, but what's happening is the folks are staring at themselves in the monitor staring at themselves in the monitor staring at themselves in the monitor, on and on, completely trapped in a reality loop that never ends.

The girl with the tray, her desperate eyes are contact-lens too green and her lips are heavy red outside the natural lip line. The blond hair is thick and teased up so the girl's shoulders don't look so big-boned. The canapés she keeps waving under all the old noses are soda crackers pooped on with meat by-products. Waving her tray, the girl wades farther up into the studio audience bleachers with her too-green eyes and big-boned hair. This is my best friend, Evie Cottrell.

This has to be Evie because here comes Manus stepping up to save her with his good looks. Manus, special police vice operative that he is, he takes one of those pooped-on soda crackers and puts it between his capped teeth. And chews. And tilts his handsome square-jawed face back and closes his eyes, Manus closes his power-blue eyes and twists his head just so much side to side and swallows.

Thick black hair like Manus has, it reminds you how people's hair is just vestigial fur with mousse on it. Such a sexy hair dog, Manus is.

The square-jawed face rocks down to give the camera a full-face, eyes-open look of complete and total love and satisfaction. So déjà vu. This was exactly the same look Manus used to give me when he'd ask if I got my orgasm.

Then Manus turns to give the exact same look to Evie, while the studio audience all looks off in another direction, watching themselves watch themselves watch themselves watch Manus smile with total and complete love and satisfaction at Evie.

Evie smiles back her red-outside-the-natural-lip-line smile at Manus, and I'm this tiny sparkling figure in the background. That's me just over Manus's shoulder, tiny me smiling away like a space heater and dropping animal matter into the Plexiglas funnel on top of the Num Num Snack Factory.

How could I be so dumb?

Let's go sailing.

Sure.

I should've known the deal was Manus and Evie all the time.

Even here, lying in a hotel bed a year after the whole story is over, I'm making fists. I could've just watched the stupid infomercial and known Manus and Evie had some tortured sick relationship they wanted to think was true love.

Okay, I did watch it. Okay, about a hundred times I watched it, but I was only watching myself. That reality loop thing.

The camera comes back to the first girl, the one onstage, and she's me. And I'm so beautiful. On television, I demonstrate the easy cleanability of the snack factory, and I'm so beautiful. I snap the blades out of the Plexiglas cover and rinse off the chewed-up animal waste under running water. And, jeez, I'm beautiful.

The disembodied voice-over is saying how the Num Num Snack Factory takes meat by-products, whatever you have—your tongues or hearts or lips or genitals—chews them up, seasons them, and poops them out in the shape of a spade or a diamond or a club onto your choice of cracker for you to eat yourself.

Here in bed, I'm crying.

Bubba-Joan Got Her Jaw Shot Off.

All these thousands of miles later, all these different people I've been, and it's still the same story. Why is it you feel like a dope if you laugh alone, but that's usually how you end up crying? How is it you can keep mutating and still be the same deadly virus?

Now, Please, Jump to Chapter Thirty-five

Chapter 7

Jump way back to the last Christmas before my accident, when I go home to open presents with my folks. My folks put up the same fake tree every year, scratchy green and making that hot poly-plastic smell that gives you a dizzy flu headache when the lights are plugged in too long. The tree's all magic and sparkle, crowded with our red and gold glass ornaments and those strands of silver plastic loaded with static electricity that people call icicles. It's the same ratty angel with a rubber doll face on top of the tree. Covering the mantel is the same spun-fiberglass *angel hair* that works into your skin and gives you an infected rash if you even touch it. It's the same Perry Como Christmas album on the stereo. This is back when I still had a face so I wasn't so confronted by singing Christmas carols.

My brother Shane's still dead so I try not to expect much attention, just a quiet Christmas. By this point, my boyfriend, Manus, was getting weird about losing his police job, and what I needed was a couple days out of the spotlight. We all talked, my mom, my dad, and me, and agreed to not buy big gifts for each other this year. Maybe just little gifts, my folks say, just stocking stuffers.

Perry Como is singing "It's Beginning to Look a Lot Like Christmas."

The red felt stockings my mom sewed for each of us, for Shane and me, are hanging on the fireplace, each one red felt with our names spelled out, top to bottom, in fancy white felt letters. Each one lumpy with the gifts stuffed inside. It's Christmas morning, and we're all sitting around the tree, my father ready with his jackknife for the knotted ribbons. My mom has a brown paper shopping bag and says, "Before things get out of hand, the wrapping paper goes in here, not all over the place."

My mom and dad sit in recliner chairs. I sit on the floor in front of the fireplace with the stockings by me. This scene is always blocked this way. Them sitting with coffee, leaned down over me, watching for my reaction. Me Indian-sitting on the floor. All of us in bathrobes and pajamas still.

Perry Como is singing "I'll Be Home for Christmas."

The first thing out of my stocking is a little stuffed koala bear, the kind that grips your pencil with its spring-loaded hands and feet. This is who my folks think I am. My mom hands me hot chocolate in a mug with miniature marshmallows floating on top. I say, "Thanks." Under the little koala is a box I take out.

My folks stop everything, lean over their cups of coffee, and just watch me.

Perry Como is singing "O Come All Ye Faithful."

The little box is condoms.

Sitting right next to our sparkling, magic Christmas tree, my father says, "We don't know how many partners you have every year, but we want you to play safe."

I stash the condoms in my bathrobe pocket and look down at the miniature marshmallows melting. I say, "Thanks."

"Those are latex," says my mom. "You need to use only a water-based sexual lubricant. If you need a lubricant at your age. Not petroleum jelly or shortenings or any kind of lotion." She says, "We didn't get you the kind made from sheep intestines because those have tiny pores that can allow the transmission of HIV."

Next inside my stocking is another little box. This is more condoms. The color marked on the box is *Nude*. This seems redundant. Next to that, the label says *odorless and tasteless*.

Oh, I could tell you all about tasteless.

"A study," my father says, "a telephone survey of heterosexuals in urban areas with a high incidence of HIV infection, showed that thirty-five percent of people are uncomfortable buying their own condoms."

And getting them from Santa Claus is better? I say, "Got it."

"This isn't just about AIDS," my mom says. "There's gonorrhea. There's syphilis. There's the human papilloma virus. That's genital warts." She says, "You do know to put the condom on as soon as the penis is erect, don't you?"

She says, "I paid a fortune for bananas out of season in case you need the practice."

This is a trap. If I say, *Oh, yeah, I roll rubbers onto new dry erections all the time*, I'll get the slut lecture from my father. But if I tell them no, we'll get to spend Christmas Day practicing to protect me from fruit.

My dad says, "There's tons more to this than AIDS." He says, "There's the herpes simplex virus two with symptoms that include small painful blisters that burst on your genitals." He looks at Mom.

"Body aches," she says.

"Yes, you get body aches," he says, "and fever. You get vaginal discharge. It hurts to urinate." He looks at my mom.

Perry Como is singing "Santa Claus Is Coming to Town."

Under the next box of condoms is another box of condoms. Jeez, three boxes should last me right into menopause.

Jump to how much I want my brother alive right now so I can kill him for wrecking my Christmas. Perry Como is singing "Up on the Housetop."

"There's hepatitis B," my mom says. To my dad she says, "What's the others?"

"Chlamydia," my father says. "And lymphogranuloma."

"Yes," my mom says, "and mucal purulent cervicitis and nongonococcal urethritis."

My dad looks at my mom and says, "But that's usually caused by an allergy to a latex condom or a spermicide."

My mom drinks some coffee. She looks down at both her hands around her cup, then looks up at me sitting here. "What your father's trying to say," she says, "is we realize now that we made some mistakes with your brother." She says, "We're just trying to keep you safe."

There's a fourth box of condoms in my stocking. Perry Como is singing "It Came upon a Midnight Clear." The box is labeled . . . *safe and strong enough even for prolonged anal intercourse . . .*

"There's granuloma inguinale," my father says to my mother, "and bacterial vaginosis." He opens one hand and counts the fingers, then counts them again, then says, "There's molluscum contagiosum."

Some of the condoms are white. Some are assorted colors. Some are ribbed to feel like serrated bread knives, I guess. Some are extra large. Some glow in the dark. This is flattering in a creepy way. My folks must think I'm wildly popular.

Perry Como is singing "O Come, O Come, Emmanuel."

"We don't want to scare you," my mom says, "but you're young. We can't expect you to just sit home nights."

"And if you ever can't sleep," my father says, "it could be pinworms."

My mom says, "We just don't want you to end up like your brother is all."

My brother's dead, but he still has a stocking full of presents and you can bet they're not rubbers. He's dead, but you can bet he's laughing his head off right now.

"With pinworms," my father says, "the females migrate down the colon to the perianal area to lay their eggs at night." He says, "If you suspect worm activity, it works best to press clear adhesive tape against the rectum, then look at the tape under a magnifying glass. The worms should be about a quarter-inch long."

My mom says, "Bob, hush."

My dad leans toward me and says, "Ten percent of the men in this country can give you these worms." He says, "You just remember that."

Almost everything in my stocking is condoms, in boxes, in little gold foil coins, in long strips of a hundred with perforations so you can tear them apart. My only other gifts are a rape whistle and a pocket-sized spray canister of Mace. That looks like I'm set for the worst, but I'm afraid to ask if there's more. There could be a vibrator to keep me at home and celibate every night. There could be dental dams in case of cunnilingus. Saran Wrap. Rubber gloves.

Perry Como is singing "Nuttin' for Christmas."

I look at Shane's stocking still lumpy with presents and ask, "You guys bought for Shane?"

If it's condoms, they're a little late.

My mom and dad look at each other. To my mom, my dad says, "You tell her."

"That's what *you* got for your brother," my mom says. "Go ahead and look."

Jump to me being confused as hell.

Give me clarity. Give me reasons. Give me answers.

Flash.

I reach up to unhook Shane's stocking from the mantel, and inside it's filled with crumpled tissue paper.

"Keep digging," my dad says.

In with the tissue, there's a sealed envelope.

"Open it," my mom says.

Inside the envelope is a printed letter with right at the top the words *Thank You*.

"It's really a gift to both our children," my dad says.

I can't believe what I'm reading.

"Instead of buying you a big present," my mom says, "we made a donation in your name to the World AIDS Research Fund."

Inside the stocking is a second letter I take out.

"That," my dad says, "is Shane's present to you."

Oh, this is too much.

Perry Como is singing "I Saw Mommy Kissing Santa Claus."

I say, "That crafty old dead brother of mine, he's so thoughtful." I say, "He shouldn't have. He really, really shouldn't have gone to all this trouble. He needs to maybe move away from denial and coping and just get on with being dead. Maybe reincarnate." I say, "His pretending he's still alive can't be healthy."

Inside, I'm ranting. What I really wanted this year was a new Prada handbag. It wasn't my fault that some hairspray can exploded in Shane's face. Boom, and he came staggering into the house with his forehead already turning black and blue. The long drive to the hospital with his one eye swoll shut and the face around it just getting bigger and bigger with every vein inside broken and bleeding under the skin, Shane didn't say a word.

It wasn't my fault how the social service people at the hospital took one look at Shane's face and came down on my father with both feet. Suspicion of child abuse. Criminal neglect. Family intervention. It wasn't any of it my fault. Police statements. A caseworker went around interviewing our neighbors, our school friends, our teachers, until everybody we knew treated me like, *You poor brave thing.*

Sitting here Christmas morning with all these gifts I need a penis to enjoy, everybody doesn't know the half of it.

Even after the police investigation was done, and nothing was proved, even then, our family was wrecked. And *everybody still thinks I'm the one who threw away the hairspray.* And since I started this, it was all my fault. The explosion. The police. Shane's running away. His death.

And it wasn't my fault.

"Really," I say, "if Shane really wanted to give me a present, he'd come back from the dead and buy me the new wardrobe he owes me. That would give me a merry Christmas. That I could really say 'thank you' for."

Silence.

As I fish out the second envelope, my mom says, "We're officially 'outing' you."

"In your brother's name," my dad says, "we bought you a membership in PFLAG.

"Pee-flag?" I say.

"Parents and Friends of Lesbians and Gays," my mom says.

Perry Como is singing "There's No Place Like Home for the Holidays."

Silence.

My mother starts up from her chair and says, "I'll go run get those bananas." She says, "Just to be on the safe side, your father and I can't wait to see you try on some of your presents."

Now, Please, Jump to Chapter Thirty-four

Chapter 8

Jump way back to the last time I ever went home to see my parents. It was my last birthday before the accident. What with Shane *still* being dead, I wasn't expecting presents. I'm not expecting a cake. This last time, I go home just to see them, my folks. This is when I still have a mouth, so I'm not so stymied by the idea of blowing out candles.

The house, the brown living room sofa and reclining chairs, everything is the same except my father's put big X's of duct tape across the inside of all the windows. Mom's car isn't in the driveway where they usually park it. The car's locked in the garage. There's a big deadbolt I don't remember being on the front door. On the front gate is a big "Beware of Dog" sign and a smaller sign for a home security system.

When I first get home, Mom waves me inside fast and says,

"Stay back from the windows, Bump. Hate crimes are up sixty-seven percent this year over last year."

She says, "After it gets dark at night, try and not let your shadow fall across the blinds so it can be seen from outside."

She cooks dinner by flashlight. When I open the oven or the fridge, she panics fast, body blocking me to one side and closing whatever I open.

"It's the bright light inside," she says. "Anti-gay violence is up over one hundred percent in the last five years."

My father comes home and parks his car a half block away. His keys rattle against the outside of the new deadbolt while Mom stands frozen in the kitchen doorway, holding me back. The keys stop, and my father knocks, three fast knocks, then two slow ones.

"That's his knock," Mom says, "but look through the peephole, anyway."

My father comes in, looking back over his shoulder to the dark street, watching. A car passes, and he says, "Romeo Tango Foxtrot six seven four. Quick, write it down."

My mother writes this on the pad by the phone. "Make?" she says. "Model?"

"Mercury, blue," my father says. "Sable."

Mom says, "It's on the record."

I say maybe they're overreacting some.

And my father says, "Don't marginalize our oppression."

Jump to what a big mistake this was, coming home. Jump to how Shane should see this, how weird our folks are being. My father turns off the lamp I turned on in the living room. The drapes on the picture window are shut and pinned together in the middle. They know all the furniture in the dark, but me, I stumble against every chair and end table. I knock a candy dish to the floor, smash, and my mother screams and drops to the kitchen linoleum.

My father comes up from where he's crouched behind the sofa and says, "You'll have to cut your mother some slack. We're expecting to get hate-crimed any day soon."

From the kitchen, Mom yells, "Was it a rock? Is anything on fire?"

And my father yells, "Don't press the panic button, Leslie. The next false alarm, and we have to start paying for them."

Now I know why they put a headlight on some kinds of vacuum cleaners. First, I'm picking up broken glass in the pitch-dark. Then I'm asking my father for bandages. I just stand in one place, keeping my cut hand raised above my heart, and wait. My father comes out of the dark with alcohol and bandages.

"This is a war we're fighting," he says, "all of us in pee-flag."

PFLAG. Parents and Friends of Lesbians and Gays. I know. I know. I know. Thank you, Shane.

I say, "You shouldn't even be in PFLAG. Your gay son is dead, so he doesn't count anymore." This sounds pretty hurtful, but I'm bleeding here. I say, "Sorry."

The bandages are tight and the alcohol stings in the dark, and my father says, "The Wilsons put a PFLAG sign in their yard. Two nights later, someone drove right through their lawn, ruined everything."

My folks don't have any PFLAG signs.

"We took ours down," my father says. "Your mother has a PFLAG bumper sticker, so we keep her car in the garage. Us taking pride in your brother has put us right on the front lines."

Out of the dark, my mother says, "Don't forget the Bradfords. They got a burning bag of dog feces on their front porch. It could've burned their whole house down with them sleeping in bed, all because they hung a rainbow PFLAG wind sock in their backyard." Mom says, "Not even their front yard, in their *back*yard."

"Hate," my father says, "is all around us, Bump. Do you know that?"

My mom says, "Come on, troops. It's chow time."

Dinner is some casserole from the PFLAG cookbook. It's good, but God only knows what it looks like. Twice, I knock over my glass in the dark. I sprinkle salt in my lap. Anytime I say a word, my folks shush me. My mom says, "Did you hear something? Did that come from outside?"

In a whisper, I ask if they remember what tomorrow is. Just to see if they remember, what with all the tension. It's not as if I'm expecting a cake with candles and a present.

"Tomorrow," my dad says. "Of course we know. That's why we're nervous as cats."

"We wanted to talk to you about tomorrow," my mom says. "We know how upset you are about your brother still, and we think it would be good for you if you'd march with our group in the parade."

Jump to another weird sick disappointment just coming over the horizon.

Jump to me getting swept up in their big compensation, their big penance for, all those years ago, my father yelling, "We don't know what kind of filthy diseases you're bringing into this house, mister, but you can just find another place to sleep tonight."

They called this tough love.

This is the same dinner table where Mom told Shane, "Dr. Peterson's office called today." To me she said, "You can go to your room and read, young lady."

I could've gone to the moon and still heard all the yelling.

Shane and my folks were in the dining room, me, I was behind my bedroom door. My clothes, most of my school clothes were outside on the clothesline. Inside, my father said, "It's not strep throat you've got, mister, and we'd like to know where you've been and what you've been up to."

"Drugs," my mom said, "we could deal with."

Shane never said a word. His face still shiny and creased with scars.

"Teenage pregnancy," my mom said, "we could deal with."

Not one word.

"Dr. Peterson," she said. "He said there's just about only one way you could get the disease the way you have it, but I told him, no, not our child, not you, Shane."

My father said, "We called Coach Ludlow, and he said you dropped basketball two months ago."

"You'll need to go down to the county health department tomorrow," my mom said.

"Tonight," my father said, "we want you out of here."

Our father.

These same people being so good and kind and caring and involved, these same people finding identity and personal fulfillment in the fight on the front lines for equality and personal dignity and equal rights for their dead son, these are the same people I hear yelling through my bedroom door.

"We don't know what kind of filthy diseases you're bringing into this house, mister, but you can just find another place to sleep tonight."

I remember I wanted to go out and get my clothes, iron them, fold them, and put them away.

Give me any sense of control.

Flash.

I remember how the front door just opened and shut, it didn't slam. With the light on in my room, all I could see was myself reflected in my bedroom window. When I turned out the light, there was Shane, standing just outside the window, looking in at me, his face all monster-movie hacked and distorted, dark and hard from the hairspray blowup.

Give me terror.

Flash.

He didn't ever smoke that I knew about, but he lit a match and put it to a cigarette in his mouth. He knocked on the window.

He said, "Hey, let me in."

Give me denial.

He said, "Hey, it's cold."

Give me ignorance.

I turned on the bedroom light so I could only see myself in the window. Then I shut the curtains. I never saw Shane again.

Tonight, with the lights off, with the curtains shut and the front door locked, with Shane gone except for the ghost of him, I ask, "What parade?"

My mom says, "It's the Gay Pride Parade."

My dad says, "We're marching with PFLAG."

And they'd like me to march with them. They'd like me to sit here in the dark and pretend it's the outside world we're hiding from. It's some hateful stranger that's going to come get us in the night. It's some alien fatal sex disease. They'd like to think it's some bigoted homophobe they're terrified of. It's not any of it their fault. They'd like me to think I have something to make up for.

I did not throw away that can of hairspray. All I did was turn out the bedroom lights. Then there were the fire engines coming in the distance. There was orange flashing across the outside of my curtains, and when I got out of bed to look, there were my school clothes on fire. Hanging dry on the clothesline and layered with air. Dresses and jumpers and pants and blouses, all of them blazing and coming apart in the breeze. In a few seconds, everything I loved, gone.

Flash.

Jump ahead a few years to me being grown up and moving out. Give me a new start.

Jump to one night, somebody calling from a pay phone to ask

my folks, were they the parents of Shane McFarland? My parents saying, *maybe*. The caller won't say where, but he says Shane is dead.

A voice behind the caller saying, *Tell them the rest.*

Another voice behind the caller saying, Tell them Miss Shane hated their hateful guts and her last words were: *This isn't over yet, not by a long shot*. Then somebody laughing.

Jump to us alone here in the dark with a casserole.

My father says, "So, honey, will you march with your mother and me?"

My mom says, "It would mean so much for gay rights."

Give me courage.

Flash.

Give me tolerance.

Flash.

Give me wisdom.

Flash.

Jump to the truth. And I say:

"No."

Now, Please, Jump to Chapter Thirty-three

Chapter 9

Where you're supposed to be is Spitefield Park, a hundred acres on the edge of town. If it were an oil well, you'd call Spitefield a gusher. It's a hundred acres of nowhere that Daisy turned into a gold mine. It's world-famous, in a quiet sort of way. The place makes money hand over fist, and more or less takes care of itself. Spitefield is a cemetery. A boneyard. What gives it a leg up on its competitors is Lady Daisy's liberal epitaph policy. Other cemeteries, bone orchards, what have you, they're run by proper world religions, obsessed with decorum. Daisy's competition wasn't ever going to let you carve on your tombstone the words:

So I'm dead.
It beats working retail at Christmas

At Spitefield Park, you can carve whatever sentiments you want. Mostly people buy graves there for their loved ones—using that term strictly as a euphemism. They pay huge sums for extra-large grave markers, granite billboards, really, that say things like:

I was a shitty husband and father.
I couldn't die fast enough

Guilt and sadness sell a lot of big-ticket caskets. Mausoleums. Solid mahogany and burnished-brass handles and great, huge wreathes of carnations. But anger . . . revenge . . . that's where the big spenders flock. The mourners, when they go to plant Grandma under a headstone that says:

Cunt

. . . they don't care if you mow the grass and maintain the lovely landscaping. Daisy made her original fortune from this type of payback. These survivors don't care if homeless people camp on the grave or off-leash dogs defecate there. Rambunctious teenagers go marauding on Halloween, pushing over a few tombstones, and nobody will raise a fuss. People who inter their dead at Spitefield Park, they never come back for a second look. They never bring flowers or miniature decorated trees on Christmas or bunches of helium balloons to bob and flutter their flashy Mylar in celebration of a dead person's birthday. Oh, but the tourists come. The you-gotta-see-this local hipsters bring their snarky tourist friends for a laugh. For an I-can't-believe-somebody-did-this tour. Art students snap the kind of ironic pictures you'd expect. No bereaved survivors check for correct spelling or dates. Sometimes they pay extra—sometimes a lot extra, that's where the pure profit is: the add-on expenses—to get names misspelled. Letters transposed. Freudian slips chiseled into marble.

She sleeps with the angles

With no overhead, the profit margin is stupendous. With such an income stream Daisy St. Patience need do nothing except count her money, and it's this cash flow from Spitefield Park that gives her some elbow room. Daisy can take her own sweet time to assemble a top-notch stable. Daisy St. Patience: Loving Do-Gooder. Empathetic Hand-Holder.

It was Daisy who went to the Blue Girls everyone had forgotten about. Candy-Striper Daisy volunteered to bring cheer to those living nightmares consigned by next-of-kin to state hospitals, to locked wards, to watching television with their runny eyes for a lifetime on account of having a lumpy head the size of a microwave oven carved from gouda cheese. The Elephant *Women*. Those twisted, shambling gals with faces like torched Halloween masks. Their smiles like lumpy, red, knobby pomegranates turned inside out. The Born-That-Way girls. The In-a-Terrible-Accident girls, and the There-But-for-the-Grace-of-God girls. Like no one you'd want to meet in a dark alley late at night. Those horror movie ladies with heartbreaking names like "Fern" and "Penny," Daisy sought them out and mentored them. These young cripples who crawled toward her on legs like boneless tentacles, and looked at her with their blue eyes set in faces like blood-red cauliflower, for them Lady Daisy lifted the hem of her own veil like a stage curtain. This is what Daisy St. Patience did after the end of the end of the last chapter. She did not don a veil and become a belly dancer. Nor did she take up playing ice hockey as a lifetime excuse to wear a goalie mask. Lady Daisy went to these wretched young ladies. Girls who, from their faces, you'd scarcely guess were still human. Daisy St. Patience reached out to gently, warmly, passionately grasp hold of their hands or claws or flippers, and she said, "I'd like to propose a partnership . . ."

Of these evolutionary dead ends, these mistakes of Mother Nature, Lady Daisy asked, "How would you like to see the world?" Adding, "And vice versa."

Now, Please, Jump to Chapter Eighteen

Chapter 10

Jump way back to a fashion shoot at this junkyard full of dirty wrecked cars where Evie and me have to climb around on the wrecks wearing Hermaun Mancing thong swimwear so narrow you have to wear a "pussy strip" of surgical tape underneath, and Evie starts in with, "About your mutilated brother . . . ?"

It's not my favorite photographer or art director, either.

And I'm going back to Evie, "Yeah?" Busy sticking out my butt.

And the photographer goes, "Evie? *That's not pouting!*"

The uglier the fashions, the worse places we'd have to pose to make them look good. Junkyards. Slaughterhouses. Sewage treatment plants. It's the ugly bridesmaid tactic where you only look good by comparison. One shoot for Industry JeansWear, I was sure we'd have to pose kissing dead bodies.

These junked cars all have rusted holes through them, serrated edges, and I'm *this close* to naked and trying to remember when was my last tetanus shot. The photographer lowers his camera and says, "I'm only wasting film until you girls decide to pull in your stomachs."

More and more, being beautiful took so much effort. Just the razor bumps would make you want to cry. The bikini waxes. Evie came out of her collagen lip injection saying she no longer had any fear of hell. The next worse thing is Manus yanking off your pussy strip if you're not close-shaved.

About hell, I told Evie, "We're shooting there tomorrow."

So, now the art director says, "Evie, could you climb up a couple cars higher on the pile?" And this is wearing high heels, but Evie goes up. Little diamonds of safety glass are scattered on everywhere you might fall.

Through her big cheesy smile, Evie says, "How exactly did your brother get mutilated?" You can only hold a real smile for so long, after that it's just teeth.

The art director steps up with his little foam applicator and retouches where the bronzer is streaked on my butt cheeks.

"It was a hairspray can somebody threw away in our family's burn barrel," I say. "He was burning the trash and it exploded."

And Evie says, "Somebody?"

And I say, "You'd think it was my mom, the way she screamed and tried to stop him bleeding."

And the photographer says, "Girls, can you go up on your toes just a little?"

Evie goes, "A big thirty-two-ounce can of HairShell hairspray? I bet it peeled half his face off."

We both go up on our toes.

I go, "It wasn't so bad."

"Wait a sec," the art director says, "I need your feet to be not so close together." Then he says, "Wider." Then, "A little wider, please." Then he hands up big chrome tools for us to hold.

Mine must weigh fifteen pounds.

"It's a ball-peen hammer," Evie says, "and you're holding it wrong."

"Honey," the photographer says to Evie, "could you hold the chain saw a bit closer to your mouth, please?"

The sun is warm on the metal of the cars, their tops crushed under the weight of being piled on top of each other. These are cars with buckled front ends you know nobody walked away from. Cars with T-boned sides where whole familes died together. Rear-ended cars with the backseats pushed up tight against the dashboard. Cars from before seat belts. Cars from before air bags. Before the Jaws of Life. Before paramedics. These are cars peeled open around their exploded gas tanks.

"This is so rich," Evie says, "how this is the place I've worked my whole life to get."

The art director says to go ahead and push our breasts against the cars.

"The whole time, growing up," Evie says, "I just thought being a woman would be . . . not such a disappointment."

All I ever wanted was to be an only child.

The photographer says, "Perfecto."

Now, Please, Jump to Chapter Thirty-two

Chapter 11

Half my life I spend hiding in the bathrooms of the rich.

Jump back to Seattle, to the time Brandy and Seth and I are on the road hunting drugs. Jump to the day after the night we went to the Space Needle, where right now Brandy is laid out flat on a master bathroom floor. First I helped her off with her suit jacket and unbuttoned the back of her blouse, and now I'm sitting on a toilet overdosing Valiums as steady as Chinese water torture into her Plumbago mouth. The thing about Valiums, the Brandy girl says, is they don't kill the pain but at least you're not pissed off about being hurt.

"Hit me," Brandy says and makes a fish lips.

The thing about Brandy is she's got such a tolerance for drugs it takes forever to kill her. That, and she's so big, most of her being muscle, it would take bottles and bottles of anything.

I drop a Valium. A little baby-blue Valium, another powder-blue Valium, Tiffany's light blue, like a gift from Tiffany's, the Valium falls end over end into Brandy's interior.

This suit I help Brandy out of, it's a Pierre Cardin Space-Age style of just bold white, the straight tube skirt being fresh and sterile to just above her knees, the jacket being timeless and clinical in its simple cut and three-quarter sleeves. Her blouse underneath is sleeveless. Her shoes are box-toe white vinyl boots. It's an outfit you'd accessorize with a Geiger counter instead of a purse.

At the Bon Marché, when she catwalks out of the fitting room, all I can do is applaud. There's going to be postpartum depression next week when she goes to take this one back.

Jump to breakfast, this morning when Brandy and Seth were flush with drug money, we were eating room service and Seth says Brandy could time-travel to Las Vegas on another planet in the 1950s and fit right in. The planet Krylon, he says, where synthetic bendable glam-bots would lipo-suck your fat and makeover you.

And Brandy says, "What fat?"

And Seth says, "I love how you could just be visiting from the distant future via the 1960s."

And I put more Premarin in Seth's next coffee refill. More Darvon in Brandy's champagne.

Jump back to us in the bathroom, Brandy and me.

"Hit me," Brandy says.

Her lips look all loose and stretched out, and I drop another gift from Tiffany's.

This bathroom we're hiding in, it goes way the other side of decorative touches. The whole deal is an undersea grotto. Even the princess phone is aqua, but when you look out the big brass porthole windows, you see Seattle from the top of Capitol Hill.

The toilet I'm sitting on, just sitting, the lid's closed under my ass *thank you*, but the toilet's a big ceramic snail shell bolted to the wall. The sink is a big ceramic half a clam bolted to the wall.

Brandy-land, sexual playground to the stars, she says, "Hit me."

Jump to when we got here and the realtor was just a big tooth. One of those football scholarships where the eyebrows grow together in the middle and they forget to get a degree in anything.

As if I can talk, me with sixteen hundred credits.

Here's this million-dollar-club realtor who got thrown his job by a grateful alumnus who just wanted a son-in-law who could stay awake through six or seven holiday bowl games. But maybe I'm being a touch judgmental.

Brandy was beside herself for feminine wetness. Here's this extra-Y-chromosome guy in a double-breasted blue serge suit, a guy whose paws make even Brandy's big hands look little.

"Mr. Parker," Brandy says, her hand hidden inside his big paw.

You can see the Henry Mancini soundtrack of love in her eyes. "We spoke this morning."

We're in the drawing room of a house on Capitol Hill. This is another rich house where everything is exactly what it looks like. The elaborate Tudor roses carved in the ceilings are plaster, not pressed tin, not fiberglass. The torsos of battered Greek nudes are marble, not marbleized plaster. The boxes in the breakfront are not enameled *in the manner of Fabergé*. The boxes are Fabergé pillboxes, and there are eleven of them. The lace under the boxes was not tatted by a machine.

Not just the spines, but the entire front and back covers of all the books on all the shelves in the library are bound in leather, and the pages are cut. You don't have to pull a single book to know this.

The realtor, Mr. Parker, his legs are still flat on the sides of his ass. In the front, there's just enough more in one pant leg to spell boxers instead of briefs.

Brandy nods my way. "This is Miss Arden Scotia, of the Denver River Logging and Paper Scotias." Another victim of the Brandy Alexander Witness Reincarnation Project.

Parker's big hand swallows my little hand, big fish and little fish, whole.

Parker's starched white shirt makes you think of eating off a clean tablecloth, so flat and stuck out you could serve drinks off the shelf of his barrel chest.

"This"—Brandy nods toward Seth—"is Miss Scotia's half-brother, Ellis Island."

Parker's big fish eats Ellis's little fish.

Brandy says, "Miss Scotia and I would like to tour the house ourselves. Ellis is mentally and emotionally disturbed."

Ellis smiles.

"We had hoped you would watch him," Brandy says.

"It's a go," Parker says. He says, "Sure thing."

Ellis smiles and tugs with two fingers at the sleeve of Brandy's suit jacket. Ellis says, "Don't leave me too long, miss. If I don't get enough of my pills, I'll have one of my fits."

"Fits?" says Parker.

Ellis says, "Sometimes, Miss Alexander, she forgets I'm waiting, and she doesn't get me any medication."

"You have fits?" Parker says.

"This is news to me," Brandy says and smiles. "You will not have a fit," Brandy tells my new half-brother. "Ellis, I forbid you to have a fit."

Jump to us camped out in the undersea grotto.

"Hit me."

The floor under Brandy's back, it's cold tile shaped like fish and laid out so they fit together, one fish tail between the heads of two fish, the way some sardines are canned, all the way across the bathroom floor.

I drop a Valium between Plumbago lips.

"Did I ever tell you how my family threw me out?" says Brandy after her little blue swallow. "My original family, I mean. My birth family. Did I ever tell you that messy little story?"

I put my head between my knees and look straight down at the queen supreme with her head between my feet.

"My throat was hurting for a couple of days, so I got out of school and everything," Brandy says. She says, "Miss Arden? Hello?"

I look down at her. It's so easy to imagine her dead.

"Miss Arden, please," she says. "Hit me?"

I drop another Valium.

Brandy swallows. "It was like I couldn't swallow for days," she says. "My throat was that sore. I could barely talk. My folks, they thought, of course, it was strep throat."

Brandy's head is almost straight under mine as I look down. Only Brandy's face is upside down. My eyes look right into the dark interior of her Plumbago mouth, dark wet going inside to her works and organs and everything behind the scenes. Brandy Alexander Backstage. Upside down she could be a complete stranger.

And Ellis was right, you only ask people about themselves so you can tell them about yourself.

"The culture," Brandy says. "The swab they did for strep throat came back positive for the clap. You know, the third Rhea sister. Gonorrhea," she says. "That little tiny gonococcus bug. I was sixteen years old and had the clap. My folks did not deal with it well."

No. No, they didn't.

"They freaked," Brandy says.

They threw him out of the house.

"They yelled about how diseased I was being," Brandy says.

Then they threw him out.

"By 'diseased' I think they meant 'gay,'" she says.

Then they threw him out.

"Miss Scotia?" she says. "Hit me."

So I hit her.

"Then they threw me out of the damn house."

Jump to Mr. Parker outside the bathroom door saying, "Miss Alexander? It's me, Miss Alexander. Miss Scotia, are you in there?"

Brandy starts to sit up and props herself on one elbow.

"It's Ellis," Mr. Parker says through the door. "I think you should come downstairs. Miss Scotia, your brother's having a seizure or something."

Drugs and cosmetics are spread out all over the aquamarine countertops, and Brandy's sprawled half naked on the floor in a sprinkling of pills and capsules and tablets.

"He's her half-brother," Brandy calls back.

The doorknob rattles. "You have to help me," Parker says.

"Stop right there, Mr. Parker!" Brandy shouts and the doorknob stops turning. "Calm yourself. Do not come in here," Brandy says. "What you need to do . . ." Brandy looks at me while she says this. "What you need to do is pin Ellis to the floor so he doesn't hurt himself. I'll be down in a moment."

Brandy looks at me and smiles her Plumbago lips into a big bow. "Parker?" she says. "Are you listening?"

"Please, hurry," comes through the door.

"After you have Ellis pinned to the floor," Brandy says, "wedge his mouth open with something. Do you have a wallet?"

There's a moment.

"It's eel skin, Miss Alexander."

"Then you must be very proud of it," says Brandy. "You're going to have to jam it between his teeth to keep his mouth open. Sit on him if you have to." Brandy, she's just smiling evil incarnate at my feet.

The shatter of some real lead crystal comes through the door from downstairs.

"Hurry!" Parker shouts. "He's breaking things!"

Brandy licks her lips. "After you have his mouth pried open, Parker, reach in and grab his tongue. If you don't, he'll choke, and then you'll be sitting on a dead body."

Silence.

"Do you hear me?" Brandy says.

"Grab his tongue?"

Something else real and expensive and far away shatters.

"Mr. Parker, honey, I hope you're bonded," the Princess Alexander says, her face all bloated red with choking back laughter. "Yes," she says, "grab Ellis's tongue. Pin him to the floor, keep his mouth open, and pull his tongue out as far as you can until I come down to help you."

The doorknob turns.

My veils are all on the vanity counter out of my reach.

The door opens far enough to hit the high-heeled foot of Brandy, sprawled giggling and half full of Valiums, there half naked in drugs on the floor. This is far enough for me to see Parker's face with its one grown-together eyebrow, and far enough for the face to see me sitting on the toilet.

Brandy screams, "I am attending to Miss Arden Scotia!"

Given the choice between grabbing a strange tongue and watching a monster poop into a giant snail shell, the face retreats and slams the door behind it.

Football scholarship footsteps charge off down the hallway.

Then pound down the stairs.

The big tooth that Parker is, his footsteps pound across the foyer to the living room.

Ellis's scream, real and sudden and far away, comes through the floor from downstairs. And, suddenly, stops.

"Now," says Brandy, "where were we?"

She lies back down with her head between my feet.

"Have you thought any more about plastic surgery?" Brandy says. Then she says, "Hit me."

Now, Please, Jump to Chapter Thirty-one

Chapter 12

bout plastic surgery, I spent a whole summer as property of La Paloma Memorial Hospital looking into what plastic surgery could do for me.

There were plastic surgeons, a lot of them, and there were the books the surgeons brought. With pictures. The pictures I saw were black-and-white, thank You, God, and the surgeons told me how after years of pain I might look.

Almost all plastic surgery starts with something called *pedicles.* Recipe to follow.

This will get gruesome. Even here in black-and-white.

For all I learned, I could be a doctor.

Sorry, Mom. Sorry, God.

Manus once said that your folks are God. You love them and want to make them happy, but you still want to make up your own rules.

The surgeons said, you can't just cut off a lump of skin one place and bandage it on another. You're not grafting a tree. The blood supply, the veins and capillaries, just wouldn't be hooked up to keep the graft alive. The lump would just die and fall off.

It's scary, but now when I see somebody blush, my reaction isn't: Oh, how cute. A blush only reminds me how blood is just under the surface of everything.

Doing dermabrasion, this one plastic surgeon told me, is about the same as pressing a ripe tomato against a belt sander. What you're paying for most is the mess.

To relocate a piece of skin, to rebuild a jaw, you have to flay a long strip of skin from your neck. Cut up from the base of your neck, but don't sever the skin at the top.

Picture a sort of banner or strip of skin hanging down loose along your neck but still attached to the bottom of your face. The skin is still attached to you, so it still gets blood. This strip of skin is still alive. Take the strip of skin and roll it into a tube or column. Leave it rolled until it heals into a long, dangling lump of flesh, hanging from the bottom of your face. Living tissue. Full of fresh, healthy blood, flapping and dangling warm against your neck. This is a pedicle.

Just the healing part, that can take months.

Jump backward to the red Fiat with Brandy behind her sunglasses and Manus locked in the trunk, and Brandy drives us to the top of Rocky Butte, the hilltop ruins of some lookout fort where if this weren't a school night kids from Parkrose and Grant and Madison high schools would be breaking beer bottles and enjoying unsafe sex up here in the old ruins.

Friday nights, this hilltop would be full of kids saying: *Look, over there, you can see my house. That blue light in the window, that's my folks watching TV.*

The ruins are just a few layers of stone blocks still on top of each other. Inside the ruins, the ground is flat and rocky, covered with broken glass and coarse orchard grass. Around us, in all directions except the road coming up, the sides of Rocky Butte are cliffs rising from the dot-to-dot streetlight grid.

You could choke on the silence.

What we need is a place to stay. Until I figure out what's next. Until we can come up with some money. We have two, maybe three days until Evie gets home and we have to be gone. Then I figure I'll just call Evie and blackmail her.

Evie owes me big.

I can get away with this.

Brandy races the Fiat into the darkest part of the ruins, then she kills the headlights and hits the brakes. Brandy and me, we stop so fast only our seat belts keep us off the dashboard.

Clatter and tintinnabulation of ringing metal against metal chimes and gongs in the car around us.

"Sorry, I guess," Brandy says. "There's shit on the floor, got under the brake pedal when I tried to stop."

Music bright as silver rolls out from under our car seats. Napkin rings and silver teaspoons rush forward against our feet. Brandy's got candlesticks between her feet. A silver platter bright with starlight is slid half out from under the front of Brandy's seat, looking up between her long legs.

Brandy looks at me. Her chin tucked down, Brandy lowers her Ray-Bans to the end of her nose and arches her penciled eyebrows.

I shrug. I get out to liberate my love cargo.

Even with the trunk open, Manus doesn't move. His knees are against his elbows, his hands clasped in his face, his feet tucked back under his butt; Manus could be a fetus in army fatigues. All around him, I hadn't noticed. I've been under a lot of stress tonight, so forgive me if I didn't notice back at Evie's house, but all around Manus flash pieces of silverware. Pirate treasure in the trunk of his Fiat, and other things.

Relics.

A long white candle, there's a candle.

Brandy slams out of her seat and comes to look, too.

"Oh, my shit," Brandy says and rolls her eyes. "*Oh, my shit.*"

There's an ashtray, no, it's a plaster cast of a little hand, right next to Manus's unconscious butt. It's the kind of cast you make in grade school when you press your hand into a pie tin of wet plaster for a Mother's Day gift.

Brandy brushes a little hair off Manus's forehead. "He's really, really cute," she says, "but I think this one's going to be brain-damaged."

It's way too much trouble to explain tonight to Brandy in writing, but Manus getting brain-damaged would be redundant.

Too bad it's just the Valiums.

Brandy takes off her Ray-Bans for a better look. She takes off her Hermès scarf and shakes her hair out full, looking good, biting her lips, wetting her lips with her tongue just in case Manus wakes up. "With cute guys," Brandy says, "it's usually better to give them barbiturates."

Guess I'll remember that.

I haul Manus up until he's sitting in the trunk with his legs hanging out over the bumper. Manus's eyes, power blue, flicker, blink, flicker, squint.

Brandy leans in to give him a good look. My brother out to steal my fiancé. At this point, I just want everybody dead.

"Wake up, honey," Brandy says with a hand cupped under Manus's chin.

And Manus squints. "Mommy?"

"Wake up, honey," Brandy says. "It's okay."

"Now?" Manus says.

"It's okay."

There's a little rushing sound, the sound of rain on the roof of a tent or a closed convertible.

"Oh, God." Brandy steps back. "Oh, sweet Christ!"

Manus blinks and peers at Brandy, then at his lap. One leg of his army fatigues goes darker, darker, darker to the knee.

"Cute," Brandy says, "but he's just peed his pants."

Jump back to plastic surgery. Jump to the happy day you're healed. You've had this long strip of skin hanging off your neck for a couple months, only it's not just one strip. There are probably more like a half dozen pedicles because you might as well do a lot at once so the plastic surgeon has more tissue to work with.

For reconstruction, you'll have these long dangling strips of skin hanging off the bottom of your face for about two months.

They say that what people notice first about you is your eyes. You'll give up that hope. You look like some meat by-product ground up and pooped out by the Num Num Snack Factory.

A mummy coming apart in the rain.

A broken piñata.

These strips of warm skin flapping around your neck are good, blood-fed, living tissue. The surgeon lifts each strip and attaches the healed end to your face. This way, the bulk of the tissue is transferred, grafted to your face without ever stopping its blood supply. They pull all this loose skin up and bunch it into the rough shape of a jaw. Your neck is the scars of where the skin used to lay. Your jaw is this mass of grafted tissue the surgeons hope will grow together and stay in place.

For another month, you and the surgeons hope. Another month, you hide in the hospital and wait.

Jump to Manus sitting in his piss and silver in the trunk of his red sports car. Potty-training flashback. It happens.

Me, I'm crouched in front of him, looking for the bulge of his wallet.

Manus just stares at Brandy. Probably thinking Brandy's me, the old me with a face.

Brandy's lost interest. "He doesn't remember. He thinks I'm his mother," Brandy says. "Sister, maybe, but mother?"

So déjà vu. Try brother.

We need a place to stay, and Manus must have a new place. Not the old place he and I shared. He lets us hide at his place, or I tell the cops he kidnapped me and burned down Evie's house. Manus won't know about Mr. Baxter and the Rhea sisters seeing me with a gun all over town.

With my finger, I write in the dirt:

we need to find his wallet.

"His pants," Brandy says, "are wet."

Now Manus peers at me, sits up, and scrapes his head on the open trunk lid. Man, oh, man, you know this hurts, still it isn't anything tragic until Brandy Alexander chimes in with her over-reaction. "Oh, you poor thing," she says.

Then Manus boo-hoos. Manus Kelley, the last person who has any right to, is crying.

I hate this.

Jump to the day the skin grafts take, and even then the tissue will need some support. Even if the grafts heal to where they look like a crude, lumpy jaw, you'll still need a jawbone. Without a mandible, the soft mass of tissue, living and viable as it is, might just reabsorb.

That's the word the plastic surgeons used.

Reabsorb.

Into my face, as if I'm just a sponge made of skin.

Jump to Manus crying and Brandy bent over him, cooing and petting his sexy hair.

In the trunk, there's a pair of bronze baby shoes, a silver chafing dish, a turkey picture made of macaroni glued to construction paper.

"You know"—Manus sniffs and wipes the back of his hand under his nose—"I'm high right now, so it's okay if I tell you this." Manus looks at Brandy bent over him and me crouched in the dirt. "First," Manus says, "your parents, they give you your life, but then they try to give you their life."

To make you a jawbone, the surgeons will break off parts of your shinbones, complete with the attached artery. First they expose the bone and sculpt it right there on your leg.

Another way is the surgeons will break several other bones, probably long bones in your legs and arms. Inside these bones is the soft cancellous bone pulp.

That was the surgeons' word and the word from the books.

Cancellous.

"My mom," Manus says, "and her new husband—my mom gets married a lot—they just bought this resort condo in Bowling River in Florida. People younger than sixty can't buy property there. That's a law they have."

I'm looking at Brandy, who's still the overreactive mother, kneeling down, brushing the hair off Manus's forehead. I'm looking over the cliff edge next to us. Those little blue lights in all the houses, that's people watching television. Tiffany's light blue. Valium blue. People in captivity.

First my best friend and now my brother is trying to steal my fiancé.

"I went to visit them at Christmas, last year," Manus says. "My mom, their condo is right on the eighth green, and they love it. It's like the whole age standard in Bowling River is fucked. My mom and stepdad are just turned sixty, so they're just youngsters. Me, all these oldsters are scoping me out like an odds-on car burglary."

Brandy licks her lips.

"According to the Bowling River age standard," Manus says, "I haven't been born yet."

You have to break out large enough slivers of this soft, bloody bone pulp. The cancellous stuff. Then you have to insert these shards and slivers of bone into the soft mass of tissue you've grafted onto your face.

Really, you don't do this, the surgeons do it all while you're asleep.

If the slivers are close enough together, they'll form fibroblast cells to bond with each other. Again, a word from the books.

Fibroblast.

Again, this takes months.

"My mom and her husband," Manus says, sitting in the open trunk of his Fiat Spider on top of Rocky Butte, "for Christmas, their biggest present to me is this box all wrapped up. It's the size of a high-end stereo system or a wide-screen television. This is what I'm hoping. I mean, it could've been anything else, and I would've liked it more."

Manus slides one foot down to the ground, then the other. On his feet, Manus turns back to the Fiat full of silver.

"No," Manus says. "They give me this shit."

Manus in his commando boots and army fatigues takes a big fat-belly silver teapot out of the trunk and looks at himself reflected fat in the convex side. "The whole box," Manus says, "is full of all this shit and heirlooms that nobody else wants."

Just like me pitching Evie's crystal cigarette box against the fireplace, Manus hauls off and fast-pitches the teapot out into the darkness. Over the cliff, out over the darkness and the lights of suburbia, the teapot flies so far that you can't hear it land.

Not turning around, Manus reaches back and grabs another something. A silver candlestick. "This is my legacy," Manus says. Pitched overhand into the darkness, the candlestick turns end over end, silent the way you imagine satellites fly.

"You know"—Manus pitches a glittering handful of napkin rings—"how your parents are sort of like God. Sure, you love them and want to know they're still around, but you never really see them unless they want something."

The silver chafing dish flies up, up, up to the stars, and then falls down to land somewhere among the blue TV lights.

And after the shards of bone have grown together to give you a new jawbone inside the lump of grafted skin, then the surgeon can try to shape this into something you can talk with and eat with and keep slathered in makeup.

This is years of pain later.

Years of living in the hope that what you'll get will be better than what you have. Years of looking and feeling worse in the hope that you might look better.

Manus grabs the candle, the white candle from the trunk.

"My mom," Manus says, "her number two Christmas present to me was a box full of all the stuff from when I was a kid that she saved." Manus says, "Check it out," and holds up the candle, "my baptism candle."

Off into the darkness Manus pitches the candle.

The bronze baby shoes go next.

Wrapped in a christening gown.

Then a scattering handful of baby teeth.

"Fuck," Manus says, "the damn tooth fairy."

A lock of blond hair inside a locket on a chain, the chain swinging and let go bola-style from Manus's hand, disappears into the dark.

"She said she was giving me this stuff because she just didn't have any room for it," Manus says. "It's not that she didn't want it."

The plaster print of the second-grade hand goes end over end, off into the darkness.

"Well, Mom, if it isn't good enough for you," Manus says, "I don't want to carry this shit around, either."

Jump to all the times when Brandy Alexander gets on me about plastic surgery, then I think of pedicles. Reabsorbtion. Fibroblast cells. Cancellous bone. Years of pain and hope, and how can I not laugh?

Laughter is the only sound left I can make that people will understand.

Brandy, the well-meaning queen supreme with her tits siliconed to the point she can't stand straight, she says: Just look to see what's out there.

How can I stop laughing?

I mean it, Shane, I don't need the attention that bad.

I'll just keep wearing my veils.

If I can't be beautiful, I want to be invisible.

Jump to the silver punch ladle flying off to nowhere.

Jump to each teaspoon, gone.

Jump to all the grade school report cards and class pictures sailed off.

Manus crumples a thick piece of paper.

His birth certificate. And chucks it out of existence. Then Manus stands rocking heel-toe, heel-toe, hugging himself.

Brandy is looking at me to say something. In the dirt, with my finger I write:

manus where do you live these days?

Little cold touches land on my hair and peachy-pink shoulders. It's raining.

Brandy says, "Listen, I don't want to know who you are, but if you could be anybody, who would you be?"

"I'm not getting old, that's for sure," Manus says, shaking his head. "No way." Arms crossed, he rocks heel-toe, heel-toe. Manus tucks his chin to his chest and rocks, looking down at all the broken bottles.

It's raining harder. You can't smell my smoky ostrich feathers or Brandy's L'Air du Temps.

"Then you're Mr. Denver Omelet," Brandy says. "Denver Omelet, meet Daisy St. Patience." Brandy's ring-beaded hand opens to full flower and lays itself across her forty-six inches of siliconed glory. "These," she says, "this is Brandy Alexander."

Now, Please, Jump to Chapter Twenty-nine

Chapter 13

I already wish I hadn't written this. Let's take that as a good sign because most truth is like that.

The part of this book that takes place in Canada is based on a road trip I took with two college friends, driving from Eugene, Oregon, to Vancouver, British Columbia. Their names were Robin and Franz. You already know my name. We were all undergraduate students at the University of Oregon. Robin bought tabs of Ecstasy for us to enjoy and to sell at nightclubs and—he hoped—pay some tuition. We drove Franz's car and hid the tabs in his ashtray, buried under some ash, never imagining that border agents might check there. We were all liberal arts majors, plodding along with crushing student loan balances, registered for the draft, that's how dumb we were. Franz didn't even know we were carrying drugs.

Not a radio song after we'd cleared the Canadian border, Robin dug the Ecstasy out of the ash. Franz was furious, yelling, "Please tell me you did *not* just use my car to smuggle drugs!" The rush we felt from not being arrested was better than any bought chemicals. Instead of packing suitcases, we went every day to the big department store on Granville Street, the Hudson's Bay Company, and bought new clothes. Each subsequent day we exchanged those clothes for even newer clothes, using that huge store as our "Canadian Closet." This being 1985, you can only imagine the billowing Hammer pants and *Flashdance* ripped tops. For daytime, preppy knit polo shirts embroidered with alligators. The Bay took back everything, though it was reeking of disco sweat and clove cigarettes. Honestly, my biggest problem was what to do with my hands while I danced.

We stayed in the Nelson Place Hotel, but we never slept. Ecstasy will do that. After the bars closed, we'd sit in our dark hotel room and tell about the strangest parts of our lives so far. When it came Franz's turn, he told about the summer his family had sent him hundreds of miles away to work for some people who ran a florist shop. That August, the florists loaded their vans before dawn and drove for hours across a desert to a desolate railroad siding in the middle of nowhere. As the sun rose, an Amtrak train called the Empire Builder arrived over the horizon and rumbled to a stop. With the sleepy passengers watching from their windows, Franz and his employers hung flowers and bunting down the length of the train. They hung a banner that read "Wedding Bells Express." At the time, Franz was only eleven or twelve years old. Even that young, he was appalled as wedding guests approached on dirt roads and began to park their pickup trucks trainside. A bride and groom climbed atop the locomotive with a wedding party of two bridesmaids and two groomsmen. Someone played bagpipes, and a minister conducted the ceremony while the delayed passengers groused. Within an hour, the train was on its way to Spokane and St. Louis. The event had happened so quickly, at such an early hour, and Franz had been so young, that by 1985 it seemed like a bad dream.

In our room of the Nelson Place Hotel, I hoped this story was only the Ecstasy happening. Franz and I didn't officially meet until college. In 1983? Was it 1984? His bad dream wasn't a dream, because a decade before we first met . . . we'd already met. The man getting married on top of that train had been my father, and my brother and I had been the two groomsmen. That had been the beginning of my father's second marriage, after divorcing my mother, and he'd wanted to put on a good show. Over a decade later, Franz and I would realize that our childhoods had had that uncomfortable hour in common. Even the bagpipe? Everything.

That's the worst aspect of being a writer: managing plausibility. Everything else about that road trip, I could use in *Invisible Monsters*. But that's the kind of actual miracle that, if I wrote it into a novel, you'd instantly cry, "Bullshit!"

Now, Please, Jump to Chapter Twenty-five

Chapter 14

In Seattle, I've been watching Brandy nap in our undersea grotto for more than one hundred and sixty years. Me, I'm sitting here with a glossy pile of brochures from surgeons showing sexual reassignment surgeries. Transitional transgender operations. Sex changes.

The color pictures show pretty much the same shot of different-quality vaginas. Camera shots focused straight into the dark vaginal introitus. Fingers with red nail polish cupped against each thigh to spread the labia. The urethral meatus soft and pink. The pubic hair clipped down to stubble on some. The vaginal depth given as six inches, eight inches, two inches. Unresected corpus spongiosum mounding around the urethral opening on some. The clitoris hooded, the frenulum of the clitoris, the tiny folds of skin under the hood that join the clitoris to the labia.

Bad, cheap vaginas with hair-growing scrotal skin used inside, still growing hair, choked with hair.

Picture-perfect, state-of-the-art vaginas lengthened using sections of colon, self-cleaning and lubricated with its own mucosa. Sensate clitorises made by cropping and rerouting bits of the glans penis. The Cadillac of vaginoplasty. Some of these Cadillacs turn out so successful the flood of colon mucosa means wearing a maxi-pad every day.

Some are old-style vaginas where you had to stretch and dilate them every day with a plastic mold. All these brochures are souvenirs of Brandy's near future.

After we saw Mr. Parker sitting on Ellis, I helped the drug-induced dead body Brandy might as well be back upstairs and took her out of her clothes again. She coughed them back up when I tried to slip any more Darvons down her throat, so I settled her back on the bathroom floor, and when I folded her suit jacket over my arm there was something cardboard tucked in the inside pocket. The Miss Rona book. Tucked in the book is a souvenir of my own future.

Kicked back on the big ceramic snail shell, I read:

I love Seth Thomas so much I have to destroy him. I overcompensate by worshipping the queen supreme. Seth will never love me. No one will ever love me ever again.

How embarrassing.

Give me needy emotional whining bullshit.

Flash.

Give me self-absorbed egocentric twaddle.

Christ.

Fuck me. I'm so tired of being me. Me beautiful. Me ugly. Blond. Brunette. A million fucking fashion makeovers that only leave me trapped being me.

Who I was before the accident is just a story now. Everything before now, before now, before now, is just a story I carry around. I guess that would apply to anybody in the world. What I need is a new story about who I am.

What I need to do is fuck up so bad I can't save myself.

Now, Please, Jump to Chapter Twenty-eight

Chapter 15

Jump way back to a fashion shoot at this slaughterhouse where whole pigs without their insides hang as thick as fringe from a moving chain. Evie and me wear Bibo Kelley stainless steel party dresses while the chain zips by behind us at about a hundred pigs an hour, and Evie says, "After your brother was mutilated, then what?"

The photographer looks at his light meter and says, "Nope. No way."

The art director says, "Girls, we're getting too much glare off the carcasses."

Each pig goes by big as a hollow tree, all red and shining inside and covered in this really nice pigskin on the outside just after someone's singed the hair off with a blowtorch. This makes me feel all stubbly by comparison, and I have to count back to my last waxing.

And Evie goes, "Your brother?"

And I'm, like, counting Friday, Thursday, Wednesday, Tuesday . . .

"How did he go from being mutilated to being dead?" Evie says.

These pigs keep going by too fast for the art director to powder down their shine. You have to wonder how pigs keep their skin so nice. If now farmers use sunblock or what. Probably, I figure it's been a month since I was as smooth as they are. The way some salons use their new lasers, even with the cooling gel, they might as well use a blowtorch.

"Space girl," Evie says to me. "Phone home."

The whole pig place is refrigerated too much to wear a stainless steel dress around. Guys in white A-line coats and boots with low heels get to spray superheated steam in where the pigs insides were, and I'm ready to trade them jobs. I'm ready to trade jobs with the pigs, even. To Evie, I say, "The police wouldn't buy the hairspray story. They were sure my father had raged on Shane's face. Or my mom had put the hairspray can in the trash. They called it 'neglect.'"

The photographer says, "What if we regroup and backlight the carcasses?"

"Too much strobe effect as they go past," the art director says.

Evie says, "Why'd the police think that?"

"Beats me," I say. "Somebody just kept making anonymous calls to them."

The photographer says, "Can we stop the chain?"

The art director says, "Not unless we can stop people from eating meat."

We're still hours away from taking a real break, and Evie says, "Somebody lied to the police?"

The pig guys are checking us out, and some are pretty cute. They laugh and slide their hands up and down fast on their shiny black steamhoses. Curling their tongues at us. Flirting.

"Then Shane ran away," I tell Evie. "Simple as that. A couple years ago, my folks got a call he was dead."

We step back as close as we can to the pigs going by, still warm. The floor seems to be really greasy, and Evie starts telling me about an idea she has for a remake of *Cinderella*, only instead of the little birds and animals making her a dress, they do cosmetic surgery. Bluebirds give her a face-lift. Squirrels give her implants. Snakes, liposuction. Plus, Cinderella starts out as a lonely little boy.

"As much attention as he got," I tell Evie, "I'd bet my brother put that hairspray can in the fire himself."

Now, Please, Jump to Chapter Twenty-six

Chapter 16

If you're an old person, older than, say, twenty-two, you're going to hate these backward parts you're forced to read, Nancy Drew–style, reflected in a mirror. As if life's not already complicated enough. Before you start feeling too sorry for yourself, please know that these parts were almost written in French. Imagine how *parlez-vous* infuriating that would be. Or in German. *Geben Sie mich viele frustrated tolerance.*

Flash.

To gauge the difference between old people and young people, weigh the amount of art versus mirrors where they live. Sure, mirrors are cheap, but you're forced to settle for what's always in them. Art, on the contrary, reflects your good taste. Most people, people with average skin and listless hair, they upgrade from mirrors to art as fast as humanly possible. Even Andy Warhol's art is better than mirrors, and Andy Warhol was wrong about so many things.

Not the least of which was his quote about being famous. The reality is that in the future everyone will get some damned privacy for fifteen minutes—and that's if they're lucky and steer clear of anything Internet.

Not even Evie Cottrell wants to be famous forever. She, who legally changed her name so that it would always end with an exclamation point, so even her driver's license says Evie! Even she took down her mirrors and hung Thomas Kinkade painting prints on those same nails. How could she resist? Each was a five-thousand-piece jigsaw puzzle she put together with glue. Such a sense of accomplishment! To spend one's life doing work of such questionable value. Each was assembled perfectly. Michelangelo never labored so hard. But after months of diligent work all you had was a friendly cottage or a comforting lighthouse. It took so much concentration to keep track of all those little pieces, it only follows that you felt overjoyed when any two of them fit together. How similar the experience is to reading this stupid book. Better left unsaid is: How like life! In the end is a garden path lined with flowers leading through a gate toward a window where a single candle burns at dusk. That cheesy comfort is more than atheists get.

Just once it would be nice to snap into place that final, vaguely swastika-shaped puzzle piece and find a person: A leprous drug dealer under a streetlight . . . A sordid orgy illuminated by flickering television porn. Nevertheless, for Evie the candle in the window was plenty. To whit, her favorite film was mostly Janet Leigh driving a 1950s car. Janet Leigh sells the car for another car. She drives all night, squinting at the glare of oncoming headlights. She has a sister who loves her and teams up with John Gavin. In Phoenix? Tucson? Wherever, it's an arid and black-and-white, Route 66 landscape. It's a very grown-up, postwar America where everyone wears a necktie even if he only pumps gas at a filling station. Everyone is tense and suspicious, and you can just smell the threat of atom bombs arriving from Russia. When Janet Leigh falls asleep in her car, a highway patrolman sends her to Anthony Perkins, who's apparently stuffed all the birds that ruined Tippi Hedren's hair and menaced Veronica Cartwright at Bodega Bay. These same birds killed Suzanne Pleshette. Anthony Perkins is our hero.

Evie's favorite part is where gentle, soft-spoken Anthony Perkins brings clean towels and a sandwich. They're both so young and alone in that lonely desert. The trick to happiness is editing. Wait a beat too long, and something dreadful always happens. When Janet Leigh and Tony Perkins sit in that motel room, eating their sandwiches and chatting with the endless night outside, that's when Evie always stops the movie. It's an absolutely charming love story. Two lonely people find one another and make small talk. "It's best to quit while you're ahead," says Evie.

Never, ever snap together two puzzle pieces unless you know exactly what you'll find five thousand pieces later. Atheists need to understand that even a wrong answer is better than no answer.

Says Evie, "If you wait too long Deborah Kerr falls off the top of the Empire State Building and—crack—breaks both legs."

Now, Please, jump to Chapter Thirty

Chapter 17

There had to be some better way to kill Brandy. To set me free. Some quick permanent closure. Some kind of cross fire I could walk away from. Evie hates me by now. Brandy looks just like I used to. Manus is still so in love with Brandy he'd follow her anywhere, even if he's not sure why. All I'd have to do is get Brandy cross-haired in front of Evie's rifle.

Bathroom talk.

Brandy's suit jacket with its sanitary little waist and mod three-quarter sleeves is still folded on the aquamarine countertop beside the big clamshell sink. I pick up the jacket, and my souvenir from the future falls out. It's a postcard of clean, sun-bleached 1962 skies and an opening-day Space Needle. You could look out the bathroom's porthole windows and see what's become of the future. Overrun with Goths wearing sandals and soaking lentils at home, the future I wanted is gone. The future I was promised. Everything I expected. The way everything was supposed to turn out. Happiness and peace and love and comfort.

When did the future, Ellis once wrote on the back of a postcard, *switch from being a promise to a threat?*

I tuck the postcard between the vaginoplasty brochures and the labiaplasty handouts stuck between the pages of the Miss Rona book. On the cover is a satellite photo of Hurricane Blonde just off the West Coast of her face. The blond is crowded with pearls, and what could be diamonds sparkle here and there.

She looks very happy. I put the book back in the inside pocket of Brandy's jacket. I pick up the cosmetics and drugs scattered across the countertops and I put them away. Sun comes through the porthole windows at a low, low angle, and the post office will be closing soon. There's still Evie's insurance money to pick up. At least a half million dollars, I figure. What you can do with all that money, I don't know, but I'm sure I'll find out.

Brandy's lapsed into major hair emergency status so I shake her.

Brandy's Aubergine Dreams eyes flicker, blink, flicker, squint.

Her hair, it's gotten all flat in the back.

Brandy comes up on one elbow. "You know," she says, "I'm on drugs so it's all right if I tell you this." Brandy looks at me bent over her, offering a hand up. "I have to tell you," Brandy says, "but I do love you." She says, "I can't tell how this is for you, but I want us to be a family."

My brother wants to marry me.

I give Brandy a hand up. Brandy leans on me, Brandy, she leans on the edge of the countertop. She says, "This wouldn't be a sister thing." Brandy says, "I still have some days left in my Real Life Training."

Stealing drugs, selling drugs, buying clothes, renting luxury cars, taking clothes back, ordering blender drinks, this isn't what I'd call Real Life, not by a long shot.

Brandy's ring-beaded hands open to full flower and spread the fabric of her skirt across her front. "I still have all my original equipment," she says.

The big hands are still patting and smoothing Brandy's crotch as she turns sideways to the mirror and looks at her profile. "It was supposed to come off after a year, but then I met you," she says. "I had my bags packed in the Congress Hotel for weeks just hoping you'd come to rescue me." Brandy turns her other side to the mirror and searches. "I just loved you so much, I thought maybe it's not too late?"

Brandy spreads pot gloss across her top lip and then her bottom lip, blots her lips on a tissue, and drops the big Plumbago kiss into the snail shell toilet. Brandy says with her new lips, "Any idea how to flush this thing?"

Hours I sat on that toilet, and no, I never saw how to flush it. I step out into the hallway so if Brandy wants to blab at me she'll have to follow.

Brandy stumbles in the bathroom doorway where the tile meets the hallway carpet. Her one shoe, the heel is broken. Her stocking is run where it rubbed the doorframe. She's grabbed at a towel rack for balance and chipped her nail polish.

Shining anal queen of perfection, she says, "Fuck."

Princess Princess, she yells after me, "It's not that I really want to be a woman." She yells, "Wait up!" Brandy yells, "I'm only doing this because it's just the biggest mistake I can think to make. It's stupid and destructive, and anybody you ask will tell you I'm wrong. That's why I have to go through with it."

Brandy says, "Don't you see? Because we're so trained to do life the right way. *To not make mistakes.*" Brandy says, "I figure, the bigger the mistake looks, the better chance I'll have to break out and live a real life."

Like Christopher Columbus sailing toward disaster at the edge of the world.

Like Fleming and his bread mold.

"Our real discoveries come from chaos," Brandy yells, "from going to the place that looks wrong and stupid and foolish."

Her imperial voice everywhere in the house, she yells, "You *do not* walk away from me when I take a minute to explain myself!"

Her example is a woman who climbs a mountain, there's no rational reason for climbing that hard, and to some people it's a stupid folly, a misadventure, a mistake. A mountain climber, maybe she starves and freezes, exhausted and in pain for days, and climbs all the way to the top. And maybe she's changed by that, but all she has to show for it is her story.

"But me," Brandy says, still in the bathroom doorway, still looking at her chipped nail polish, "I'm making the same mistake only so much worse, the pain, the money, the time, and being dumped by my old friends, and in the end my whole body is my story."

A sexual reassignment surgery is a miracle for some people, but if you don't want one, it's the ultimate form of self-mutilation.

She says, "Not that it's bad being a woman. This might be wonderful, *if I wanted to be a woman*. The point is," Brandy says, "being a woman is the last thing I want. It's just the biggest mistake I could think to make."

So it's the path to the greatest discovery.

It's because we're so trapped in our culture, in the being of being human on this planet with the brains we have, and the same two arms and two legs everybody has. We're so trapped that any way we could imagine to escape would be just another part of the trap. Anything we want, we're trained to want.

"My first idea was to have one arm and one leg amputated, the left ones, or the right ones"—she looks at me and shrugs—"but no surgeon would agree to help me."

She says, "I considered AIDS, for the experience, but then everybody had AIDS and it looked so mainstream and trendy." She says, "That's what the Rhea sisters told my birth family, I'm pretty sure. Those bitches can be so possessive."

Brandy pulls a pair of white gloves out of her handbag, the kind of gloves with a white pearl button on the inside of each wrist. She works each hand into a glove and does the button. White is not a good color choice. In white, her hands look transplanted from a giant cartoon mouse.

"Then I thought, a sex change," she says, "a sexual reassignment surgery. The Rheas," she says, "they think they're using me, but really I'm using them for their money, for their thinking they were in control of me and this was all their idea."

Brandy lifts her foot to look at the broken heel, and she sighs. Then she reaches down to take off the other shoe.

"None of this was the Rhea sisters' pushing. It wasn't. It was just the biggest mistake I could make. The biggest challenge I could give myself."

Brandy snaps the heel off her one good shoe, leaving her feet in two ugly flats.

She says, "You have to jump into disaster with both feet."

She throws the broken heels into the bathroom trash.

"I'm not straight, and I'm not gay," she says. "I'm not bisexual. I want out of the labels. I don't want my whole life crammed into a single word. A story. I want to find something else, unknowable, someplace to be that's not on the map. A real adventure."

A sphinx. A mystery. A blank. Unknown. Undefined. Unknowable. Indefinable. Those were all the words Brandy used to describe me in my veils. Not just a story that goes and then, and then, and then, and then until you die.

"When I met you," she says, "I envied you. I coveted your face. I thought that face of yours will take more guts than any sex change operation. It will give you bigger discoveries. It will make you stronger than I could ever be."

I start down the stairs. Brandy in her new flats, me in my total confusion, we get to the foyer, and through the drawing room doors you can hear Mr. Parker's long, deep voice belching over and over, "That's right. Just do that."

Brandy and me, we stand outside the doors a moment. We pick the lint and toilet paper off each other, and I fluff up the flat back of Brandy's hair. Brandy pulls her pantyhose up her legs a little and tugs down the front of her jacket.

The postcard and the book tucked inside her jacket, the dick tucked in her pantyhose, you can't tell either one's there.

We throw open the drawing room double doors and there's Mr. Parker and Ellis. Mr. Parker's pants are around his knees, his bare hairy ass is stuck up in the air. The rest of his bareness is stuck in Ellis's face. Ellis Island, formerly Independent Special Contract Vice Operative Manus Kelley.

"Oh, yes. Just do that. That's so good."

Ellis's getting an A in job performance, his hands are cupped around Parker's football scholarship power-clean bare buns, pulling everything he can swallow into his square-jawed Nazi-poster-boy face. Ellis grunting and gagging, making his comeback from forced retirement.

Now, Please, Jump to Chapter Twenty-four

Chapter 18

We all know the scene in the classic movie, the David Lynch masterpiece, but Daisy's version was better. How Daisy St. Patience remembered the movie, it wasn't even sepia-toned. The setting was still an auditorium filled with row upon row of tiered seats, standing-room-only crowded, that full house of straightlaced, Victorian nobility. Ladies in bustles. Men in tall silk hats. Everyone hushed with anticipation. They were all staring intently at a screen of cloth stretched over a lightweight frame, the type of screen used to separate beds in old hospital wards. But when that screen slid aside to reveal an almost naked figure . . . Daisy's interpretation was better.

To start with, there was music. An unseen hand pressed an offstage button, and a thumping bass beat shook that staid auditorium. The house lights dimmed. From loudspeakers, a voice shouted, "Ladies and gentlemen, the Pathological Society of London brings you the sexy . . . the sin-sational . . . the searing-hot, one-and-only . . . the Elephant Man!"

In Lady Daisy's revision Joseph Merrick made his entrance in a burst of blue smoke bomb, wearing a skintight California highway patrolman's buff-color uniform. A brown stripe running down the outside of each thigh. Twenty-one, twenty-two years old. He'd wear a giant-sized pair of mirrored aviator sunglasses in perfect proportion to his huge Elephant Man head. His every seam was cleverly held together with Velcro; he'd wear nothing you couldn't get off with a firm yank. He'd wear a banana hammock engineered for maximum flop. And boots. Sexy black leather boots.

One nipple was pierced, pinned through with a polished policeman's badge on his otherwise bare torso.

No, when Joseph Merrick was presented to the Pathological Society of London in 1884 he didn't need to dance—but he did. That was the fantasy of Daisy St. Patience. No working the brass pole, not for him, but Daisy imagined him wearing a black Chippendales bow tie. This Elephant Man augmented his tan with baby oil. Who's to say what really went down? History tells us the Elephant Man didn't sport sexy Speedo tan lines—those sexy runway lines that point the shortcut to some sexy Elephant Man groin, groin, groin. Rumor has it he didn't shave his legs or wax his chest, not even while he was touring the European Continent. Again, history records that he was twenty-one, twenty-two years old. Who's to say Joseph Merrick didn't get his elephant ears pierced for some hot saddle plugs? A gold ring glinting in his sexy navel. Odds are excellent that he got his lopsided Elephant Man chest inked with a couple of tribal tats. In Daisy's version, Joe Merrick wore the effects of his Proteus syndrome and neurofibromatosis like a hot-pink thong, bumping and grinding his G-stringed self to invade the personal space of those esteemed scientist voyeurs. No passive object for critical gaze, he rotated his deformed hips. Shimmying and finger-snapping. Flexing his washboard elephant abs. No cowering victim, he flexed his fibroid-distorted self and returned their aghast stares with his sexy Elephant Man smile. He grinned his bulbous Elephant Man face like he'd been growing his big forehead lump since he was a three-year-old kid in Leicestershire, pumping up his skull and practicing moves in front of a mirror for today's command performance. His skeleton might've been tortured, but his capped teeth looked perfect, blazing white in the spotlight. Delivering it home, hot, to those whale-boned mamas. Bringing them the ol' razzle-dazzle with his Elephant Man jazz hands, he did his smooth moonwalk. Working his mutilations with the arrogance of a *Playgirl* centerfold, Merrick executed perfect backflips. He did handstands and shook his junk in everyone's cookie-cutter Victorian face. So close they could feel the heat coming off his Elephant Man thighs, he was just boom, boom, boom to the scorching mix of Donna Summer and Lady Gaga. Strutting the sexy curvature of his twisted spine, he pumped his bony cock-eyed pelvis. Unmistakable. Sans apology. His every knotted muscle said: *Here, this is what it is to be alive.* His thrusting crotch said: *Come and get it!*

Showing his audience no mercy, Merrick was all: *Deal with it, bitches.*

He was sweating now, flaunting his Elephant Man nipples and his bushy Elephant Man armpit hair. He sidled up to rub his pheromone-drenched elephant skin, all Brillo Pad–wet, against folks seated along the aisle. Dry-humping the shoulders of elegant gents, he shook his elephant ass cheeks like two scoops of lizard ice cream.

In Daisy's version, barely legal Joe Merrick, almost-elephant-jailbait, he sold the audience his bad attitude self. Like a flaming banquet of all-you-can eat birth defects. Like a visitor from the planet of Worst-Case Scenario. He made those eminent Victorian ladies want nothing more than to be the mama of his Elephant Man babies. Outsider sexy, he made everyone present forget the tragedy they'd been sold about his Elephant Man life.

Elephant Joe. The Elephant Dude. He worked that Bloomsbury crowd for all the pound notes they could tuck into his G-string. He lap-danced the blushing bachelorettes until they spilled their Long Island iced teas, intentionally, just to hide the overly excited wet soaking through their hoop skirts. The telephone had barely been invented, but already people were trying to slip Joseph Merrick their unlisted numbers.

No, the way Daisy told the story, he didn't just stand there like an object for physicians to stare at. Nobody screamed. Nobody wept quietly into their handkerchiefs, or barfed.

People whistled and stomped. They swooned. People chanted, in unison, "Elephant MAN . . . elephant MAN . . . elephant MAN!"

That was what happened when Joseph Merrick was presented at Pathological Society of London in 1884. According to Daisy St. Patience, he had thick, flowing, shoulder-length blond hair.

And if that's not *exactly* how it actually happened, says Daisy . . . well, that's the way it should've.

Now, Please, Jump to Chapter Thirty-six

Chapter 19

My dress I carry my ass around Evie's wedding in is tighter than skintight. It's what you'd call bone-tight. It's that knockoff print of the Shroud of Turin, most of it brown and white, draped and cut so the shiny red buttons all button through the stigmata. Then I'm wearing yards and yards of black silk gloves bunched up on my arms. My heels are nosebleed-high. I wrap Brandy's half mile of black tulle studded with sparkle up around my scar tissue, over the shining cherry pie where my face used to be, wrapped tight, until only my eyes are out. It's a look that's bleak and morbid. The feeling is we've got a little out of control.

It takes more effort to hate Evie than it used to. My whole life is moving farther away from any reason to hate her. It's moving far away from reason itself. It takes a cup of coffee and a Dexedrine capsule to feel even vaguely pissed about anything.

Brandy, she wears the knockoff Bob Mackie suit with the little peplum skirt and the big, I don't know, and the thin, narrow I couldn't care less. She wears a hat, since it's a wedding, after all. Got some shoes on her feet made from the skin of some animal. Accessorized including jewelry, you know, stones dug out of the earth, polished and cut to reflect light, set in alloys of gold and copper, atomic weight, melted and beat with hammers, all of it so labor-intensive. Meaning, all of Brandy Alexander.

Ellis, he wears a double-breasted, whatever, a suit, a single vent in the back, black. He looks the way you'd imagine yourself dead in a casket if you're a guy, not a problem for me, since Ellis has outlived his role in my life.

Ellis's strutting around now that he's proved he can seduce something in every category. Not that knobbing Mr. Parker makes him King of Fag Town, but now he's got Evie under his belt, and maybe enough time's gone by Ellis can go back on duty, get his old beat back in Washington Park.

So we take the gold-engraved wedding invitation that I stole, Brandy and Ellis each take a Percodan, and we go to Evie's wedding reception moment.

Jump to eleven o'clock ante meridiem at the baronial West Hills manor house of crazy Evie Cottrell, gun-happy Evie, newly united Mrs. Evelyn Cottrell Skinner, as if I could care at this point. And. This is oh so dazzling. Evie, she could be the wedding cake, in tier on tier of sashes and flowers rising around her big hoop skirt, up and up to her cinched waist, then her big Texas breasts popped out the top of a strapless bodice. There's so much of her to decorate, the same as Christmas at a shopping mall. Silk flowers are bunched at one side of her waist. Silk flowers over both ears anchor a veil thrown back over her blond on blond sprayed-up hair. In that hoop skirt and those pushed-up Texas grapefruits, the girl walks around riding her own parade float.

Full of champagne and Percodan interactions, Brandy is looking at me.

And I'm amazed I never saw it before, how Evie was a man. A big blonde, the same as she is here, but with one of those ugly wrinkled, you know, scrotums.

Ellis is hiding from Evie, trying to scope out if her new husband has yet another notch in his special contract vice operative résumé. Ellis, how this story looks from his point of view is he's still major sport bait winning proof he can bust any man after the long fight. Everybody here thinks the whole story is about them. Definitely that goes for everybody in the world.

Oh, and this is gone way beyond sorry, Mom. Sorry, God. At this point, I'm not sorry for anything. Or anybody.

No, really, everybody here's just itching to be cremated.

Jump to upstairs. In the master bedroom, Evie's trousseau is laid out ready to be packed. I brought my own matches this time, and I light the hand-torn edge of the gold-engraved invitation, and I carry the invitation from the bedspread to the trousseau to the curtains. It's the sweetest of moments when the fire takes control, and you're no longer responsible for anything.

I take a big bottle of Chanel No. 5 from Evie's bathroom and a big bottle of Joy and a big bottle of White Shoulders, and I slosh the smell of a million parade float flowers all over the bedroom.

The fire, Evie's wedding inferno, finds the trail of flowers in alcohol and chases me out into the hallway. That's what I love about fire, how it would kill me as quick as anybody else. How it can't know I'm its mother. It's so beautiful and powerful and beyond feeling anything for anybody, that's what I love about fire.

You can't stop any of this. You can't control. The fire in Evie's clothes is just more and more every second, and now the plot moves along without you pushing.

And I descend. Step-pause-step. The invisible showgirl. For once, what's happening is what I want. Even better than I expected. Nobody's noticed.

Our world is speeding straight ahead into the future. Flowers and stuffed mushrooms, wedding guests and string quartet, we're all going there together on the planet Brandy Alexander. In the front hall, there's the Princess Princess thinking she's still in control.

The feeling is of supreme and ultimate control over all. Jump to the day we'll all be dead and none of this will matter. Jump to the day another house will stand here and the people living there won't know we ever happened.

"Where did you go?" Brandy says.

The immediate future, I would tell her.

Now, Please, Jump to Chapter Twenty-three

Chapter 20

"My life," Brandy says. "I'm dying, and I'm supposed to see my whole life."

Nobody's dying here. Give me denial.

Evie's shot her wad, dropped the rifle, and gone outside.

The police and paramedics are on their way, and the rest of the wedding guests are outside fighting over the wedding gifts, who gave what and who now has the right to take it back. All of it good messy fun.

Blood is pretty much all over Brandy Alexander, and she says, "I want to see my life."

From some back room, Ellis says, "You have the right to remain silent."

Jump to me, I let go from holding Brandy's hand, my hand warm red with blood-borne pathogens, I write on the burning wallpaper.

Your Name Is Shane McFarland.

You Were Born Twenty-Four Years Ago.

You Have A Sister, One Year Younger.

The fire's already eating my top line.

You Got Gonorrhea From A Special Contract Vice Operative And Your Family Threw You Out.

You Met Three Drag Queens Who Paid You To Start A Sex Change Because You Couldn't Think Of Anything You Wanted Less.

The fire's already eating my second line.

You Met Me.

I Am Your Sister, Shannon McFarland.

Me writing the truth in blood just minutes ahead of the fire eating it.

You Loved Me Because Even If You Didn't Recognize Me, You Knew I Was Your Sister. On Some Level, You Knew Right Away So You Loved Me.

We traveled all over the West and grew up together again.

I've hated you for as long as I can remember.

And You Are Not Going To Die.

I could've saved you.

And you are not going to die.

The fire and my writing are now neck-and-neck.

Jump to Brandy half-bled on the floor, most of her blood wiped up by me to write with, Brandy squints to read as the fire eats our whole family history, line by line. The line *And You Are Not Going To Die* is almost at the floor, right in Brandy's face.

"Honey," Brandy says, "Shannon, sweetness, I knew all that. It was Miss Evie's doing. She told me about you being in the hospital. About your accident."

Such a hand model I am already. And such a rube.

"Now," Brandy says. "Tell me everything."

I write: *I've Been Feeding Ellis Island Female Hormones For The Past Eight Months.*

And Brandy laughs blood. "Me too!" she says.

How can I not laugh?

"Now," Brandy says, "quick, before I die, what else?"

I write: *Everybody Just Loved You More After The Hairspray Accident.*

And:

And I Did Not Make That Hairspray Can Explode.

Brandy says, "I know. *I did it.* I was so miserable being a normal average child. I wanted something to save me. I wanted the opposite of a miracle."

From some other room, Ellis says, "Anything you say can and may be used against you in a court of law." And on the baseboard, I write:

The Truth Is I Shot Myself In The Face.

There's no more room to write, no more blood to write with, and nothing left to say, and Brandy says, "You shot your own face off?"

I nod.

"That," says Brandy, "that, I didn't know."

Now, Please, Jump to Chapter Twenty-two

Chapter 21

Jump back to the La Paloma emergency room. The intravenous morphine. The tiny operating-room manicure scissors cut Brandy's suit off. My brother's unhappy penis there blue and cold for the whole world to see. The police photos, and Sister Katherine screaming, "Take your pictures! Take your pictures now! He's still losing blood!"

Jump to surgery. Jump to post-op. Jump to me taking Sister Katherine aside, little Sister Katherine hugging me so hard around the knees I almost buckle to the floor. She looks at me, both of us stained with the blood, and I ask her in writing:

please.

do this one special thing for me. please. if you really want to make me happy.

Jump to Evie installed talk-show–style under the hot track lights, downtown at Brumbach's, chatting with her mother and Manus and her new husband about how she met Brandy years before all of us, in some transgender support group. About how everybody needs a big disaster every now and then.

Jump to someday down the road soon when Manus will get his breasts.

Jump to me kneeling beside my brother's hospital bed. Shane's skin, you don't know where the faded blue hospital gown ends and Shane begins, he's so pale. This is my brother, thin and pale with Shane's thin arms and pigeon chest. The flat auburn hair across his forehead, this is who I remember growing up with. Put together out of sticks and bird bones. The Shane I'd forgotten. The Shane from before the hairspray accident. I don't know why I forgot, but Shane had always looked so miserable.

Jump to our folks at home at night, showing home movies against the side of their white house. The windows from twenty years ago lined up perfect with the windows now. The grass lined up with the grass. The ghosts of Shane and me as toddlers running around, happy with each other.

Jump to the Rhea sisters crowded around the hospital bed. Hairnets pulled on over their wigs. Surgical masks on their faces. They're wearing those faded green scrub suits, the Rheas have those Duchess of Windsor costume jewelry brooches pinned on their scrubs: leopards shimmering with diamond and topaz spots. Hummingbirds with pavé emerald bodies.

Me, I just want Shane to be happy. I'm tired of being me, hateful me.

Give me release.

I'm tired of this world of appearances. Pigs that only look fat. Families that look happy.

Give me deliverance.

From what only looks like generosity. What only looks like love.

Flash.

I don't want to be me anymore. I want to be happy, and I want Brandy Alexander back. Here's my first real dead end in my life. There's nowhere to go, not the way I am right now, the person I am. Here's my first real beginning.

As Shane sleeps, the Rhea sisters all crowd around, decorating him with little gifts. They're misting Shane with L'Air du Temps as if he were a Boston fern.

New earrings. A new Hermès scarf around his head.

Cosmetics are spread in perfect rows on a surgical tray that hovers next to the bed, and Sofonda says, "Moisturizer!" and holds her hand out, palm up.

"Moisturizer," Kitty Litter says, and slaps the tube into Sofonda's palm.

Sofonda puts her hand out and says, "Concealer!"

And Vivienne slaps another tube into her palm and says, "Concealer."

Shane, I know you can't hear, but that's okay, since I can't talk.

With short, light strokes, Sofonda uses a little sponge to spread concealer on the dark bags under Shane's eyes. Vivienne pins a diamond stickpin on Shane's hospital gown.

Miss Rona saved your life, Shane. The book in your jacket pocket, it slowed the bullet enough that only your boobs exploded. It's just a flesh wound, flesh and silicone.

Florists come in with sprays of irises and roses and stock.

Your silicone broke, Shane. The bullet popped your silicone so they had to take it out. Now you can have any sized breasts you want. The Rheas have said so.

"Foundation!" Sofonda says, blending the foundation into Shane's hairline.

She says, "Eyebrow pencil!" with sweat beading on her forehead.

Kitty hands over the pencil, saying, "Eyebrow pencil."

"Blot me!" Sofonda says.

And Vivienne blots her forehead with a sponge.

Sofonda says, "Eyeliner! *Stat!*"

And I have to go, Shane, while you're still asleep. But I want to give you something. I want to give you life. This is my third chance, and I don't want to blow it. I could've opened my bedroom window. I could've stopped Evie shooting you. The truth is I didn't, so I'm giving you *my* life because I don't want it anymore.

I tuck my clutch bag under Shane's big ring-beaded hand. You see, the size of a man's hands are the one thing a plastic surgeon can't change. The one thing that will always give away a girl like Brandy Alexander. There's just no way to hide those hands.

This is all my identification, my birth certificate, my everything. You can be Shannon McFarland from now on. My career. The ninety-degree attention. It's yours. All of it. Everyone. I hope it's enough for you. It's everything I have left.

"Base color!" Sofonda says, and Vivienne hands her the lightest shade of Aubergine Dreams eye shadow.

"Lid color!" Sofonda says, and Kitty hands her the next eye shadow.

"Contour color!" Sofonda says, and Kitty hands her the darkest shade.

Shane, you go back to my career. You make Sofonda get you a top contract, no local charity benefit runway shit. You're Shannon fucking McFarland now. You go right to the top. A year from now, I want to turn on the TV and see you drinking a diet cola naked in slow motion. Make Sofonda get you big national contracts.

Be famous. Be a big social experiment in getting what you don't want. Find value in what we've been taught is worthless. Find good in what the world says is evil. I'm giving you my life because

I want the whole world to know you. I wish the whole world would embrace what it hates.

Find what you're afraid of most and go live there.

"Lash curler!" says Sofonda, and she curls Shane's sleeping eyelashes.

"Mascara!" she says, combing mascara into the lashes.

"Exquisite," says Kitty.

And Sofonda says, "We're not out of the woods yet."

Shane, I'm giving you my life, my driver's license, my old report cards, because you look more like me than I can ever remember looking. Because I'm tired of hating and preening and telling myself old stories that were never true in the first place. I'm tired of always being me, me, me first.

Mirror, mirror on the wall.

And please don't come after me. Be the new center of attention. Be a big success, be beautiful and loved and everything else I wanted to be. I'm over that now. I just want to be invisible. Maybe I'll become a belly dancer in my veils. Become a nun and work in a leper colony where nobody is complete. I'll be an ice hockey goalie and wear a mask. Those big amusement parks will only hire women to wear the cartoon character costumes, since folks don't want to chance a strange molester guy hugging their kid. Maybe I'll be a big cartoon mouse. Or a dog. Or a duck. I don't know, but

I'm sure I'll find out. There's no escaping fate, it just keeps going. Day and night, the future just keeps coming at you.

I stroke Shane's pale hand.

I'm giving you my life to prove to myself I can, I really can love somebody. Even when I'm not getting paid, I can give love and happiness and charm. You see, I can handle the baby food and the not talking and being homeless and invisible, but I have to know that I can love somebody. Completely and totally, permanently and without hope of reward, just as an act of will, I will love somebody.

I lean in, as if I could kiss my brother's face.

I leave my purse and any idea of who I am tucked under Shane's hand. And I leave behind the story that I was ever this beautiful, that I could walk into a room deep-fried in a tight dress and everybody would turn and look at me. A million reporters would take my picture. And I leave behind the idea that this attention was worth what I did to get it.

What I need is a new story.

What the Rhea sisters did for Brandy Alexander.

What Brandy's been doing for me.

What I need to learn to do for myself. To write my own story.

Let my brother be Shannon McFarland.

I don't need that kind of attention. Not anymore.

"Lip liner!" Sofonda says.

"Lip gloss!" she says.

She says, "We've got a bleeder!"

And Vivienne leans in with a tissue to blot the extra Plumbago off Shane's chin.

Sister Katherine brings me what I asked for, please, and it's the pictures, the eight-by-ten glossies of me in my white sheet. They aren't good or bad, ugly or beautiful. They're just the way I look. The truth. My future. Just regular reality. And I take off my veils, the cut-work and muslin and lace, and leave them for Shane to find at his feet.

I don't need them at this moment, or the next, or the next, forever.

Sofonda sets the makeup with powder and then Shane's gone. My brother, thin and pale, sticks and bird bones and miserable, is gone.

The Rhea sisters slowly peel off their surgical masks.

"Brandy Alexander," says Kitty, "queen supreme."

"Total quality girl," Vivienne says.

"Forever and ever," says Sofonda, "and that's enough."

Completely and totally, permanently and without hope, forever and ever I love Brandy Alexander.

And that's enough.

(The end)

Chapter 22

Jump to this one time, nowhere special, just Brandy almost dead on the floor and me kneeling over her with my hands covered in her Princess Alexander partytime blood.

Brandy yells, "Evie!"

And Evie's burned-up head sticks back in through the front doorway. "Brandy, sugar," Evie says, "this all's been the best disaster you've ever pulled off!"

To me, Evie runs up and kisses me with her nasty melted lipstick and says, "Shannon, I just can't thank you enough for spicing up my boring old home life."

"Miss Evie," Brandy says, "you can act like anything, but, girl, you just totally missed shooting the bulletproof part of my vest."

Jump to the truth. I'm the stupid one.

Jump to the truth. I shot myself. I let Evie think it was Manus and Manus think it was Evie. Probably it was their suspicion of each other that drove them apart. It drove Evie to keep a loaded rifle around in case Manus came after her. The same fear made Manus carry a butcher knife the night he came over to confront her.

The truth is nobody here is as stupid or evil as I let on. Except me. The truth is I drove out away from the city on the day of the accident. With my driver's-side window rolled halfway up, I got out and I shot through the glass. On the way back into town, on the freeway, I got in the exit lane for Growden Avenue, the exit for La Paloma Memorial Hospital.

The truth is I was addicted to being beautiful, and that's not something you just walk away from. Being addicted to all that attention, I had to quit cold turkey. I could shave my head, but hair grows back. Even bald, I might still look too good. Bald, I might get even more attention. There was the option of getting fat or drinking out of control to ruin my looks, but I wanted to be ugly, and I wanted my health. Wrinkles and aging looked too far off. There had to be some way to get ugly in a flash. I had to deal with my looks in a fast, permanent way or I'd always be tempted to go back.

You know how you look at ugly hunchback girls, and they are so lucky. Nobody drags them out at night so they can't finish their doctoral thesis papers. They don't get yelled at by fashion photographers if they get infected ingrown bikini hairs. You look at burn victims and think how much time they save not looking in mirrors to check their skin for sun damage.

I wanted the everyday reassurance of being mutilated. The way a crippled deformed birth-defected disfigured girl can drive her car with the windows open and not care how the wind makes her hair look, that's the kind of freedom I was after.

I was tired of staying a lower life-form just because of my looks. Trading on them. Cheating. Never getting anything real accomplished, but getting the attention and recognition anyway. Trapped in a beauty ghetto is how I felt. Stereotyped. Robbed of my motivation.

In this way, Shane, we are very much brother and sister. This is the biggest mistake I could think would save me. I wanted to give up the idea I had any control. Shake things up. To be saved by chaos. To see if I could cope, I wanted to force myself to grow again. To explode my comfort zone.

I slowed down for the exit and pulled over onto the shoulder, what they call the breakdown lane. I remember thinking, How apropos. I remember thinking, This is going to be so exciting. My makeover. Here was my life about to start all over again. I could be a great brain surgeon this time around. Or I could be an artist. Nobody would care how I'd look. People would just see my art, what I made instead of just how I looked, and people would love me.

What I thought last was, at last I'll be growing again, mutating, adapting, evolving. I'll be physically challenged.

I couldn't wait. I got the gun from the glove compartment. I wore a glove against powder burns, and held the gun at arm's length out my broken window. It wasn't even like aiming, with the gun only about two feet away. I might've killed myself that way, but by now that idea didn't seem very tragic.

This makeover would make piercings and tattoos and brandings look so lame, all those little fashion revolts so safe that they themselves only become fashionable. Those little paper tiger attempts to reject looking good that only end up reinforcing it.

The shot, it was like getting hit hard is what I remember. The bullet. It took a minute before I could focus my eyes, but there was my blood and snot, my drool and teeth all over the passenger seat. I had to open the car door and get the gun from where I'd dropped it outside the window. Being in shock helped. The gun and the glove are in a storm drain in the hospital parking lot where I dropped them, in case you want proof.

Then the intravenous morphine, the tiny operating-room manicure scissors cut my dress off, the little patch panties, the police photos. Birds ate my face. Nobody ever suspected the truth.

The truth is I panicked a little after that. I let everybody think the wrong things. The future is not a good place to start lying and cheating all over again. None of this is anybody's fault except mine. I ran because just getting my jaw rebuilt was too much temptation to revert, to play that game, the looking good game. Now my whole new future is still out there waiting for me.

The truth is, being ugly isn't the thrill you'd think, but it can be an opportunity for something better than I ever imagined.

The truth is I'm sorry.

Now, Please, Jump to Chapter Twenty-one

Chapter 23

Jump to Brandy and me, we can't find Ellis anywhere. Evie and all the Texas Cottrells can't find their groom, either, everybody laughing that nervous laughter. What bridesmaid has run off with him, everybody wants to know. Ha, ha.

I tug Brandy toward the door, but she shushes me. Ellis and the groom both missing . . . a hundred Texans drinking hard . . . that ridiculous bride in her big drag wedding dress . . . this is just too much fun for Brandy to walk out now.

Jump to Evie riding her big parade float out of the butler's pantry, her hands all fisted up, her veil and hair flying straight out behind her. Evie's shouting about how she done found her butt-sucking fag-assed new husband face-downed enjoying butt sex with everybody's old boyfriend in the butler's pantry.

Oh, Ellis.

I remember all his porno magazines, and all the details of anal, oral, rimming, fisting, felching. You could put yourself in the hospital trying to self-suck.

Oh, this is dazzling.

Of course, Evie's answer to everything is to heft her hoop skirt and run upstairs after a rifle except by now most of her bedroom is a Chanel No. 5 perfumed wall of flames Evie has to ride her parade float right into. Everybody cell-phones 911 for help. Nobody's bothered enough to go into the butler's pantry and check out the action. Folks don't want to know what might be going on in there.

Go figure, but Texans seem to be a lot more comfortable around disastrous house fires than they are around anal sex.

I remember my folks. Scat and water sports. Sado and masochism.

Waiting for Evie to burn to death, everybody gets a fresh drink and goes to stand in the foyer at the foot of the stairs. You hear loud spanking from the butler's pantry. The painful kind where you spit on your hand first.

Brandy, the socially inappropriate thing she is, Brandy starts laughing. "This is going to be messy good fun," Brandy tells me out the side of her Plumbago mouth. "I put a handful of Bilax bowel evacuant in Ellis's last drink."

Oh, Ellis.

With all that's going on, Brandy could've gotten away if she hadn't started laughing.

You see, since right then, Evie steps out of that wall of flame at the top of the stairs. A rifle in her hands, her wedding dress burned down to the steel hoops, the silk flowers in her hair burned down to their wire skeletons, all her blond hair burned off, Evie does her slow step-pause-step down the stairs with a rifle pointed right at Brandy Alexander.

With everybody looking up the stairs at Evie wearing nothing but wire and ashes, sweat and soot smeared all over her luscious hourglass transgender bod, we all watch Evelyn Cottrell in her big incorporated moment, and Evie screams, "You!"

She screams at Brandy Alexander down the barrel of the rifle, "You did it to me again. Another fire!"

Step-pause-step.

"I thought we were best friends," she says. "Sure, yes, I slept with your boyfriend, but *who hasn't*?" Evie says, with the gun and everything.

Step-pause-step.

"It's just not enough for you to be the best and most beautiful," Evie says. "Most people, if they looked as good as you, they'd tread water for the rest of their lives."

Step-pause-step.

"But no," Evie says, "here you have to destroy everyone else."

The second-floor fire inches down the foyer wallpaper, and wedding guests are scrambling for their wraps and bags, all of them headed outdoors with the wedding gifts, the silver and the crystal.

You hear that butt-slapping sound from the butler's pantry.

"Shut up in there!" Evie yells. Back to Brandy, Evie says, "So maybe I'll spend some years in prison, but you'll have a big head start on me in hell!"

You hear the rifle cock.

The fire inches down the walls.

"Oh, God, yes, Jesus Christ," Ellis yells. "Oh, God, I'm coming!"

Brandy stops laughing. Bigger and prettier than ever, looking regal and annoyed and put-upon as if this is all a big joke, Brandy Alexander lifts a giant hand and looks at her watch.

And I'm about to become an only child.

And I could stop everything at this moment. I could throw off my veil, tell the truth, save lives. I'm me. Brandy's innocent. Here's my second chance. I could've opened my bedroom window years ago and let Shane inside. I could've not called the police all those times to suggest Shane's accident wasn't. What stands in my way is the story of how Shane burned my clothes. How being mutilated made Shane the center of attention. And if I throw off my veil now, I'll just be a monster, a less than perfect, mutilated victim. I'll be only how I look. Just the truth, the whole truth, and nothing but the truth. Honesty being the most boring thing on the planet Brandy Alexander.

And. Evie aims.

"Yes!" Ellis yells from the pantry. "Yes, do it, big guy! Give it to me! Shoot it!"

Evie squints down the barrel.

"Now!" Ellis is yelling. "Shoot it right in my mouth!"

Brandy smiles.

And I do nothing.

And Evie shoots Brandy Alexander right in the heart.

Now, Please, Jump to Chapter Twenty

Chapter 24

The man at General Delivery who asked to see my ID pretty much had to take my word for it. The picture on my driver's license might as well be Brandy's. This means a lot of writing on scraps of paper for me to explain how I look now. This whole time I'm in the post office, I'm looking sideways to see if I'm a cover girl up on the FBI's most wanted poster board.

Almost half a million dollars is about twenty-five pounds of ten- and twenty-dollar bills in a box. Plus, inside with the money is a pink stationery note from Evie saying blah, blah, blah, I will kill you if I ever see you again. And I couldn't be happier.

Before Brandy can see who it's addressed to, I claw off the label.

One part of being a model is my phone number was unlisted so I wasn't in any city for Brandy to find. I was nowhere. And now we're driving back to Evie. To Brandy's fate. The whole way back, me and

Ellis, we're writing postcards from the future and slipping them out the car windows as we go south on Interstate 5 at a mile and a half every minute. Three miles closer to Evie and her rifle every two minutes. Ninety miles closer to fate every hour.

Ellis writes: *Your birth is a mistake you'll spend your whole life trying to correct.*

The electric window of the Lincoln Town Car hums down a half inch, and Ellis drops the card out into the I-5 slipstream.

I write: *You spend your entire life becoming God and then you die.*

Ellis writes: *When you don't share your problems, you resent hearing the problems of other people.*

I write: *All God does is watch us and kill us when we get boring. We must never, ever be boring.*

Jump to us reading the real estate section of the newspaper, looking for big open houses. We always do this in a new town. We sit at a nice sidewalk café and drink cappuccino with chocolate sprinkles and read the paper, then Brandy calls all the realtors to find which open houses have people still living in them. Ellis makes a list of houses to hit tomorrow.

We check into a nice hotel, and we take a catnap. After midnight Brandy wakes me up with a kiss. She and Ellis are going out to sell the stock we picked up in Seattle. Probably they're screwing. I don't care.

"And no," Brandy says. "Miss Alexander will not be calling the Rhea sisters while she's in town. Anymore, she's determined the only vagina worth having is the kind you buy yourself."

Ellis is standing in the open doorway to the hotel hallway, looking like a superhero that I want to crawl into bed and save me. Still, since Seattle, he's been my brother. And you can't be in love with your brother.

Brandy says, "You want the TV remote control?" Brandy turns on the television, and there's Evie scared and desperate with her big pumped-up rainbow hair in every shade of blond. Evelyn Cottrell, Inc., everybody's favorite write-off, is stumbling through the studio audience in her sequined dress begging folks to eat her meat by-products.

Brandy changes channels.

Brandy changes channels.

Brandy changes channels.

Evie is everywhere after midnight, offering what she's got on a silver tray. The studio audience ignores her, watching themselves on the monitor, trapped in the reality loop of watching themselves watch themselves, trying the way we do every time we look in a mirror to figure out exactly who that person is.

That loop that never ends. Evie and me, we did this infomercial. How could I be so dumb? We're so totally trapped in ourselves.

The camera stays on Evie, and what I can almost hear Evie saying is, Love me.

Love me, love me, love me, love me, love me, love me, love me, I'll be anybody you want me to be. Use me. Change me. I can be thin with big breasts and big hair. Take me apart. Make me into anything, but just love me.

Jump way back to one time, Evie and me did this fashion shoot in a junkyard, in a slaughterhouse, in a mortuary. We'd go anywhere to look good by comparison, and what I realize is mostly what I hate about Evie is the fact that she's so vain and stupid and needy. But what I hate most is how she's just like me. What I really hate is me, so I hate pretty much everybody.

Jump to the next day we hit a few houses, a mansion, a couple palaces, and a chateau full of drugs. Around three o'clock we meet a realtor in the baronial dining room of a West Hills manor house. All around us are caterers and florists. The dining room table is spread and heaping with silver and crystal, tea sets, samovars, candelabras, stemware. A woman in dowdy scarecrow social-secretary tweeds is unwrapping these gifts of silver and crystal and making notes in a tiny red book.

A constant stream of arriving flowers eddies around us, buckets of irises and roses and stock. The manor house is sweet with the smell of flowers and rich with the smell of little puff pastries and stuffed mushrooms.

Not our style. Brandy looks at me. Way too many folks around.

But the realtor's already there, smiling. In a drawl as flat and drawn-out as the Texas horizon, the realtor introduces herself as Mrs. Leonard Cottrell. And she is so happy to meet us.

This Cottrell woman takes Brandy by the elbow and steers her around the baronial first floor while I decide to fight or flight.

Give me terror.

Flash.

Give me panic.

Flash.

This has to be Evie's mother, oh, you know it is. And this must be Evie's new house. And I'm wondering how it is we came here. Why today? What are the chances?

The realty Cottrell steers us past the tweedy social secretary and all the wedding gifts. "This is my daughter's house. But she spends almost all her days in the furniture department at Brumbach's, downtown. So far we've gone along with her little obsessions, but enough's enough, so now we're gonna marry her off to some jackass."

She leans in close. "It was more difficult than you'd ever imagine, trying to settle her down. You know, she burned down the last house we bought her."

Beside the social secretary, there's a stack of gold-engraved wedding invitations. These are the regrets. Sorry, but we can't make it.

There seem to be a lot of regrets. Nice invitations, though, gold engraved, hand-torn edges, a three-fold card with a dried violet inside. I steal one of the regrets, and I catch up with the realty Cottrell woman and Brandy and Ellis.

"No," Brandy's saying. "There are too many people around. We couldn't view the house under these conditions."

"Between you and me," says the realty Cottrell, "the biggest wedding in the world is worth the cost if we can shove Evie off onto some poor man."

Brandy says, "We don't want to keep you."

"But, then," the Cottrell woman says, "there's this subgroup of 'men' who like their 'women' the way Evie is now."

Brandy says, "We really must be going."

And Ellis says, "Men who like insane women?"

"Why, it plumb broke our hearts the day Evan came to us. Sixteen years old, and he says, 'Mommy, Daddy, I want to be a girl,'" says Mrs. Cottrell.

"But we paid for it," she says. "A tax deduction is a tax deduction. Evan wanted to be a world-famous fashion model, he told us. He started calling himself Evie, and I canceled my subscription to *Vogue* the next day. I felt it had done enough damage to my family."

Brandy says, "Well, congratulations," and starts tugging me toward the front door.

And Ellis says, *"Evie was a man?"*

Evie was a man. And I just have to sit down. Evie was a man. And I saw her implant scars. Evie was a man. And I saw her naked in fitting rooms.

Give me a complete late-stage revision of my adult life.

Flash.

Give me anything in this whole fucking world that is exactly what it looks like!

Flash!

Evie's mother looks hard at Brandy. "Have you ever done any modeling?" she says. "You look so much like a friend of my son's."

"Your daughter," Brandy growls.

And I finger the invitation I stole. The wedding, the union of Miss Evelyn Cottrell and Mr. Allen Skinner, is tomorrow. At eleven ante meridiem, according to the gold engraving. To be followed by a reception at the bride's home.

To be followed by a house fire.

To be followed by a murder.

Dress formal.

Now, Please, Jump to Chapter Nineteen

Chapter 25

Where you're supposed to be is the weekly Dangerous Writing workshop in Tom Spanbauer's tiny living room in 1991 with writing students and half-written novels all over the house. It costs twenty dollars to attend each Thursday night even if you bring a bottle of wine, which a lot of people do, even if you come on weekends to help Tom clear the rusty junk and thorny blackberries from his property. Which I do. Monica Drake is also here, and because she can't afford to pay the tuition in cash, each week she brings Tom a table lamp, a clock, some piece of furniture in trade. Tom's house is filling up while Monica's is almost empty.

For twenty dollars, Tom Spanbauer tells us, "Establish your authority on the page, and you can make anything happen."

For another twenty, he tells us, "No Latinates!"

Tom tells us, "Unpack your objects." And we love Tom so much that we print his advice on buttons, like big campaign buttons, we can wear pinned to our shirts. We're not teenagers; we're thirty, thirty-two, thirty-five years old. What's even more amazing is . . . we do wear these buttons. In exchange for our cash and our lamps and clearing blackberries, Tom gives us copies of a short story called "The Harvest" by a writer named Amy Hempel. It demonstrates every excellent thing he hopes we'll learn. Monica is the star of our Thursday nights. Suzy Vitello is a star. Erin Leonard and Joanna Rose and Rick Thompson are stars. Candace Mulligan is a star, but we all want to play the role of Amy Hempel.

I've given up all hope of ever being published so I'm writing a loopy tale about a fashion model without a face. My inspiration is the loopy descriptions that narrators read off note cards during fashion shows: a hundred adjectives in search of a noun. "A sumptuous crimson melding of shimmering perfumed extravagance demanding unequaled glamour, demanding liquid romance, ensuring lucid transcendent . . ." Oh, you get the picture. I pronounce *hyperbole* as "hiper-bowl." I pronounce *Hermés*, the Italian fashion house, as "her-mees"; I'm so obviously stupid that Tom is delighted. I bring in the first draft of a chapter about cosmetic reconstructive surgery, and Erin Leonard brings me a magazine article by a young woman who, as a child, lost much of her face to cancer. Her name is Lucy Grealy, and she's written the most extraordinary memoir called *Autobiography of a Face*, which I don't read, not for years and years, then only after I've invented my goofus road trip novel which no one wants to publish. In the interim, I write *Fight Club*. I write *Survivor*. Jump to ten years gone by, and I fly to New York to read my work at the KGB literary bar in the East Village. A decade after those twenty-dollar lessons, two pretty women walk into the bar. Like the lead-in to a joke, two pretty women walk into the KGB Bar, and one of them is Amy Hempel and the friend accompanying her is—the only person she could possibly be in this strange, magical, dreamy, miraculous, impossible world—Lucy Grealy.

Now, Please, Jump to Chapter Forty-two

Chapter 26

Jump to one time, nowhere special, just Brandy and me shopping along a main street of stores in some Idaho town with a Sears outlet, a diner, a day-old bakery store, and a realtor's office with our own Mr. White Westinghouse gone inside to hustle some realtor. We go into a secondhand dress shop. This is next door to the day-old bargain bakery, and Brandy says how her father used to pull this stunt with pigs just before he took them to market. She says how he used to feed them expired desserts he bought by the truckload from this kind of bakery outlet. Sunlight comes down on us through clean air. Bears and mountains are within walking distance.

Brandy looks at me over a rack of secondhand dresses. "You know about that kind of scam? The one with the pigs, sweetness?" she says.

He used to stovepipe potatoes, her father. You hold the burlap bag open and stand a length of stovepipe inside. All around the pipe, you put big potatoes from this year's crop. Inside the pipe you put last year's soft, bruised, cut, and rotting potatoes so folks can't see them from through the burlap. You pull the stovepipe out, and you stitch the bag shut tight so nothing inside can shift. You sell them roadside with your kids helping, and even at a cheap price, you're making money.

We had a Ford that day in Idaho. It was brown inside and out.

Brandy pushes the hangers apart, checking out every dress on the rack, and says, "You ever hear of anything in your whole life so underhanded?"

Jump to Brandy and me in a secondhand store on that same main street, behind a curtain, crowded together in a fitting room the size of a phone booth. Most of the crowding is a ball gown Brandy needs me to help get her into, a real Grace Kelly of a dress with Charles James written all over it. Baffles and plenums and all that high-stressed skeletoning engineered inside a skin of shot-pink organza or ice-blue velveteen.

These most incredible dresses, Brandy tells me, the constructed ball gowns, the engineered evening dresses with their hoops and strapless bodices, their stand-up horseshoe collars and flaring shoulders, nipped waists, their stand-away peplums and bones, they never last very long. The tension, the push and pull of satin and crepe de Chine trying to control the wire and boning inside, the battle of fabric against metal, this tension will shred them. As the outsides age, the fabric, the part you can see, as it gets weak, the insides start to poke and tear their way out.

Princess Princess, she says, "It will take at least three Darvons to get me into this dress."

She opens her hand, and I shake out the prescription.

Her father, Brandy says, he used to grind his beef with crushed ice to force it full of water before he sold it. He'd grind beef with what's called bull meal to force it full of cereal.

"He wasn't a bad person," she says. "Not outside of following the rules a little too much."

Not the rules about being fair and honest, she says, so much as the rules about protecting your family from poverty. And disease.

Some nights, Brandy says, her father used to creep into her room while she was asleep.

I don't want to hear this. Brandy's diet of Provera and Darvon has side-effected her with this kind of emotional bulimia where she can't keep down any nasty secret. I smooth my veils over my ears. *Thank you for not sharing.*

"My father used to sit on my bed some nights," she says, "and wake me up."

Our father.

The ball gown is resurrected glorious on Brandy's shoulders, brought back to life, larger than life and fairy-tale impossible to wear anyplace in the past fifty years. A zipper thick as my spine goes up the side to just under Brandy's arm. The panels of the bodice pinch Brandy off at her waist and explode her out the top, her breasts, her bare arms and long neck. The skirt is layered pale yellow silk faille and tulle. It's so much gold embroidery and seed pearls would make any bit of jewelry too much.

"It's a palace of a dress," Brandy says, "but even with the drugs, it hurts."

The broke ends of the wire stays poke out around the neck, poke in at the waist. Panels of plastic whalebone, their corners and sharp edges jab and cut. The silk is hot, the tulle, rough. Just her breathing in and out makes the clashing steel and celluloid tucked inside, hidden, just Brandy being alive makes it bite and chew at the fabric and her skin.

Jump to at night, Brandy's father, he used to say, Hurry. Get dressed. Wake your sister.

Me.

Get your coats on and get in the back of the truck, he'd say.

And we would, late after the TV stations had done the national anthem and gone off the air. Concluded their broadcast day. Nothing was on the road except us, our folks in the cab of the pickup and us two in the back, Brandy and his sister, curled on our sides against the corrugated floor of the truck bed, the squeak of the leaf springs, the hum of the driveline coming right into us. The potholes bounce our pumpkin heads hard on the floor of the bed. Our hands clamp tight over our faces to keep from breathing the sawdust and dried manure blowing around, left over. Our eyes shut tight to keep out the same. We were going we didn't know where, but tried to figure out. A right turn, then a left turn, then a long straight stretch going we didn't know how fast, then another right turn would roll us over on our left sides. We didn't know how long. You couldn't sleep.

Wearing the dress to shreds and holding very still, Brandy says, "You know, I've been on my own pretty much since I was sixteen."

With every breath, even her taking shallow Darvon-overdosed little gulps of air, Brandy winces. She says, "There was an accident when I was fifteen, and at the hospital, the police accused my father of abusing me. It just went on and on. I couldn't tell them anything because there was nothing to tell."

She inhales and winces. "The interviews, the counseling, the intervention therapy, it just went on and on."

The pickup truck slowed and bounced off the edge of the blacktop, onto gravel or washboard dirt, and the whole truck bounced and rattled a while farther, then stopped.

This is how poor we were.

Still in the truck bed, you took your hands off your face, and we'd be stopped. The dust and manure would settle. Brandy's father would drop the tailgate of the truck, and you'd be on a dirt road alongside a looming broken wall of boxcars laying this way and that off their tracks. Boxcars would be broken open. Flatcars would be rolled over with their loads of logs or two-by-fours scattered. Tanker cars buckled and leaking. Hoppers full of coal or wood chips would be heaved over and dumped out in black or gold piles. The fierce smell of ammonia. The good smell of cedar. The sun would be just under the horizon with light coming around to us from underneath the world.

There'd be lumber to load on the truck. Cases of instant butterscotch pudding. Cases of typing paper, toilet paper, double-A batteries, toothpaste, canned peaches, books. Crushed diamonds of safety glass'd be everywhere around car carriers tipped sideways with the brand-new cars inside wrecked, with their clean black tires in the air.

Brandy lifts the gown's neckline and peeks inside at her Estraderm patch on one breast. She peels the backing off another patch and pastes it on her other breast, then takes another stabbing breath and winces.

"The whole mess died down after about three months, the whole child abuse investigation," Brandy says. "Then one basketball practice, I'm getting out of the gym and a man comes up. He's with the police, he says, and this is a confidential follow-up interview."

Brandy inhales, winces. She lifts the neckline again and takes out a Methadone Disket from between her breasts, bites off half of it, and drops the rest back inside.

The fitting room is hot and small with the two of us and that huge civil engineering project of a dress packed together.

Brandy says, "Darvon." She says, "Quick, please." And she snaps her fingers.

I fish out another red and pink capsule, and she gulps it dry.

"This guy," Brandy says, "he asks me to get in his car, to talk, just to talk, and he asks if I have anything I'd like to say that maybe I was too afraid to tell any of the child service people."

The dress is coming apart, the silk opening at every seam, the tulle busting out, and Brandy says, "This guy, this detective, I tell him, 'No,' and he says, 'Good.' He says he likes a kid who can keep a secret."

At a train wreck you could pick up pencils two thousand at a time. Lightbulbs still perfect and not rattling inside. Key blanks by the hundreds. The pickup truck could only hold so much, and by then other trucks would be arrived with people shoveling grain into car backseats and people watching us with our piles of too much as we decided what we needed more, the ten thousand shoelaces or one thousand jars of celery salt. The five hundred fan belts all one size we didn't need but could resell, or the double-A batteries. The case of shortening we couldn't use up before it went rancid or the three hundred cans of hairspray.

"The police guy," Brandy says, and every wire is rising out of her tight yellow silk, "he puts his hand on me, right up the leg of my shorts, and he says we don't have to reopen the case. We don't have to cause my family any more problems." Brandy says, "This detective says the police want to arrest my father for suspicion. He can stop them, he says. He says, it's all up to me."

Brandy inhales and the dress shreds, she breathes and every breath makes her naked in more places.

"What did I know?" she says. "I was fifteen. I didn't know anything."

In a hundred torn holes, bare skin shows through.

At the train wreck, my father said security would be here any minute.

How I heard this was: We'd be rich. We'd be secure. But what he really meant was we'd have to hurry or we'd get caught and lose it all.

Of course I remember.

"The police guy," Brandy says, "he was young, twenty-one or twenty-two. He wasn't some dirty old man. It wasn't horrible," she says, "but it wasn't love."

With more of the dress torn, the skeleton springs apart in different places.

"Mostly," Brandy says, "it made me confused for a long time."

That's my growing up, those kind of train wrecks. Our only dessert from the time I was six to the time I was nine was butterscotch pudding. It turns out I loathe butterscotch. Even the color. Especially the color. And the taste. And smell.

How I met Manus was when I was eighteen a great-looking guy came to the door of my parents' house and asked, did we ever hear back from my brother after he ran away?

The guy was a little older, but not out of the ballpark. Twenty-five, tops. He gave me a card that said *Manus Kelley. Independent Special Contract Vice Operative.* The only thing else I noticed was he didn't wear a wedding ring. He said, "You know, you look a lot like your brother." He had a glorious smile and said, "What's your name?"

"Before we go back to the car," Brandy says, "I have to tell you something about your friend. Mr. White Westinghouse."

Formerly Mr. Chase Manhattan, formerly Nash Rambler, formerly Denver Omelet, formerly Independent Special Contract Vice Operative Manus Kelley. I do the homework: Manus is thirty years old. Brandy's twenty-four. When Brandy was sixteen, I was fifteen. When Brandy was sixteen, maybe Manus was already part of our lives.

I don't want to hear this.

The most beautiful ancient perfect dress is gone. The silk and tulle have slipped, dropped, slumped to the fitting room floor, and the wire and boning is broken and sprung away, leaving just some red marks already fading on Brandy's skin with Brandy left standing way too close to me in just her underwear.

"It's funny," Brandy says, "but this isn't the first time I've destroyed somebody's beautiful dress," and a big Aubergine Dreams eye winks at me. Her breath and skin feel warm, she's that close.

"The night I ran away from home," Brandy says, "I burned almost every stitch of clothing my family had hanging on the clothesline."

Brandy knows about me, or she doesn't know. She's confessing her heart, or she's teasing me. If she knows, she could be lying to me about Manus. If she doesn't know, then the man I love is a freaky creepy sexual predator.

Either Manus or Brandy is being a sleazy liar to me, me, the paragon of virtue and truth here. Manus or Brandy, I don't know who to hate.

Me and Manus or me and Brandy. It wasn't horrible, but it wasn't love.

Now, Please, Jump to Chapter Seventeen

Chapter 27

Daisy St. Patience only started Spitefield Park because her parents died. If it softens the blow, please know that they died in their sleep. Simply drifted away . . . sorry, Mom, sorry, Dad. The culprit was a faulty pilot light on their furnace. The first cold night of October, and the batteries in their smoke detector had long before preceded them in death. Nobody felt any pain except for Daisy, who knew exactly what words she wanted carved on their tombstone, but no cemetery would allow it. The inscription wasn't even the worst message that sprang to mind. Go shopping for tombstones, and you, too, will be impressed by the limited selection.

Lady Daisy realized she wasn't the only one of anything. Other like-minded bereaved must have had money to spend with mixed feelings. The land was cheap, and she was a gal with half a face for the sympathy vote. Daisy St. Patience, her least favorite movie was where Judy Garland does all of that full-color singing and dancing just to end up back in dreary black-and-white. Her dog is the only person who shows any gumption. Before the story even starts, he bites Margaret Hamilton off-screen. The dog rescues Jack Haley and draws the green curtain aside to expose the shenanigans of Frank Morgan. MGM spent a fortune. Yet after weeping buckets of glycerin and being clutched by winged monkeys Judy Garland is happy to wake up in a dirty bed surrounded by men. Nuh-uh. No way. To Daisy that didn't read as enlightenment.

Daisy St. Patience fixed the pilot light. She sold her parents' house and put the money toward a good surveyor to eyeball the plot lines. The long-term truth is that people's hearts change across time. Not just the hearts of the wildly vindictive. Even the widower whose wife was laid to rest beneath a granite marker that said:

I couldn't be bothered to shave my legs

A year later, even he phoned back to sheepishly inquire about the cost of a new stone.

Again, as Harriet Beecher Stowe asked, "Dude, why can't you do *both*?" Why can't a novel do this? You're not dead until you're dead.

What never failed to boggle Daisy was how Judy Garland had only just arrived in this glorious colorful place and she immediately wanted to run back to some boring pig farm. The fact that everyone else loved that film . . . what did that say about people? It says that most people can tolerate being over the rainbow for only about thirty seconds. Regret, Daisy knew, was the only confirmation of a well-lived life. If you didn't occasionally go too far, you weren't going anywhere. It was the dog—smart dog! good boy!—who chased the Siamese cat and baited Judy Garland to leave that dumb hot-air balloon which was taking her home. Time and time again, that dog did everything in its power to give Judy a better life.

In the alternate version of that movie, the way Daisy remembered it, when Judy awoke in Kansas, all giddy to be home in that tiresome dust and dirt, in the Daisy St. Patience Preferred Text Director's Cut, that little dog bit Judy Garland. It jumped into that windblown bed and sank its teeth right in her ingrate ass.

Now, Please, Jump to Chapter Nine

Chapter 28

So this is life in the Brandy Alexander Witness Reincarnation Project.

In Santa Barbara, Manus who was Denver taught us how to get drugs. The three of us were squeezed into that Fiat Spider from Portland to Santa Barbara, and Brandy just wanted to die. All the time, holding both hands pressed on her lower back, Brandy kept saying, "Stop the car. I got to stretch. I am spaz-am-ing. We have to stop."

It took us two days to drive from Oregon to California, and the two states are right next door to each other. Manus being all the time looking at Brandy, listening to her, in love with her so obviously I only wanted to kill them in worse and more painful ways.

In Santa Barbara, we're just into town when Brandy wants to get out and walk a little. Trouble is, this is a really good neighborhood in California. Right up in the hills over Santa Barbara. You walk around up here, the police or some private security patrol cruises you and wants to know who you are and see some ID, please.

Still, Brandy, she's spasming again, and the hysterical princess has one leg over the door, half climbed out of the Spider before Denver Omelet will even stop. What Brandy wants are the Tylox capsules she left in Suite 15-G at the Congress Hotel.

"You can't be beautiful," Brandy says about a thousand times, "until you feel beautiful."

Up here in the hills, we pull up curbside to an OPEN HOUSE sign. The house looking down on us is a big hacienda, Spanish enough to make you want to dance the flamenco on a table, swing on a wrought-iron chandelier, wear a sombrero and a bandolier.

"Here," Denver says to her. "Get yourselves pretty, and I'll show you how we can scam some prescription painkillers."

Jump back to the three days we hid out in Denver's apartment until we could get some cash together. Brandy, she's cooked up some new plan. Before she goes under the knife she's decided to find her sister.

The me who wants to dance on her grave.

"A vaginoplasty is pretty much forever," she says. "It can wait while I figure some things out."

She's decided to find her sister and tell her everything, about the gonorrhea, about why Shane's not dead, what happened, everything. Make a clean break of it. Probably she'd be surprised how much her sister already knows.

I just want to be out of town in case a felony arson arrest warrant is in the pipeline, so I threaten Denver, if he won't come with us, I'll run to the police and accuse him. Of arson, of kidnapping, of attempted murder. To Evie, I mail a letter.

To Brandy, I write:

let's drive around some. see what happens. chill.

This seems a little labor-intensive, but we've all got something to run from. And when I say we, I mean everybody in the world. So Brandy thinks we're on tour to find her sister, and Denver's come along by blackmail. My letter to Evie's sitting in her mailbox at the end of her driveway leading up to her burned-up ruins of a house. Evie's in Cancún, maybe.

The letter to Evie says:

To Miss Evelyn Cottrell,

Manus says he shot me and you helped him 'cuz of your filthy relationship. In order for you to stay out of PRISON, please seek an insurance settlement for the damage to your home and personal property as soon as possible. Convert this entire settlement into United States funds, tens and twenties, and mail them to me care of General Delivery in Seattle, Washington. I am the person you are responsible for being without a fiancé, your former best friend, no matter what lies you tell yourself. Send the money and I will consider the matter dealt with and will not go to the police and have you arrested and sent to PRISON, where you will have to fight day and night for your dignity and life but no doubt lose them both. Yes, and I've had major reconstructive surgery, so I look even better than myself, and I have Manus Kelley with me and he still loves me and says he hates you and will testify against you in court that you're a bitch.

Signed, Me

Jump to above the edge of the Pacific Ocean, parked curbside at the Spanish hacienda OPEN HOUSE. Denver tells Brandy and me how to go upstairs while he keeps the realtor busy. The master bedroom will have the best view, that's how to find it. The master bathroom will have the best drugs.

Sure, Manus used to be a police vice detective, if you consider wagging your butt around the bushes in Washington Park wearing a Speedo bikini a size too small and hoping some lonely sex hound will whip his dick out, if that's detective work, then, sure, Manus was a detective.

Because beauty is power the way money is power the way a loaded gun is power. And Manus with his square-jawed, cheek-boned good looks could be a Nazi recruiting poster.

While Manus was still fighting crime, I found him cutting the crust off a slice of bread one morning. Bread without crust made me remember being little. This was so sweet, but I thought he was making me toast. Then Manus goes to in front of a mirror in the apartment we used to share, wearing his white Speedo, and he asks, if I were a gay guy would I want to bang him up the butt? Then he changed to a red Speedo and asked again. You know, he says, really stuff his poop chute? Plow the cowboy? It's not a morning I would want on video.

"What I need," Manus said, "is for my basket to look big, but my ass to look adolescent." He takes the slice of bread and stuffs it inside between himself and the crotch of the Speedo. "Don't worry, this is how underwear models get a better look," he says. "You get a smooth unoffensive bulge this way." He stands sideways to the mirror and says, "You think I need another slice?"

His being a detective meant he crunched around in good weather, in his sandals and his lucky red Speedo, while two plain-clothes men nearby in a parked car waited for somebody to take the bait. This happened more than you'd imagine. Manus was a one-man campaign to clean up Washington Park. He'd never been this successful as a regular policeman and this way nobody ever shot at him.

It all felt very Bond, James Bond. Very cloak-and-dagger. Very spy versus spy. Plus he was getting a great tan. Plus he got to tax-deduct his gym membership and his buying new Speedos.

Jump to the realtor in Santa Barbara shaking my hand and saying my name, Daisy St. Patience, over and over the way you do when you want to make a good impression but not looking at me in my veils. He's looking at Brandy and Denver.

Charmed, I'm sure.

The house is just what you'd expect from the outside. There's a big scarred mission-style trestle table in the dining room, under a wrought-iron chandelier you could swing on. Laid across the table is a silver-embroidered, fringed Spanish shawl.

We represent a television personality who wishes to remain nameless, Denver tells the realtor. We're an advance team scouting for a weekend home for this nameless celebrity. Miss Alexander, she's an expert in product toxicity, you know, the lethal fumes and secretions given off by homes.

"New carpet," Denver says, "will exude poisonous formaldehyde for up to two years after it's been laid."

Brandy says, "I know that feeling."

It got so that when Manus's crotch wasn't leading men to their doom, Manus was three-piece-suited in court on the witness stand, saying how the defendant approached him in some lurid exposed public masturbating way and asked for a cigarette.

"Like anybody could look at me and think I smoke," Manus would say.

You didn't know what vice he objected to more.

After Santa Barbara, we drove to San Francisco and sold the Fiat Spider. Me, I'm writing on cocktail napkins all the time: *maybe your sister's in the next city. she could be anywhere.*

In the Santa Barbara hacienda, Brandy and me found Benzedrine and Dexedrine and old Quaaludes and Soma and some

Dialose capsules that turned out to be a fecal softener. And some Solaquin Forte cream that turned out to be a skin bleach.

In San Francisco, we sold the Fiat and some drugs and bought a big red *Physicians' Desk Reference* book so we wouldn't be stealing worthless fecal softeners and skin bleaches. In San Francisco, old people are all over selling their big rich houses full of drugs and hormones. We had Demerol and Darvocet-Ns. Not the puny little Darvocet-N 50s. Brandy was feeling beautiful with me trying to OD her on big Darvocet 100-milligram jobbers.

After the Fiat, we rented a big Seville convertible. Just between us, we were the Zine kids:

Me, I was Comp Zine.

Denver was Thor Zine.

Brandy, Stella Zine.

It was in San Francisco I started Denver on his own secret hormone therapy to destroy him.

Manus's detective career had started to peter out when his arrest rate dropped to one per day, then one per week, then zero, then still zero. The problem was the sun, the tanning, and the fact he was getting older and he was a known bait, none of the older men he had already arrested went near him. The younger men just thought he was too old.

So Manus got bold. More and more his Speedos got smaller, which wasn't a good look, either. The pressure was on to replace him with a new model. So now he'd have to start conversations. Talk. Be funny. Really work at meeting guys. Develop a personality, and still the younger men, the only ones who didn't run when they saw him, a younger man would still decline when Manus suggested they take a walk back into the trees, into the bushes.

Even the most horny young men with their eyes scamming everybody else would say, "Uh, no thanks."

Or, "I just want to be alone right now."

Or worse, "Back off, you old troll, or I'll call a cop."

After San Francisco and San Jose and Sacramento, we went to Reno and Brandy turned Denver Omelet into Chase Manhattan. We zigzagged everywhere I thought we'd find enough drugs. Evie's money could wait.

Jump to Las Vegas and Brandy turns Chase Manhattan into Eberhard Faber. We drive the Seville down the gut of Las Vegas. All that spasming neon, the red chase lights going one direction, white chase lights going the other direction. Las Vegas looks the way you'd imagine heaven must look at night. We never put the top up on the Seville, had it two weeks, never put the top up.

Cruising the gut of Las Vegas, Brandy sat on the boot with her ass up on the trunk lid and her feet on the backseat, wearing this strapless metallic brocade sheath as pink as the burning center of a road flare with a bejeweled bodice and a detachable long silk taffeta cape with balloon sleeves.

With her looking that good, Las Vegas with all its flash and dazzle was just another Brandy Alexander–brand fashion accessory.

Brandy puts her arms up, wearing these long pink opera gloves, and just howls. She just looks and feels so good at that moment. And the detachable long silk taffeta cape with balloon sleeves, it detaches.

And sails off into Las Vegas traffic.

"Go around the block," Brandy screams. "That cape has to go back to Bullock's in the morning."

After Manus's detective career started downhill, we'd have to work out in the gym every day, twice on some days. Aerobics, tanning, nutrition, every station of the cross. He was a bodybuilder, if what that means is you drink your meal-replacement shakes right out of the blender six times a day over the kitchen sink. Then Manus would get swimwear through the mail you couldn't buy in this country, little pouches on strings and microfilament technology he'd put on the moment we got home from the gym, then follow me around asking, did I think his butt looked too flat?

If I was a gay guy, did I think he needed to trim back his pubic hair? Me being a gay guy, would I think he looked too desperate? Too aloof? Was his chest big enough? Too big, maybe?

"I'd hate for guys to think I'm just a big dumb cow is all," Manus would say.

Did he look, you know, too gay? Gay guys only wanted guys who acted straight.

"I don't want guys to see me as a big passive bottom," Manus would say. "It's not like I'd just flop there and let just any guy bone me."

Manus would leave a ring of shaved hairs and bronzer scum around the bathtub and expect me to scrub.

Always in the background was the idea of going back to an assignment where people shot at you, criminals with nothing to lose if you got killed.

And maybe Manus could bust some old tourist who found the cruisy part of Washington Park by accident, but most days the precinct commander was on him to start training a younger replacement.

Most days, Manus would untangle a silver metallic tiger-stripe string bikini out of the knotted mess in his underwear drawer. He'd strain his ass into this little A-cup nothing and look at himself in the mirror sideways, frontways, backward, then tear it off and leave the stretched, dead little animal print on the bed for me to find. This would go on through zebra stripes, tiger stripes, leopard spots, then cheetah, panther, puma, ocelot, until he ran out of time.

"These are my lucky lifeguard 'kinis," he'd tell me. "Be honest."

And this is what I kept telling myself was love.

Be honest? I wouldn't know where to start. I was so out of practice.

After Las Vegas, we rented one of those family vans. Eberhard Faber became Hewlett Packard. Brandy wore a long white cotton piqué dress with open strappy sides and a high slit up the skirt that was totally inappropriate for the entire state of Utah. We stopped and tasted the Great Salt Lake.

This just seemed like the thing to do.

I was always writing in the sand, writing in the dust on the car: *maybe your sister is in the next town.*

Writing: *here, take a few more Vicodins.*

It was after Manus couldn't get guys to approach him for sex that he started into buying man-on-man sex magazines and going out to gay clubs.

"Research," he'd say.

"You can come with," he'd tell me, "but don't stand too close, I don't want to send out the wrong signal."

After Utah, Brandy turned Hewlett Packard into Harper Collins in Butte. There in Montana, we rented a Ford Probe and Harper drove with me squashed in the backseat, and every once in a while Harper would say, "We're going one hundred and ten miles an hour."

Brandy and me, we'd shrug.

Speeding didn't seem like anything in a place as big as Montana.

maybe your sister's not even in the united states, I wrote in lipstick on a bathroom mirror in a motel in Great Falls.

So to keep Manus's job, we went out to gay bars, and I sat alone and told myself that it was different for men, the good looks thing was. Manus flirted and danced and sent drinks down the bar to whoever looked like a challenge. Manus would slip onto the barstool next to mine and whisper out the side of his mouth.

"I can't believe he's with that guy," he'd say.

Manus would nod just enough for me to figure out which guy.

"Last week, he wouldn't give me the time of day," Manus would rant under his breath. "I wasn't good enough, and that trashy, bottle-blond piece of garbage is supposed to be better?"

Manus would hunch over his drink and say, "Guys are so fucked up."

And I'd be, like, no duh.

And I told myself it was okay. Any relationship I could be in would have these rough times.

Jump to Calgary, Alberta, where Brandy ate Nebalino suppositories wrapped in gold foil because she thought they were Almond Roca. She got so ripped, she turned Harper Collins into Addison Wesley. Most of Calgary, Brandy wore a white, quilted ski jacket with a faux-fur collar and a white bikini bottom by Donna Karan. The look was fun and spirited and we felt light and popular.

Evenings called for a black-and-white-striped floor-length coat dress that Brandy could never keep buttoned up, with black wool hot pants on underneath. Addison Wesley turned into Nash Rambler, and we rented another Cadillac.

Jump to Edmonton, Alberta, Nash Rambler turned into Alfa Romeo. Brandy wore these crinoline shorty-short square dance petticoats over black tights tucked into cowboy boots. Brandy wore this push-up bustier made of leather with local cattle brands burned all over it.

In a nice hotel bar in Edmonton, Brandy says, "I hate it when you can see the seam in your martini glass. I mean, I can feel the mold line. It's so cheap."

Guys all over her. Like spotlights, I remember that kind of attention. That whole country, Brandy never had to buy her own drinks, not once.

Jump to Manus losing his assignment as an independent special contract vice operative to the detective division of the Metropolitan Police Department. My point is, he never really got over it.

He was running out of money. It's not like there was a lot in the bank to begin with. Then the birds ate my face.

What I didn't know is, there was Evie Cottrell living alone in her big lonesome house with all her Texas land and oil money, saying, hey, she had some work that needed doing. And Manus with his driving need to prove he can still pee on every tree. That mirror-mirror kind of power. The rest you already know.

Jump to us on the road, after the hospital, after the Rhea sisters, and I keep slipping the hormones, the Provera and Climara and Premarin, into what he ate and drank. Whiskey and estradiol. Vodka and ethinyl estradiol. It was so easy it was scary. He was all the time making big cow eyes at Brandy.

We were all running from something. Vaginoplasty. Aging. The future.

Jump to Los Angeles.

Jump to Spokane.

Jump to Boise and San Diego and Phoenix.

Jump to Vancouver, British Columbia, where we were Italian expatriates speaking English as a second language until there wasn't a native tongue among us.

"You have two of the breasts of a young woman," Alfa Romeo told a realtor I can't remember in which house.

From Vancouver, we reentered the United States as Brandy, Seth, and Bubba-Joan via the Princess Princess's very professional mouth. All the way to Seattle, Brandy read to us how a little Jewish girl with a mysterious muscle disease turned herself into Rona Barrett.

All of us looking at big rich houses, picking up drugs, renting cars, buying clothes, and taking clothes back.

"Tell us a gross personal story," Brandy says en route to Seattle. Brandy all the time being the boss of me. Being *this close* to death herself.

Rip yourself open.

Tell me my life story before I die.

Sew yourself shut.

Now, Please, Jump to Chapter Fifteen

Chapter 29

Jump to this one time, nowhere special, just Brandy and me in the speech therapist office when Brandy catches me with my hands up under my veil, touching the seashells and ivory of my exposed molars, stroking the embossed leather of my scar tissue, dry and polished from my breath going back and forth across it. I'm touching the saliva where it dries sticky and raw down the sides of my neck, and Brandy says not to watch myself too close.

"Honey," she says, "times like this, it helps to think of yourself as a sofa or a newspaper, something made by a lot of other people but not made to last forever."

The open edge of my throat feels starched and plastic, ribbed-knitted and stiff with sizing and interfacing. It's the same feel as the top edge of a strapless dress or maillot, held up with wire or plastic stays sewn inside. Hard but warm the way pink looks. Bony but covered in soft, touchable skin.

This kind of acute traumatic mandibulectomy without reconstruction, before decannulation of the tracheostomy tube can lead to sleep apnea, the doctors said. This was them talking to each other during morning rounds.

And people find *me* hard to understand.

What the doctors told me was unless they rebuilt me some kind of jaw, at least some kind of flap, they said, I could die anytime I fell asleep. I could just stop breathing and not wake up. A quick, painless death.

On my pad with my pen, I wrote:

don't tease.

Us in the speech therapist office, Brandy says, "It helps to know you're not any more responsible for how you look than a car is," Brandy says. "You're a product just as much. A product of a product of a product. The people who design cars, they're products. Your parents are products. Their parents were products. Your teachers, products. The minister in your church, another product," Brandy says.

Sometimes your best way to deal with shit, she says, is to not hold yourself as such a precious little prize.

"My point being," Brandy says, "is you can't escape the world, and you're not responsible for how you look, if you look beauticious or butt-ugly. You're not responsible for how you feel or what you say or how you act or anything you do. It's all out of your hands," Brandy says.

The same way a compact disk isn't responsible for what's recorded on it, that's how we are. You're about as free to act as a programmed computer. You're about as one-of-a-kind as a dollar bill.

"There isn't any real *you* in *you*," she says. "Even your physical body, all your cells will be replaced within eight years."

Skin, bones, blood, and organs transplant from person to person. Even what's inside you already, the colonies of microbes and bugs that eat your food for you, without them you'd die. Nothing of you is all-the-way yours. All of you is inherited.

"Relax," Brandy says, "Whatever you're thinking, a million other folks are thinking. Whatever you do, they're doing, and none of you is responsible. All of you is a cooperative effort."

Up under my veil, I finger the wet poking stub of a tongue from some vandalized product. The doctors suggested using part of my small intestine to make my throat longer. They suggested carving the shinbones, the fibulas of this human product I am, shaping the bones and grafting them to build me, build the product, a new jawbone.

On my pad, I wrote:

the leg-bone connected to the head-bone?

The doctors didn't get it.

Now hear the word of the Lord.

"You're a product of our language," Brandy says, "and how our laws are and how we believe our God wants us. Every bitty molecule about you has already been thought out by some million people before you," she says. "Anything you can do is boring and old and perfectly okay. You're safe because you're so trapped inside your culture. Anything you can conceive of is fine *because you can conceive of it.* You can't imagine any way to escape. There's no way you can get out," Brandy says.

"The world," Brandy says, "is your cradle and your trap."

This is after I backslid. I wrote to my booker at the agency and asked about my chances of getting hand or foot work. Modeling watches and shoes. My booker had sent me some flowers in the hospital early on. Maybe I could pick up assignments as a leg model. How much Evie had blabbed to them, I didn't know.

To be a hand model, he wrote back, you have to wear a size seven glove and a size five ring. A foot model must have perfect toenails and wear a size six shoe. A leg model can't play any sports. She can't have any visible veins. Unless your fingers and toes still look good printed in a magazine at three times their normal size, or billboarded at two hundred times their size, he wrote, don't count on body part work.

My hand's an eight. My foot, a seven.

Brandy says, "And if you can find any way out of our culture, then that's a trap, too. Just wanting to get out of the trap reinforces the trap."

The books on plastic surgery, the pamphlets and brochures, all promised to help me live a more normal, happy life; but less and less this looked like what I'd want. What I wanted looked more and more like what I'd always been trained to want. What everybody wants.

Give me attention.

Flash.

Give me beauty.

Flash.

Give me peace and happiness, a loving relationship, and a perfect home.

Flash.

Brandy says, "The best way is not to fight it, just go. Don't be trying all the time to fix things. What you run from only stays with you longer. When you fight something, you only make it stronger."

She says, "Don't do what you want." She says, "Do what you don't want. Do what you're trained not to want."

It's the opposite of following your bliss.

Brandy tells me, "Do the things that scare you the most."

Now, Please, Jump to Chapter Fourteen

Chapter 30

You won't catch Manus bowing down, making himself a slave to the golden calf of total accuracy. You, who are always trying to get everything "right," he could teach you a thing or ten. For example: don't be in such an all-fired hurry to get everything wrapped up.

Witness how Manus recounts the story of his all-time favorite movie: Billy Zane is riding a boat with Dolores Claiborne. Also aboard are Kate Winslet and that demented kid from *Gilbert Grape*. The lavish interiors are spectacular, but the exteriors make the boat look a little computer-generated—genuinely video-gamey—not that you could do much better. The boat, itself, wow, this boat is gigantic, plowing through the North Atlantic, escorted by leaping porpoises, but most of what you'll notice is how much air pollution it generates. It's as if the entire reason for this trip is to draw a fat line of coal smoke between Southampton and Ellis Island.

Inside the grand salon, Billy Zane gives Kate Winslet a big blue diamond and slugs her in the chops. The kid from *Gilbert Grape* draws a naked picture of her boobs. This, this *is just not Kate Winslet's day*! Finally, an iceberg takes a bite out of the boat's hull, well below the waterline. It's exactly like *Jaws* but in slow motion and with ice. This grand metaphor—it's sinking fast. As the boat stands straight up in the water, panic ensues. This gesture mimics, strangely, the moment Kate Winslet stood on her tiptoes, ballerina-style, and fell down drunk. To save two thousand Irish people from drowning, Kate shoots Billy Zane and stuffs his corpse in the leak. Nobody sees that coming. At this point there's still three days to kill before anyone will see the Statue of Liberty; most of the actors are playing a card game called "bridge." Hereabouts, usually Manus gets up to use the bathroom or microwave a snack. When he comes back to watch, the boat is swarming with vampires. Sometimes Manus channel-surfs, splicing in the better parts of other films. Martians blast the boat with death rays. Charleton Heston tries to rescue Ava Gardner but is washed away to a martyr's offscreen death. The kid from *Gilbert Grape* dies every time—BUT NEVER SOON ENOUGH.

As far as Manus is concerned, Bill Paxton should've made *Aliens II* and quit while he was ahead. Instead, Paxton finds the naked drawing of Kate Winslet locked in an underwater safe. This is not what he wanted. He wanted the big blue diamond that a littering old woman doesn't think to recycle. She simply heaves it into the ocean, where human beings throw all their Styrofoam cups and used diapers. Bankrupt, Bill Paxton smiles at a skinny blond girl.

That . . . that's the wonderful freedom you had when you were six years old, before you caved in to logic. You had authority but you forgot it. There is no *truth.* Not really. There's only *the best truth.*

The happy ending is that, time and time again, Manus falls asleep.

Now, Please, Jump to Chapter Three

Chapter 31

When you go out with a drunk, you'll notice how a drunk fills your glass so he can empty his own. As long as you're drinking, drinking is okay. Two's company. Drinking is fun. If there's a bottle, even if your glass isn't empty, a drunk, he'll pour a little in your glass before he fills his own.

This only looks like generosity.

That Brandy Alexander, she's always on me about plastic surgery. Why don't I, you know, just look at what's out there? With her chest siliconed, her hips liposucked, the 46-16-26 Katty Kathy hourglass thing she is, the fairy godmother makeover, my fair lady, *Pygmalion* thing she is, my brother back from the dead, Brandy Alexander is very invested in plastic surgery.

And vice versa.

Bathroom talk.

Brandy's still laid out on the cold tile floor, high atop Capitol Hill in Seattle. Mr. Parker has come and gone. Just Brandy and me all afternoon. I'm still sitting on the open end of a huge ceramic snail shell bolted to the wall. Trying to kill her in my half-assed way. Brandy's auburn head of hair is between my feet. Lipsticks and Demerols, blushes and Percocet 5, Aubergine Dreams and Nembutal Sodium capsules are spread out all over the aquamarine countertops around the vanity sink.

My hand, I've been holding a handful of Valiums so long my palm has gone Tiffany's light blue. Just Brandy and me all afternoon with the sun coming in at lower and lower angles through the big brass porthole windows.

"My waist," Brandy says. The Plumbago mouth looks a little too blue, Tiffany's light blue, if you ask me. Overdose baby blue. "Sofonda said I had to have a sixteen-inch waist," Brandy says. "I said, 'Miss Sofonda, I am big-boned. I am six feet tall. No way am I getting down to a sixteen-inch waistline."

Sitting on the snail shell, I'm only half listening.

"Sofonda," Brandy says, "Sofonda says, there's a way, but I have to trust her. When I wake up in the recovery room, I'll have a sixteen-inch waist."

It's not like I haven't heard this story in a dozen other bathrooms. Another bottle off the countertop, Bilax capsules, I look it up in the *Phyicians' Desk Reference* book.

Bilax capsules. A bowel evacuant.

Maybe I should drop a few of these into that nonstop mouth between my feet.

Jump to Manus watching me do that infomercial. We were so beautiful. Me with a face. Him not so full of conjugated estrogens.

I thought we were a real love relationship. I did. I was very invested in love, but it was just this long, long sex thing that could end at any moment because, after all, it's just about getting off. Manus would close his power-blue eyes and twist his head just so, side to side, and swallow.

And, Yes, I'd tell Manus. I came right when he did.

Pillow talk.

Almost all the time, you tell yourself you're loving somebody when you're just using them.

This only looks like love.

Jump to Brandy on the bathroom floor, saying, "Sofonda and Vivienne and Kitty were all with me at the hospital." Her hands curl up off the tile, and she runs them up and down the sides of her blouse. "All three of them wore those baggy green scrub suits, wearing hairnets over their wigs and with those Duchess of Windsor costume jewelry brooches pinned on their scrub suits," Brandy says. "They were flying around behind the surgeon and the lights, and Sofonda was telling me to count backwards from one hundred. You know . . . 99 . . . 98 . . . 97 . . ."

The Aubergine Dreams eyes close. Brandy, pulling long, even breaths, says, "The doctors, they took out the bottom rib on each side of my chest." Her hands rub where, and she says, "I couldn't sit up in bed for two months, but I had a sixteen-inch waist. I still have a sixteen-inch waist."

One of Brandy's hands opens to full flower and slides over the flat land where her blouse tucks into the belt of her skirt. "They cut out two of my ribs, and I never saw them again," Brandy says. "There's something in the Bible about taking out your ribs."

The creation of Eve.

Brandy says, "I don't know why I let them do that to me."

And Brandy, she's asleep.

Jump back to the night Brandy and I started this road trip, the night we left the Congress Hotel with Brandy driving the way you can only drive at two-thirty A.M. in an open sports car with a loaded rifle and an overdosed hostage. Brandy hides her eyes behind Ray-Bans so she can drive in a little privacy. Instant glamour from another planet in the 1950s, Brandy pulls an Hermès scarf over her auburn hair and ties it under her chin.

All I can see is myself reflected in Brandy's Ray-Bans, tiny and horrible. Still strung out and pulled apart by the cold night air around the windshield. Bathrobe still dragging shut in the car door. My face, you touch my blasted, scar-tissue face and you'd swear you were touching chunks of orange peel and leather.

Driving east, I'm not sure what we're running from. Evie or the police or Mr. Baxter or the Rhea sisters. Or nobody. Or the future. Fate. Growing up, getting old. Picking up the pieces. As if by running we won't have to get on with our lives. I'm with Brandy right now because I can't imagine getting away with this without Brandy's help. Because, right now, I need her.

Not that I really love her. Him. Shane.

Already the word "love" is sounding pretty thin.

Hermès scarf on her head, Ray-Bans on her head, makeup on her face, I look at the queen supreme in the pulse-pulse, then pulse-pulse, then pulse-pulse of oncoming headlights. What I see when I look at Brandy, this is what Manus saw when he took me sailing.

Right now, looking at flashes of Brandy beside me in Manus's car, I know what it is I loved about her. What I love is myself. Brandy Alexander just looks exactly the way I looked before the accident. Why wouldn't she? She's my brother, Shane. Shane and I were almost the same height, born one year apart. The same coloring. The same features. The same hair, only Brandy's hair is in better shape.

Add to this her lipo, her silicone, her trachea shave, her brow shave, her scalp advance, her forehead realignment, her rhino contouring to smooth her nose, her maxomilliary operations to shape her jaw. Add to all that years of electrolysis and a handful of hormones and antiandrogens every day, and it's no wonder I didn't recognize her.

Plus the idea my brother's been dead for years. You just don't expect to meet dead people.

What I love is myself. I was so beautiful.

My love cargo, Manus Locked in the Trunk, Manus Trying to Kill Me, how can I keep thinking I love Manus? Manus is just the last man who thought I was beautiful. Who kissed me on the lips. Who touched me. Manus is just the last man who ever told me he loved me.

You count down the facts and it's so depressing.

I can only eat baby food.

My best friend screwed my fiancé.

My fiancé almost stabbed me to death.

I've set fire to a house and been pointing a rifle at innocent people all night.

My brother I hate has come back from the dead to upstage me.

I'm an invisible monster, and I'm incapable of loving anybody. You don't know which is worse.

Jump to me wetting a washcloth in the vanity sink. In the undersea bathroom grotto even the towels and washcloths are aqua and blue, with a scalloped shell motif along the hems. I put the cold wet washcloth on Brandy's forehead and wake her up, so's she can take more pills. Die in the car instead of this bathroom.

I haul Brandy to her feet and stuff the princess back into her suit jacket.

We have to walk her around before anybody sees her this way.

I strap her high heels back on her feet. Brandy, she leans on me. She leans on the edge of the countertop. She picks up a handful of Bilax capsules and squints down at them.

"My back is killing me," Brandy says. "Why'd I ever let them give me such big tits?"

The queen supreme looks ready to swallow a handful of anything.

I shake my head no.

Brandy squints at me. "But I need these."

In the *Physicians' Desk Reference*, I show her Bilax, bowel evacuant.

"Oh." Brandy turns her hand over to spill the Bilax into her purse, and some capsules fall but some stick to the sweat on her palm. "After they give you the tits, your nipples are cockeyed and way too high," she says. "They use a razor to shave the nipples off, and they relocate them."

That's her word.

Relocate.

The Brandy Alexander Nipple Relocation Program.

My dead brother, the late Shane, shakes the last bowel evacuant off her damp palm. Brandy says, "I have no sensation in my nipples."

Off the counter, I get my veils and put layer after layer over my head.

Thank you for not sharing.

We walk up and down the second-floor hallways until Brandy says she's ready for the stairs. Step at a time, quiet, we go down to the foyer. Across the foyer, through the double doors closed on the drawing room, you can hear Mr. Parker's deep voice saying something soft, over and over.

Brandy leaning on me, we tiptoe a slow three-legged race across the foyer, from the foot of the stairs to the drawing room doors. We crack the doors open some inches and poke our faces through the crack.

Ellis is laid out on the drawing room carpet.

Mr. Parker is sitting on Ellis's chest with a size seventeen wingtip planted on each side of Ellis's head.

Ellis's hands slap Parker's big ass, claw at the back of the double-breasted jacket. The single vent in Mr. Parker's jacket is torn open along the seam up the middle of his back to his collar.

Mr. Parker's hands, the heel of one hand crams a soggy, gnawed eel-skin wallet between Ellis's capped teeth.

Ellis's face is dark red and shining the way you'd look if you got the cherry pie in the pie-eating contest. A runny finger-painting mess of nosebleed and tears, snot and drool.

Mr. Parker, his hair is fallen over his eyes. His other hand is a fist around five inches of Ellis's pulled-out tongue.

Ellis is slapping and gagging between Mr. Parker's thick legs.

Broken Ming vases and other collectibles are all around them on the floor.

Mr. Parker says, "That's right. Just do that. That's nice. Just relax."

Brandy and me, watching.

Me wanting Ellis destroyed, this is all just too perfect to spoil.

I tug on Brandy. Brandy, honey. We better walk you back upstairs. Rest you some more. Give you a nice fresh handful of Benzedrine spansules.

Now, Please, Jump to Chapter Twelve

Chapter 32

What you get with the Rhea sisters is three skin-and-bone white men who sit around a suite at the Congress Hotel all day in nylon slips with the shoulder straps fallen off one shoulder or the other, wearing high heels and smoking cigarettes. Kitty Litter, Sofonda Peters, and the Vivacious Vivienne VaVane, their faces shining with moisturizer and egg-white facials, they listen to that step-two-three cha-cha music you only hear on elevators anymore. The Rhea sister hair, their hair is short and flat with grease and matted down bristling with bobby pins, flat on their heads. Maybe they have a wig cap stretched on over the pins if it's not summer outside. Most of the time, they don't know what season it is. The blinds aren't ever open, and there are maybe a dozen of those cha-cha records stacked on the automatic record changer.

All the furniture is blond, and the big four-legged RCA Philco console stereo. The stereo, you could plow a field with that old needle, and the metal tone arm weighs about two pounds.

May I present them:

Kitty Litter.

Sofonda Peters.

The Vivacious Vivienne VaVane.

Aka the Rhea sisters when they're onstage, these are her family, Brandy Alexander told me in the speech therapist office. Not the first time we met, this wasn't the time I cried and told Brandy how I lost my face. This wasn't the second time, either, the time Brandy brought her sewing basket full of ways to hide my being a monster. This was one of the other tons of times we snuck off while I was still in the hospital. The speech therapist office was just where we'd meet.

"Usually," Brandy tells me, "Kitty Litter is bleaching and tweezing away unwanted facial hair. This unsightly hair thing can tie up a bathroom for hours, but Kitty would wear her Ray-Bans inside out, she loves looking at her reflection so much."

The Rheas, they made Brandy what she is. Brandy, she owes them everything.

Brandy would lock the speech therapist door, and if somebody would knock, Brandy and me, we'd fake loud orgasm noises. We'd scream and yip and slap the floor. I'd clap my hands to make that special spanking sound that everybody knows. Whoever knocks, they'd go away fast.

Then we'd go back to just us using up makeup and talking.

"Sofonda," Brandy would tell me, "Sofonda Peters, she's the

brains, Sofonda is. Miss Peters is all day with her porcelain nails stuck in the rotary-dial Princess phone to an agent or a merchandiser, selling, selling, selling."

Somebody would knock on the speech therapist door, so I'd give out with a cat scream and slap my thigh.

The Rhea sisters, Brandy would tell me, she'd be dead without them. When they'd found her, the princess queen supreme, she'd been a size twenty-six, lip-synching at amateur-night open-mike shows. Lip-synching "Thumbelina."

Her hair, her figure, her hippy, hippy-forward Brandy Alexander walk, the Rhea sisters invented all that.

Jump to two fire engines passing me in the opposite direction as I drive the freeway toward downtown, away from Evie's house on fire. In the rearview mirror of Manus's Fiat Spider, Evie's house is a smaller and smaller bonfire. The peachy-pink hem of Evie's bathrobe is shut in the car door, and the ostrich feathers whip me in the cool night air pouring around the convertible's windshield.

Smoke is all I smell like. The rifle on the passenger seat is pointing at the floor.

There's not one word from my love cargo in the trunk.

And there's only one place left to go.

No way could I call and just ask the operator to ring Brandy. No way would the operator understand me, so we're on our way downtown to the Congress Hotel.

Jump to how all the Rhea sister money comes from a doll named Katty Kathy. This is what else Brandy told me between faking orgasms in the speech therapist office. She's a doll, Katty Kathy is one of those foot-high flesh-tone dolls with the impossible measurements. What she would be as a real woman is 46-16-26. As a real woman, Katty Kathy could buy a total of nothing off the rack. You know you've seen this doll. Comes naked in a plastic bubble pack for a dollar, but her clothes cost a fortune, that's how realistic she is. You can buy about four hundred tiny fashion separates that mix and match to create three tasteful outfits. In that way, the doll is incredibly lifelike. Chilling, even.

Sofonda Peters came up with the idea. Invented Katty Kathy, made the prototype, sold the doll, and cut all the deals. Still, Sofonda is about married to Kitty and Vivian and there's enough money to support them all.

What sold Katty Kathy is that she's a talking doll, but instead of a string, she's got this little gold chain coming out of her back. You pull her chain, and she says:

"That dress is fine, I mean, if that's *really* how you want to look."

"Your heart is my piñata."

"Is that what you're going to wear?"

"I think it would be good for our relationship if we dated other people."

"Kiss kiss."

And, "Don't touch my hair!"

The Rhea sisters, they made a bundle. Katty Kathy's little bolero jacket alone, they have that jacket sewn in Cambodia for a dime and sell it here in America for sixteen dollars. People pay that.

Jump to me parking the Fiat with its trunk full of my love cargo on a side street, and me walking up Broadway toward the doorman at the Congress Hotel. I'm a woman with half a face arriving at a luxury hotel, one of those big glazed terra-cotta palace hotels built a hundred years ago, where the doormen wear tailcoats with gold braid on the shoulders. I'm wearing a peignoir set and a bathrobe. No veils. Half the bathrobe has been shut in a car door, dragging on the freeway for the past twenty miles. My ostrich feathers smell like smoke, and I'm trying to keep it a big secret that I have a rifle tucked up crutchlike under my arm.

Yeah, and I lost a shoe, one of those high-heeled mules, too.

The doorman in his tailcoat doesn't even look at me. Yeah, and my hair, I see it reflected in the big brass plaque that says The Congress Hotel. The cool night air has pulled my butter crème frosting hairdo out into a ratted stringy mess.

Jump to me at the front desk of the Congress Hotel where I try and make my eyes alluring. They say what people notice first about you is your eyes. I have the attention of what must be the night auditor, the bellman, the manager, and a clerk. First impressions are so important. It must be the way I'm dressed or the rifle. Using the hole that's the top of my throat, my tongue sticking out of it and all the scar tissue around it, I say, "Gerl terk nahdz gah sssid."

Everybody is just flash-frozen by my alluring eyes.

I don't know how, but then the rifle's up on the desk, pointing at nobody in particular.

The manager steps up in his navy blue blazer with its little brass *Mr. Baxter* name tag, and he says, "We can give you all the money in the drawer, but no one here can open the safe in the office."

The gun on the desk points right at the brass *Mr. Baxter* name tag, a fact that hasn't gone unnoticed. I snap my fingers and point at a piece of paper for him to give me. With the guest pen on a chain, I write:

which suite are the rhea sisters in? don't make me knock on every door on the fifteenth floor. it's the middle of the night.

"That would be Suite 15-G," says Mr. Baxter, both his hands full of cash I don't want and reached out across the desk toward me. "The elevators," he says, "are to your right."

Jump to me being Daisy St. Patience the first day Brandy and I sat together. The day of the frozen turkey after the whole summer I waited for somebody to ask me what happened to my face, and I told Brandy everything.

Brandy, when she sat me in the chair still hot from her ass and she locked the speech therapist door that first time, she named me out of my future. She named me Daisy St. Patience and never wanted to know what name I walked in the door with. I was the rightful heir to the international fashion house the House of St. Patience.

Brandy, she just talked and talked. We were running out of air, she talked so much, and I don't mean just we, Brandy and me. I mean the world. The world was running out of air, Brandy talked that much. The Amazon Basin just could not keep up.

"Who you are moment to moment," Brandy said, "is just a story."

What I needed was a new story.

"Let me do for you," Brandy said, "what the Rhea sisters did for me."

Give me courage.

Flash.

Give me heart.

Flash.

So jump to me being Daisy St. Patience going up in that elevator, and Daisy St. Patience walking down that wide carpeted hallway to Suite 15-G. Daisy knocks and nobody answers. Through the door, you can hear that cha-cha music.

The door opens six inches, but the chain is on so it stops.

Three white faces appear in the six-inch gap, one on top of the other, Kitty Litter, Sofonda Peters, and the Vivacious Vivienne VaVane, their faces shining with moisturizer. Their short dark hair is matted down flat with bobby pins and wig caps.

The Rhea sisters.

Who's who, I don't know. The drag queen totem pole in the door crack says:

"Don't take the queen supreme from us."

"She's all we have to do with our lives."

"She isn't finished yet. We're not half done, and there's just so much more we have to do on her."

I give them a peekaboo pink chiffon flash of the rifle, and the door slams.

Through the door, you can hear the chain come off. Then the door opens all the way.

Jump to one time, late one night, driving between Nowhere, Wyoming, and WhoKnowsWhere, Montana, when Seth says how your being born makes your parents God. You owe them your life, and they can control you.

"Then puberty makes you Satan," he says, "just because you want something better."

Jump to inside suite 15-G with its blond furniture and the bossa-nova cha-cha music and cigarette smoke, and the Rhea sisters are flying around the room in their nylon slips with the shoulder straps off one shoulder or the other. I don't have to do anything but point the rifle.

"We know who you are, Daisy St. Patience," one of them says, lighting a cigarette. "With a face like that, you're all Brandy talks about anymore."

All over the room are these big, big 1959 spatter-glaze ashtrays, so big you only have to empty them every couple years.

The one with the cigarette gives me her long hand with its porcelain nails and says, "I'm Pie Rhea."

"I'm Die Rhea," says another one, near the stereo.

The one with the cigarette, Pie Rhea, says, "Those are our stage names." She points at the third Rhea, over on the sofa, eating Chinese out of a takeaway carton. "That," she says and points, "this Miss Eating Herself to Fat, you can call her Gon Rhea."

With her mouth full of nothing you'd want to see, Gon Rhea says, "Charmed, I'm sure."

Putting her cigarette everywhere but in her mouth, Pie Rhea says, "The queen just does not need your problems, not tonight." She says, "We're all the family the top girl needs."

On the stereo is a picture in a silver frame of a girl, beautiful in front of seamless paper, smiling into an unseen camera, an invisible photographer telling her:

Give me passion.

Flash.

Give me joy.

Flash.

Give me youth and energy and innocence and beauty.

Flash.

"Brandy's first family, her birth family, didn't want her, so we adopted her," says Die Rhea. Pointing her long finger at the picture smiling on the blond stereo, Die Rhea says, "Her birth family thinks she's dead."

Jump to one time back when I had a face and I did this magazine cover shoot for *BabeWear* magazine.

Jump back to Suite 15-G and the picture on the blond stereo is me, my cover, the *BabeWear* magazine cover, framed with Die Rhea pointing her finger at me.

Jump back to us in the speech therapist office with the door locked and Brandy saying how lucky she was the Rhea sisters found her. It's not everybody who gets a second chance to be born again and raised a second time, but this time by a family that loves her.

"Kitty Litter, Sofonda, and Vivienne," Brandy says, "I owe them everything."

Jump to Suite 15-G and Gon Rhea waving her chopsticks at me and saying, "Don't you try and take her from us. We're not finished with her yet."

"If Brandy goes with you," says Pie Rhea, "she can pay for her own conjugated estrogens. And her vaginoplasty. And her labiaplasty. Not to mention her scrotal electrolysis."

To the picture on the stereo, to the smiling stupid face in the silver frame, Die Rhea says, "None of that is cheap." Die Rhea lifts the picture and holds it up to me, my past looking me eye to eye, and Die Rhea says, "This, this is how Brandy wanted to look, like her bitch sister. That was two years ago, before she had laser surgery to thin her vocal cords and then her trachea shave. She had her scalp advanced three centimeters to give her the right hairline. We paid for her brow shave to get rid of the bone ridge above her eyes that the Miss Male used to have. We paid for her jaw contouring and her forehead feminization."

"And," Gon Rhea says with her mouth full of chewed-up Chinese, "and every time she came home from the hospital with her forehead broken and realigned or her Adam's apple shaved down to a ladylike nothing, who do you think took care of her for those two years?"

Jump to my folks asleep in their bed across mountains and deserts away from here. Jump to them and their telephone and years ago some crazy man, some screeching awful pervert, calling them and screaming that their son was dead. Their son they didn't want, Shane, he was dead of AIDS and this man wouldn't say where or when and then he laughed and hung up.

Jump back to inside Suite 15-G and Die Rhea waving an old picture of me in my face and saying, "This is how she wanted to look, and tens of thousands of Katty Kathy dollars later, this is how she looks."

Gon Rhea says, "Hell. Brandy looks *better* than that."

"We're the ones who love Brandy Alexander," says Pie Rhea.

"But you're the one Brandy loves because you *need* her," says Die Rhea.

Gon Rhea says, "The one you love and the one who loves you are never, ever the same person." She says, "Brandy will leave us if she thinks you need her, but we need her, too."

The one I love is locked in the trunk of a car outside with a stomach full of Valiums, and I wonder if he still has to pee. My brother I hate is come back from the dead. Shane's being dead was just too good to be true.

First the exploding hairspray can didn't kill him.

Then our family couldn't just forget him.

Now even the deadly AIDS virus has failed me.

My brother is nothing but one bitter fucking disappointment after another.

You can hear a door opening and shutting somewheres, then another door, then another door opens and Brandy's there saying, "Daisy, honey," and steps into the smoke and cha-cha music wearing this amazing sort of Bill Blass First Lady type of traveling suit made out of solid kelly green trimmed with white piping and green high heels and a really smart green purse. On her head is an eco-incorrect tasty sort of spray of rain-forest-green parrot feathers made into a hat, and Brandy says, "Daisy, honey, don't point a gun at the people who I love."

In each of Brandy's big ring-beaded hands is a sassy off-white American Tourister luggage. "Give us a hand, somebody. These are just the royal hormones." She says, "My clothes I need are in the other room."

To Sofonda, Brandy says, "Miss Pie Rhea, I have just got to get."

To Kitty, Brandy says, "Miss Die Rhea, I've done everything we can do for now. We've done the scalp advancement, the brow lift, the brow bone shave. We've done the trachea shave, the nose contouring, the jawline contouring, the forehead realignment . . . "

Like it's any wonder I didn't recognize my old mutilated brother.

To Vivienne, Brandy says, "Miss Gon Rhea, I've got months left on my Real Life Training and I'm not spending them holed up here in this hotel."

Jump to us driving away with the Fiat Spider just piled with luggage. Imagine desperate refugees from Beverly Hills with seventeen pieces of matched luggage migrating cross-country to start a new life in the Okie Midwest. Everything very elegant and tasteful, one of those epic Joad family vacations, only backward. Leaving a trail of cast-off accessories, shoes and gloves and chokers and hats to lighten their load so's they can cross the Rocky Mountains, that would be us.

This is after the police showed up, no doubt after the hotel manager called and said a mutilated psycho with a gun was menacing everybody up on the fifteenth floor. This is after the Rhea sisters ran all Brandy's luggage down the fire stairs. This is after Brandy says she has to go, she needs to think about things, you know, before her big surgery. You know. The transformation.

This is after I keep looking at Brandy and wondering, *Shane?*

"It's just such a big commitment," Brandy says, "being a girl, you know. Forever."

Taking the hormones. For the rest of her life. The pills, the patches, the injections, for the rest of her life. And what if there was someone, just one person who would love her, who could make her life happy, just the way she was, without the hormones and makeup and the clothes and shoes and surgery? She has to at least look around the world a little. Brandy explains all this, and the Rhea sisters start to cry and wave and pile the American Touristers into the car.

And the whole scene would be just heartbreaking, and I would be boo-hooing, too, if I didn't know Brandy was my dead brother and the person he wants to love him is me, his hateful sister, already plotting to kill him. Yes. Plotting me, plotting to kill Brandy Alexander. Me with nothing left to lose, plotting my big revenge in the spotlight.

Give me violent revenge fantasies as a coping mechanism.

Flash.

Just give me my first opportunity.

Flash.

Brandy behind the wheel, she turns to me, her eyes all spidery with tears and mascara, and says, "Do you know what the Benjamin Standards guidelines are?"

Brandy starts the car and puts it in gear. She drops the parking brake and cranes her neck to see for traffic. She says, "I have to live one whole year on hormones in my new gender role before my vaginoplasty. They call it Real Life Training."

Brandy pulls out into the street and we're almost escaped. Police SWAT teams in chic basic black accessorized with tear gas and semiautomatic weapons are charging in past the doorman holding the door in his gold braid. The Rheas run after us, waving and throwing kisses and doing pretty much ugly bridesmaid behavior until they stumble, panting, in the street, their high heels shot to hell.

There's a moon in the sky. Office buildings are canyoned along either side of the street. There's still Manus in the trunk, and we're already putting gross distance between me and my getting caught.

Brandy puts her big hand open on my leg and squeezes.

Arson, kidnapping, I think I'm up to murder. Maybe all this will get me just a glimmer of attention, not the good, glorious kind, but still the national media kind.

MONSTER GIRL SLAYS SECRET BROTHER GAL PAL

"I've got eight months left to my RLT year," Brandy says. "Think you can keep me busy for the next eight months?"

Now, Please, Jump to Chapter Eleven

Chapter 33

Jump to the moment around one o'clock in the morning in Evie's big silent house when Manus stops screaming and I can finally think.

Evie is in Cancún, probably waiting for the police to call her and say: *Your house sitter, the monster without a jaw, well, she's shot your secret boyfriend to death when he broke in with a butcher knife is our best guess.*

You know that Evie's wide awake right now. In some Mexican hotel room, Evie's trying to figure out if there's a three-hour or a four-hour time difference between her big house where I'm stabbed to death, dead, and Cancún, where Evie's supposed to be on a catalogue shoot. It's not like Evie is entered in the biggest brain category. Nobody shoots a catalogue in Cancún in the peak season, especially not with big-boned cowgirls like Evie Cottrell.

But me being dead, that opens up a whole world of possibility.

I'm an invisible nobody sitting on a white damask sofa facing another white sofa across a coffee table that looks like a big block of malachite from Geology 101.

Evie slept with my fiancé, so now I can do anything to her.

In the movie, where somebody is invisible all the sudden—you know, a nuclear radiation fluke or a mad scientist recipe—and you think, what would I do if I was invisible . . . ? Like go into the guy's locker room at Gold's Gym or, better yet, the Oakland Raiders' locker room. Stuff like that. Scope things out. Go to Tiffany's and shoplift diamond tiaras and stuff.

Just by his being so dumb, Manus could've stabbed me, tonight, thinking I was Evie, thinking Evie shot me, while I was asleep in the dark in her bed.

My dad, he'd go to my funeral and talk to everybody about how I was always about to go back to college and finish my personal fitness training degree and then no doubt go on to medical school. Dad, Dad, Dad, Dad, Daddy, I couldn't get past the fetal pig in Biology 101. Now I'm the cadaver.

Sorry, Mom. Sorry, God.

Evie would be right next to my mom, next to the open casket. Evie would stagger up leaning on Manus. You know, Evie would've found something totally grotesque for the undertaker to dress me in. So Evie throws an arm around my mom, and Manus can't get away from the open casket fast enough, and I'm lying there in this blue velveteen casket like the interior of a Lincoln Town Car. Of course, thank you, Evie, I'm wearing this concubine evening wear Chinese yellow silk kimono slit up the side to my waist with black fishnet stockings and red Chinese dragons embroidered across the pelvic region and my breasts.

And red high heels. And no jawbone.

Of course, Evie says to my mom: "She always loved this dress. This kimono was her favorite." Sensitive Evie would say, "Guess this makes you oh for two."

I could kill Evie.

I would pay snakes to bite her.

Evie would be wearing this little black cocktail number with an asymmetrical hemline satin skirt and a strapless bodice by Rei Kawakubo. The shoulders and sleeves would be sheer black chiffon. Evie, you know she has jewelry, big emeralds for her too-green eyes and a change of accessories in her black clutch bag so she can wear this dress later, dancing.

I hate Evie.

Me, I'm rotting with my blood pumped out in this slutty Suzie Wong Tokyo Rose concubine drag dress where it didn't fit so they had to pin all the extra together behind my back.

I look like shit, dead.

I look like dead shit.

I would stab Evie right now over the telephone.

No, really, I'd tell Mrs. Cottrell as we placed Evie's urn in a family vault somewhere in Godawful, Texas. Really, Evie wanted to be cremated.

Me, at Evie's funeral, I'd be wearing this tourniquet-tight black leather minidress by Gianni Versace with yards and yards of black silk gloves bunched up on my arms. I'd sit next to Manus in the back of the mortuary's big black Caddy, and I'd have on this wagon wheel of a black Christian Lacroix hat with a black veil you could take off later and go to a swell auction preview or estate sale or something and then, lunch.

Evie, Evie would be dirt. Okay, ashes.

Alone in her living room, I pick up a crystal cigarette box off the table that looks like a block of malachite, and I overhand fast-pitch this little treasure against the fireplace bricks. There's a smash with cigarettes and matches everywhere.

Bourgeois dead girl that I am, I wish all of the sudden I hadn't done this, and I kneel down and start to pick up the mess. The glass and cigarettes. Only Evie . . . a cigarette box. It's just so *last-generational*.

And matches.

A little tug hits my finger, and I'm cut on a shard so thin and clear it's invisible.

Oh, this is dazzling.

Only when the blood comes out to outline the shard in red, only then can I see what cut me. It's my blood on the broken glass I pull out. My blood on a book of matches.

No, Mrs. Cottrell. No, really, Evie wanted to be cremated.

I get up out of my mess, and run around leaving blood on every light switch and lamp, turning them all off. I run past the coat closet, and Manus calls, "Please," but what I have in mind is too exciting.

I turn out all the first-floor lights, and Manus calls. He has to go to the bathroom, he calls. "Please."

Evie's big plantation house with its big pillars in front is all the way dark as I feel my way back to the dining room. I can feel the doorframe and count ten slow, blind footsteps across the Oriental carpet to the dining room table with its lace tablecloth.

I light a match. I light one of the candles in the big silver candelabra.

Okay, it's so Gothic Novel, but I light all five candles in the silver candelabra so heavy it takes both hands for me to lift.

Still wearing my satin peignoir set and ostrich feather bathrobe, what I am is the ghost of a beautiful dead girl carrying this candle thing up Evie's long circular staircase. Up past all the oil paintings, then down the second-floor hallway. In the master bedroom, the beautiful ghost girl in her candlelit satin opens the armoires and the closets full of her own clothes, stretched to death by the giant evil Evie Cottrell. The tortured bodies of dresses and sweaters and dresses and slacks and dresses and jeans and gowns and shoes and dresses, almost everything mutilated and misshapen and begging to be put out of its misery.

The photographer in my head says: Give me anger.

Flash.

Give me vengeance.

Flash.

Give me total and complete justified retribution.

Flash.

The already dead ghost I am, the not-occurring, the completely empowered invisible nothing I've become, I wave the candelabra past all that fabric and:

Flash.

What we have is Evie's enormous fashion inferno.

Which is dazzling.

Which is just too much fun! I try the bedspread, it's this antique Belgian lace duvet, and it burns.

The drapes, Miss Evie's green velvet portieres, they burn.

Lampshades burn.

Big shit. The chiffon I'm wearing, it's burning, too. I slap out my smoldering feathers and step backward from Evie's master bedroom fashion furnace and into the second-floor hallway.

There are ten other bedrooms and some bathrooms, and I go room to room. Towels burn. Bathroom inferno! Chanel No. 5, it burns. Oil paintings of racehorses and dead pheasants burn. The reproduction Oriental carpets burn. Evie's bad dried flower arrangements, they're these little tabletop infernos. Too cute! Evie's Katty Kathy doll, it melts, then it burns. Evie's collection of big carnival stuffed animals—Cootie, Poochie, Pam-Pam, Mr. Bunnits, Choochie, Poo Poo, and Ringer—it's a fun-fur holocaust. Too sweet. Too precious.

Back in the bathroom, I snatch one of the few things not on fire:

A bottle of Valiums.

I start down the big circular staircase. Manus, when he broke in to kill me, he left the front door open, and the second-floor inferno sucks a cool breeze of night air up the stairs around me. Blowing my candles out. Now the only light is the inferno, a giant space heater smiling down on me, me deep-fried in my eleven herbs and spices of singed chiffon.

The feeling is that I've just won some major distinguished award for a major lifetime achievement.

Like, here she is, Miss America.

Come on down.

And this kind of attention, I still love it.

At the closet door, Manus is whining about how he can smell smoke, and please, please, please don't let him die. As if I could even care right now.

No, really, Manus wanted to be cremated.

On the telephone message pad, I write:

in a minute i'll open the door, but i still have the gun. before that, i'm shoving valiums under the door. eat them. do this or I'll kill you.

And I put the note under the door.

We're going out to his car in the driveway. I'm taking him away. He'll do everything I want, or wherever we end up, I'll tell the police that he broke into the house. He set the fire and used the rifle to kidnap me. I'll blab everything about Manus and Evie and their sick love affair.

The word "love" tastes like earwax when I think it about Manus and Evie.

I slam the butt of the rifle against the closet door, and the rifle goes off. Another inch, and I'd be dead. With me dead outside the locked door, Manus would burn.

"Yes," Manus screams. "I'll do anything. Just, please, don't let me burn to death or shoot me. Anything, just open the door!"

With my shoe, I shove the poured-out Valiums through the crack under the closet door. With the rifle out in front of me, I unlock the door and stand back. In the light from the upstairs fire, you can see how the house is filling up with smoke. Manus stumbles out, power-blue-bug-eyed with his hands in the air, and I march him out to his car with the rifle pressed against his back. Even at the end of a rifle, Manus's skin feels tight and sexy. Beyond this, I have no plan. All I know is I don't want anything resolved for a while. Wherever we end up, I just won't go back to normal.

I lock Manus in the trunk of his Fiat Spider. A nice car, it's a nice car, red, with the convertible top down. I slam the butt of the rifle against the trunk lid.

Nothing comes back from my love cargo. Then I wonder if he still has to pee.

I toss the rifle into the passenger seat and I go back into Evie's plantation inferno. In the foyer, only now it's a chimney, it's a wind tunnel with the cold air rushing in the front door and up into the heat and light above me. The foyer still has that desk with the gold saxophone telephone. Smoke is everywhere, and a chorus of every smoke detector siren sirening is so loud it hurts.

It's just plain mean, making Evie in Cancún lie awake so long for her good news.

So I call the number she left. You know Evie picks up on the first ring.

And Evie says, "Hello?"

There's nothing but the sound of everything I've done, the smoke detectors and the flames, the tinkle of the chandelier as the breeze chimes through it, that's all there is to hear from her end of the conversation.

Evie says, "Manus?"

Somewhere, the dining room maybe, the ceiling crashes down and sparks and embers rush out the dining room doorway and over the foyer floor.

Evie says, "Manus, don't play games. If this is you, I said I didn't want to see you anymore."

And right then:

Crash.

A half ton of sparkling, flashing, white-light, hand-cut Austrian crystal, the big chandelier drops from the center of the foyer ceiling and explodes too close.

Another inch, and I'd be dead.

How can I not laugh? I'm already dead.

"Listen, Manus," Evie says. "I told you not to call me or I'll tell the police about how you put my best friend in the hospital without a face. You got that?"

Evie says, "You just went too far. I'll get a restraining order if I have to."

Manus or Evie, I don't know who to believe, all I know is my feathers are on fire.

Now, Please, Jump to Chapter Ten

Chapter 34

Jump to around midnight in Evie's house, where I catch Seth Thomas trying to kill me.

The way my face is without a jaw, my throat just ends in sort of a hole with my tongue hanging out. Around the hole, the skin is all scar tissue: dark red lumps and shiny the way you'd look if you got the cherry pie in a pie-eating contest. If I let my tongue hang down, you can see the roof of my mouth, pink and smooth as the inside of a crab's back, and hanging down around the roof is the white vertebrae horseshoe of the upper teeth I have left.

There are times to wear a veil and there are not. Other than this, I'm stunning when I meet Seth Thomas breaking into Evie's big house at midnight.

What Seth sees coming down the big circular staircase in Evie's foyer is me wearing one of Evie's peachy-pink satin and lace peignoir sets pieced on the bias. Evie's bathrobe is this peachy-pink retro Zsa Zsa number that hides me the way cellophane hides a frozen turkey. At the cuffs and along the front of the bathrobe is the peachy-pink ozone haze of ostrich feathers that match the feathers on the high-heeled mules I'm wearing.

Seth is just frozen at the foot of Evie's big circular staircase with Evie's best sixteen-inch carving knife in his hand. A pair of Evie's control-top pantyhose is pulled down over Seth's head. You can see Evie's hygienic cotton crotch sitting across Seth's face. The pantyhose legs drape the way a cocker spaniel's ears would look down the front of his otherwise mix-and-match army fatigues ensemble.

And I am a vision. Descending step by step toward the point of the carving knife, with the slow step-pause-step of a showgirl in a big Vegas revue.

Oh, I am just that fabulous. So sex furniture.

Seth's standing there, looking up, having a moment, afraid for the first time in his life because I'm holding Evie's rifle. The butt is planted against my shoulder, and the barrel is out in both hands in front of me. The sight's cross-haired right in the middle of Evie Cottrell's cotton crotch.

This is just Seth and me in Evie's foyer with its beveled glass windows broken around the front door and Evie's Austrian crystal chandelier that sparkles like so much costume jewelry for a house. The only other thing is a little desk in that Frenchy provincial white and gold.

On the little French desk is a *très* ooh-la-la telephone where the receiver is as big as a gold saxophone and sits in a gold cradle on top of an ivory box. In the middle of the push-button circle is a cameo. So chic, Evie probably thinks.

With the knife out in front of him, Seth goes, “I’m not going to hurt you.”

I’m doing that slow step-pause-step down the stairs.

Seth says, “Let’s not anybody get killed, here.”

And it’s so déjà vu.

This was the exact way Manus Kelley would ask if I’d gotten my orgasm. Not the words, but the voice.

Seth says through Evie’s crotch, “All’s I did was sleep with Evie.”

So déjà vu.

Let’s go sailing. It’s the exact same voice.

Seth drops the carving knife and the tip of the blade sticks mumblety-peg straight down next to his combat boot in Evie’s foyer parquet floor. Seth says, “If Evie says it was me that shot you, she was lying.”

On the desk next to the telephone is a pad and pencil for taking down messages.

Seth says, “I knew the second I heard about you in the hospital that it was Evie’s doing.”

Balancing the rifle with one arm, on the pad, I write:

take off your pantyhose.

“I mean, you can’t kill me,” Seth says. Seth’s pulling at the waistband of his pantyhose. “I’m just the reason why Evie shot you.”

I step-pause-step the last ten feet to Seth and hook the end of the rifle barrel on the pantyhose waistband and pull them off

Seth's square-jawed face. Seth Thomas, who would be Alfa Romeo in Vancouver, British Columbia. Alfa Romeo, who was Nash Rambler, formerly Bergdorf Goodman, formerly Neiman Marcus, formerly Saks Fifth Avenue, formerly Christian Dior.

Seth Thomas, who a long time before was named Manus Kelley, my fiancé from the infomercial. I couldn't tell you this until now because I want you to know how discovering this felt. In my heart. My fiancé wanted to kill me. Even when he's that much an asshole, I loved Manus. I still love Seth. A knife, it felt like a knife, and I'd discovered that despite everything that's happened, I still had an endless untapped potential for getting hurt.

It's from this night we started on the road together and Manus Kelley would someday become Seth Thomas. In between, in Santa Barbara and San Francisco and Los Angles and Reno and Boise and Salt Lake City, Manus was other men. Between that night and now, tonight, me in bed in Seattle still in love with him, Seth was Lance Corporal and Chase Manhattan. He was Dow Corning and Herald Tribune and Morris Code.

All courtesy of the Brandy Alexander Witness Reincarnation Project, as she calls it.

Different names, but all these men started out as Manus Trying to Kill Me.

Different men, but there's always the same special police vice operative good looks. The same power-blue eyes. Don't shoot— Let's go sailing—it's the same voice. Different haircuts but it's always the same thick black sexy dog hair.

Seth Thomas is Manus. Manus cheated on me with Evie, but I still love him so much I'll hide any amount of conjugated estrogen in his food. So much I'll do anything to destroy him.

You'd think I'd be smarter now after, what? Sixteen hundred college credits. I should be smarter. I could be a doctor by now.

Sorry, Mom. Sorry, God.

Jump to me not feeling anything but stupid, trying to balance one of Evie's gold saxophone telephones against my ear. Brandy Alexander, the inconvenient queen she is, isn't listed in the phone book. All I know is she lives downtown at the Congress Hotel in a corner suite with three roommates:

Kitty Litter.

Sofonda Peters.

And the Vivacious Vivienne VaVane.

Aka the Rhea sisters, three drag guys who worship the quality queen deluxe but would kill each other for more closet space. The Brandy queen told me that much.

It should be Brandy I talk to, but I call my folks. What's gone on is I lock my killer fiancé in the coat closet, and when I go to put him inside there's more of my beautiful clothes but all stretched out three sizes. Those clothes were every penny I ever made. After all that, I have to call somebody.

For so many reasons, no way can I just go back to bed. So I call, and my call goes out across mountains and deserts to where my father answers, and in my best ventriloquist voice, avoiding the consonants you really need a jaw to say, I tell him, "Gflerb sorlfd qortk, erd sairk. Srd. Erd, korts derk sairk? Kirdo!"

Anymore, the telephone is just not my friend.

And my father says, "Please don't hang up. Let me get my wife."

Away from the receiver, he says, "Leslie, wake up, we're being hate-crimed finally."

And in the background is my mother's voice saying, "Don't even talk to them. Tell them we loved and treasured our dead homosexual child."

It's the middle of the night here. They must be in bed.

"Lot. Ordilj," I say. "Serta ish ka alt. Serta ish ka alt!"

"Here," my father says as his voice drifts away. "Leslie, you give them what-for."

The gold saxophone receiver feels heavy and stagy, a prop, as if this call needs any more drama. From back in the coat closet, Seth yells, "Please. Don't be calling the police until you've talked to Evie."

Then from the telephone, "Hello?" And it's my mother.

"The world is big enough we can all love each other." she says, "There's room in God's heart for all His children. Gay, lesbian, bisexual, and transgendered. Just because it's anal intercourse doesn't mean it's not love."

She says, "I hear a lot of hurt from you. I want to help you deal with these issues."

And Seth yells, "I wasn't going to kill you. I was here to confront

Evie because of what she did to you. I was only trying to protect myself."

On the telephone, a two-hour drive from here, there's a toilet flush, then my father's voice. "You still talking to those lunatics?"

And my mother, "It's so exciting! I think one of them says he's going to kill us."

And Seth yells, "It had to be Evie who shot you."

Then in the telephone is my father's voice, roaring so loud that I have to hold the receiver away from my ear, he says, "You, you're the one who should be dead." He says, "You killed my son, you goddamned perverts."

And Seth yells, "What I had with Evie was just sex."

I might as well not even be in the room, or just hand the phone to Seth.

Seth says, "Please don't think for one minute that I could just stab you in your sleep."

And in the phone, my father shouts, "You just try it, mister. I've got a gun here and I'll keep it loaded and next to me day and night." He says, "We're through letting you torture us." He says, "We're proud to be the parents of a dead gay son."

And Seth yells, "Please, just put the phone down."

And I go, "Aht! Oahk!"

But my father hangs up.

My inventory of people who can save me is down to just me. Not my best friend. Or my old boyfriend. Not the doctors or the nuns. Maybe the police, but not yet. It isn't time to wrap this whole mess into a neat legal package and get on with my less-than life. Hideous and invisible forever and picking up pieces.

Things are still all messy and up in the air, but I'm not ready to settle them. My comfort zone was getting bigger by the minute. My threshold for drama was bumping out. It was time to keep pushing the envelope. It felt like I could do anything, and I was only getting started.

My rifle was loaded, and I had my first hostage.

Now, Please, Jump to Chapter Eight

Chapter 35

Jump back to when I first got out of the hospital without a career or a fiancé or an apartment, and I had to sleep at Evie's big house, her real house where even she didn't like to live, it was so lonely, stuck way out in some rain forest with nobody paying attention.

Jump to me being on Evie's bed, on my back that first night, but I can't sleep.

Wind lifts the curtains, lace curtains. All Evie's furniture is that curlicue Frenchy provincial stuff painted white and gold. There isn't a moon, but the sky is full of stars, so everything—Evie's house, the rose hedges, the bedroom curtains, the backs of my hands against the bedspread—is all either black or gray.

Evie's house was what a Texas girl would buy if her parents kept giving her about ten million dollars all the time. It's like the Cottrells know Evie will never make the big-time runways. So Evie, she lives here. Not New York. Not Milan. The suburbs, right out in the nowhere of professional modeling. This is pretty far from doing the Paris collections. Being stuck in nowhere is the excuse Evie needs, living here is, for a big-boned girl who'd never be a big-time success anywhere.

The doors are locked tonight. The cat is inside. When I look, the cat looks back at me the way dogs and some cars look when people say they're smiling.

Just that afternoon, Evie was on the telephone begging me to check myself out of the hospital and come visit.

Evie's house was big—white with hunter-green shutters, a three-story plantation house fronted with big pillars. Needlepoint ivy and climbing roses—yellow roses—were climbed up around the bottom ten feet of each big pillar. You'd imagine Ashley Wilkes mowing the grass here, or Rhett Butler taking down the storm windows, but Evie, she has these minimum-wage slave Laotians who refuse to live in.

Jump to the day before, Evie driving me from the hospital. Evie really is Evelyn Cottrell, Inc. No, really. She's traded publicly now. Everybody's favorite write-off. The Cottrells made a private stock offering in her career when Evie was twenty-one, and all the Cottrell relatives with their Texas land and oil money are heavily invested in Evie's being a model failure.

Most times it was an embarrassment going to modeling look-see auditions with Evie. Sure, I'd get work, but then the art director or the stylist would start screaming at Evie that, no, in his expert opinion she was not a perfect size six. Most times, some assistant stylist had to wrestle Evie out the door. Evie would be screaming back over her shoulder about how I shouldn't let them treat me like a piece of meat. I should just walk out.

"Fuck 'em," Evie's screaming by this point. "Fuck 'em all."

Me, I'm not angry. I'd be getting strapped into this incredible leather corset by Poupie Cadole and leather pants by Chrome Hearts. Life was good back then. I'd have three hours of work, maybe four or five.

At the photo studio doorway, before she'd get thrown out of the shoot, Evie would swing the assistant stylist into the doorjamb, and the little guy would just crumple up at her feet. It's then Evie would scream, "You people can all suck the crap out of my sweet Texas ass." Then she'd go out to her Ferrari and wait the three or four or five hours so she could drive me home.

Evie, that Evie was my best friend in the whole world. Moments like that, Evie was fun and quirky, almost like she had a life of her own.

Okay, so I didn't know about Evie and Manus and their complete and total love and satisfaction. So kill me.

Jump to before that, Evie calling me at the hospital and begging me, please, could I discharge myself and come stay at her house, she was so lonely, please.

My health insurance had a two-million-dollar lifetime ceiling, and the meter had just run and run all summer. No social service contact had the guts to transition me into God only knows where.

Begging me on the telephone, Evie said she had plane reservations. She was going to Cancún for a catalogue shoot so would I, could I, please, just house-sit for her?

When she picked me up, on my pad I wrote:

is that my halter top? you know you're stretching it.

"You'll need to feed my cat is all," Evie says.

i don't like being alone so far out from town, I write. *i don't know how you can live here.*

Evie says, "It's not living alone if you keep a rifle under the bed."

I write:

i know girls who say that about their dildos.

And Evie says, "Gross! I'm not that way at all with my rifle!"

So jump to Evie being flown off to Cancún, Mexico, and when I go to look under her bed, there's the thirty-aught rifle and scope. In her closets are what's left of my clothes, stretched and tortured to death and hanging there on wire hangers, dead.

Then jump to me in Evie's bed that night. It's midnight. The wind lifts the bedroom curtains, lace curtains, and the cat jumps up on the windowsill to see who's just pulled up in the gravel driveway. With the stars behind it, the cat looks back at me. Downstairs, you hear a window break.

Now, Please, Jump to Chapter Seven

Chapter 36

Where you're supposed to be is a big wedding at the big Duomo in Milan, Italy, a location roughly midwayish between Armani and Intimissimi, a very private wedding with hydrocephalics and parastremmatic dwarves all over the cathedral.

This is less of a dead end in the narrative than it is a cul-de-sac. You, the put-upon reader, you just want to get through this story, only the author keeps putting plot obstacles in your way. How similar this process is to when feng shui experts hang wind chimes and place rocks to cause ripples in fast streams of running water. As if to say, *Slow down!* All of those hindrances, like the bones in a trout, they make you take time and actually taste something. It's why heat-and-serve fish sticks are so immensely popular. And Danielle Steel. For people with so little free time that they're forced to wolf down their leisure activities.

On the bride's side of the church are seated mostly young women. Of the bridesmaids, one has two arms and two legs, most of a whole extra person, growing out of her stomach. A legitimate medical condition, it's called an "epigastric parasite" by doctors. As you can imagine, she finds shopping for prêt-à-porter clothing impossible. Another bridesmaid clearly lives with Milroy disease: the lymph nodes in her legs never developed, resulting in feet the size of suitcases on legs like tree trunks. The third bridesmaid boasts no nose and both her eyes are squeezed together in the same socket. In other words, Cyclopia. Standing at the altar, they look nothing short of—spectacular. Dressed to the nines, as people say.

Among the bride's guests are those people with no arms, girls born with the condition phocomelia, and only their hands emerging from their shoulders. Others resemble mermaids: their legs fused together by the birth defect sirenomelia. Still others have their fingers fused into two fleshy pincers, their legs withered and useless. Textbook examples of Ectrodactyly syndrome.

The bride herself wears a veil. For the moment she's a secret monster, like the majority of us.

The groom is someone discerning. A connoisseur who won't settle for one-size-fits-all beauty. He's someone who can appreciate a cubist face. They found each other through a matchmaking service called Fascination. In truth, it's more of an escort service. It's *Pretty Woman* but with a less conventional definition of pretty. You know the trope about men? How they'll pay twice as much for the experience of sex with a one-legged woman. Well, can you imagine how much they'll pay for sex with someone who has three extra arms and a dorsal fin? Want to venture a guess about the going rate for sex with someone who has two heads? In ballpark figures: they'll pay a lot.

This is the unconventional family assembled by Daisy St. Patience from the abandoned people whom no one else wanted. And not just any people. Daisy can spot a silicone hump from a thousand paces, that's how good the money is. People tired of trying to look beautiful, they'll go the other route. They find backalley cosmetic surgeons to undo what nature unfortunately got right. Average people will pay to look like melted candles. Like a walking red-brown pile of swollen livers with a few sharp teeth and whiskers jutting out. Daisy St. Patience of all people understands this impulse. Everything is revisions, edits, rewrites. She's not so much a pimp as she is a gallery owner, giving artists a place to showcase their work, introducing them to wealthy patrons.

Somewhere else, an ornithologist is sorting through the bones around the base of an eagle nest, and she finds one containing teeth . . . molars, the metal fillings made by a dentist. It's part of the mandible bone of a human female, approximately twenty-two years old. A mystery. The tree containing that nest is growing in Spitefield; that's how small this world gets.

All of which brings us here to wedded bliss. On cue, the groom pinches the hem of the bride's veil and lifts it. A stage curtain rising to reveal horrors unimaginable. Terrors of beauty you could never dream to afford. The bride's bouquet traces a slow arc through the air, thrown and sailing, thrown and tumbling toward a sea of waving claws, paws, fins, human beaks, prehensile tongues, tails, hooves, and stumps.

The bride? She's Daisy St. Patience, living happily ever after. In the mirror around the edges of this chapter, would you just look at the expression on your face.

The happy couple, they kiss.

There isn't a dry eye in the house.

Now, Please, Jump to Chapter Twenty-seven

Chapter 37

Jump back to the day Brandy chucks a handful of shimmering nothing into the air above my head, and the speech therapist office around me turns gold.

Brandy says, "This is cotton voile."

She throws another handful of fog, and the world blurs behind gold and green.

"Silk georgette," Brandy says.

She throws a handful of sparkle, and the world, Brandy sitting in front of me with her wicker sewing basket open in her lap. The two of us alone, locked in the speech therapist office. The poster of a kitten on the cinder-block wall. All this goes star-filter soft and bright, every sharp edge erased or smeared behind the green and gold, and the fluorescent light coming through in broken exploded bits.

"Veils," Brandy says as each color settles over me. "You need to look like you're keeping secrets," she says. "If you're going to do the outside world, Miss St. Patience, you need to not let people see your face," she says.

"You can go anywhere in the world," Brandy goes on and on.

You just can't let people know who you really are.

"You can live a completely normal, regular life," she says.

You just can't let anybody get close enough to you to learn the truth.

"In a word," she says, "veils."

Take-charge princess who she is, Brandy Alexander never does ask my real name. The name who I was born. Miss Bossy Pants right away gives me a new name, a new past. She invents another future for me with no connections, except to her, a cult all by herself.

"Your name is Daisy St. Patience," she tells me. "You're the lost heiress to the House of St. Patience, the very haute couture fashion showroom, and this season we're doing hats," she says. "Hats with veils."

I ask her, "Jsfssjf ciacb sxi?"

"You come from escaped French aristocrat blood," Brandy says.

"Gwdcn aixa gklgfnv?"

"You grew up in Paris, and went to a school run by nuns," Brandy says.

Hard at work, planning stylist that she is, Brandy Alexander is already pulling tulle out of her purse, pink tulle and lace and crochet doily netting, and settling it over my head.

She says, "You don't have to wear makeup. You don't even have to wash. A good veil is the equivalent of mirrored sunglasses, but for your whole head."

A good veil is the same as staying indoors, Brandy tells me. Cloistered. Private. She throws sheer yellow chiffon. She drapes red patterned nylon over me. In the way our world is, everybody shoulder to shoulder, people knowing everything about you at first glance, a good veil is your tinted limousine window. The unlisted number for your face. Behind a good veil, you could be anyone. A movie star. A saint. A good veil says:

We Have Not Been Properly Introduced.

You're the prize behind door number three.

You're the lady or the tiger.

In our world where nobody can keep a secret anymore, a good veil says:

Thank You For NOT Sharing.

"Don't worry," Brandy says. "Other people will fill in the blanks."

The same as how they do with God, she says.

What I never told Brandy is I grew up near a farm. This was a farm that grew pigs. Daisy St. Patience used to come home from school every sunny afternoon and had to feed the pigs with her brother.

Give me homesickness.

Flash.

Give me nostalgic childhood yearnings.

Flash.

What's the word for the opposite of glamour?

Brandy never asked about my folks, were they living or dead, and why weren't they here to gnash their teeth.

"Your father and mother, Rainier and Honoraria St. Patience, were assassinated by fashion terrorists," she says.

B.B., before Brandy, my father took his pigs to market every fall. His secret is to spend all summer driving his flatbed truck around Idaho and the other upper left-hand corner states, stopping at all the day-old bakery outlets selling expired snack foods, individual fruit pies and cupcakes with creamy fillings, little loaves of sponge cake injected with artificial whipped cream, and lumps of devil's food cake covered with marshmallow and shredded coconut dyed pink. Old birthday cakes that didn't sell. Stale cakes wishing *Congratulations. Happy Mother's Day. Be My Valentine.* My father still brings it all home, heaped in a dense sticky pile or heat-sealed inside cellophane. That's the hardest part, opening these thousands of old snacks and dropping them to the pigs.

My father who Brandy didn't want to hear about, his secret is to feed the pigs these pies and cakes and snacks the last two weeks before they go to market. The snacks have no nutrition, and the pigs gobble them until there isn't an expired snack left within five hundred miles.

These snacks don't have any real fiber to them so every fall, every three-hundred-pound pig goes to market with an extra ninety pounds in its colon. My father makes a fortune at auction, and who knows how long after that, but the pigs all take a big sugary crap when they see inside whatever slaughterhouse where they end up.

I say, "Kwvne wivnuw fw sojaoa."

"No," Brandy says and puts up her foot-long index finger, six cocktail rings stacked on just this one finger, and she presses her jeweled hot dog up and down across my mouth the moment I try and say anything.

"Not a word," Brandy says. "You're still too connected to your past. Your saying anything is pointless."

From out of her sewing basket, Brandy draws a streamer of white and gold, a magic act, a layer of sheer white silk patterned with a Greek key design in gold she casts over my head.

Behind another veil, the real world is that much farther away.

"Guess how they do the gold design," Brandy says.

The fabric is so light my breath blows it out in front; the silk lays across my eyelashes without bending them. Even my face, where every nerve in your body comes to an end, even my face can't feel it.

It takes a team of kids in India, Brandy says, four- and five-year-old kids sitting all day on wooden benches, being vegetarians, they have to tweeze out most of about a zillion gold threads to leave the pattern of just the gold left behind.

"You don't see kids any older than ten doing this job," Brandy says, "because by then most kids go blind."

Just the veil Brandy takes out of her basket must be six feet square. The precious eyesight of all those darling children, lost. The precious days of their fragile childhood spent tweezing silk threads out.

Give me pity.

Flash.

Give me empathy.

Flash.

Oh, I wish I could make my poor heart just bust.

I say, "Vswf siws cm eiuvn sincs."

No, it's okay, Brandy says. She doesn't want to reward anybody for exploiting children. She got it on sale.

Caged behind my silk, settled inside my cloud of organza and georgette, the idea that I can't share my problems with other people makes me not give a shit about their problems.

"Oh, and don't worry," Brandy says. "You'll still get attention. You have a dynamite tits-and-ass combo. You just can't talk to anybody."

People just can't stand not knowing something, she tells me. Especially men can't bear not climbing every mountain, mapping everywhere. Labeling everything. Peeing on every tree and then never calling you back.

"Behind a veil, you're the great unknown," she says. "Most guys will fight to know you. Some guys will deny you're a real person, and some will just ignore you."

The zealot. The atheist. The agnostic.

Even if somebody is only wearing an eye patch, you always want to look. To see if he's faking. The man in the Hathaway shirt. Or to see the horror underneath.

The photographer in my head says:

Give me a voice.

Flash.

Give me a face.

Brandy's answer was little hats with veils. And big hats with veils. Pancake hats and pillbox hats edged all around with clouds of tulle and gauze. Parachute silk or heavy crepe or dense net dotted with chenille pom-poms.

"The most boring thing in the entire world," Brandy says, "is nudity."

The second most boring thing, she says, is honesty.

"Think of this as a tease. It's lingerie for your face," she says. "A peekaboo nightgown you wear over your whole identity."

The third most boring thing in the entire world is your sorry-assed past. So Brandy never asked me anything. Bulldozer alpha bitch she can be, we meet again and again in the speech therapist office and Brandy tells me everything I need to know about myself.

Now, Please, Jump to Chapter Six

Chapter 38

Jump way back to the last Thanksgiving before my accident when I go home to eat dinner with my folks. This is back when I still had a face so I wasn't so confronted by solid food. On the dining room table, covering it all over, is a tablecloth I don't remember, a really nice dark blue damask with a lace edge. This isn't something I'd expect my mom to buy, so I ask, did somebody give this to her?

Mom's just pulling up to the table and unfolding her blue damask napkin with everything steaming between us: her, me, and my dad. The sweet potatoes under their layer of marshmallows. The big brown turkey. The rolls are inside a quilted cozy sewed to look like a hen. You lift the wings to take a roll out. There's the cut-glass tray of sweet pickles and celery filled with peanut butter.

"Give what?" my mom says.

The new tablecloth. It's really nice.

My father sighs and plunges a knife into the turkey.

"It wasn't going to be a tablecloth at first," Mom says. "Your father and I pretty much dropped the ball on our original project."

The knife goes in again and again and my father starts to dismember our dinner.

My mom says, "Do you know what the AIDS memorial quilt is all about?"

Jump to how much I hate my brother at this moment.

"I bought this fabric because I thought it would make a nice panel for Shane," Mom says. "We just ran into some problems with what to sew on it."

Give me amnesia.

Flash.

Give me new parents.

Flash.

"Your mother didn't want to step on any toes," Dad says. He twists a drumstick off and starts scraping the meat onto a plate. "With gay stuff you have to be so careful since everything means something in secret code. I mean, we didn't want to give people the wrong idea."

My mom leans over to scoop yams onto my plate, and says, "Your father wanted a black border, but black on a field of blue would mean Shane was excited by leather sex, you know, bondage and discipline, sado- and masochism." She says, "Really these panels are to help the people left behind."

"Strangers are going to see us and see Shane's name," my dad says. "We didn't want them thinking things."

The dishes all start their slow clockwise march around the table. The stuffing. The olives. The cranberry sauce.

"I wanted pink triangles but all the panels have pink triangles," my mom says. "It's the symbol for Nazi homosexuals." She says, "Your father suggested black triangles, but that would mean Shane was a lesbian. It looks like the female pubic hair. The black triangle does."

My father says, "Then I wanted a green border, but it turns out that would mean Shane was a male prostitute."

My mom says, "We almost chose a red border, but that would mean fisting. Brown would mean either scat or rimming, we couldn't figure which."

"Yellow," my father says, "means watersports."

"A lighter shade of blue," Mom says, "would mean just regular oral sex."

"Regular white," my father says, "would mean anal. White could also mean Shane was excited by men wearing underwear." He says, "I can't remember which."

My mother passes me the quilted chicken with the rolls still warm inside.

We're supposed to sit and eat with Shane dead all over the table in front of us.

"Finally we just gave up," my mom says, "and I made a nice tablecloth out of the material."

Between the yams and the stuffing, Dad looks down at his plate and says, "Do you know about rimming?"

I know it isn't table talk.

"And fisting?" my mom asks.

I say, I know. I don't mention Manus and his vocational porno magazines.

We sit there, all of us around a blue shroud with the turkey more like a big dead baked animal than ever, the stuffing chock-full of organs you can still recognize, the heart and gizzard and liver, the gravy thick with cooked fat and blood. The flower centerpiece could be a casket spray.

"Would you pass the butter, please?" my mother says. To my father she says, "Do you know what felching is?"

This, it's too much. Shane's dead, but he's more the center of attention than he ever was. My folks wonder why I never come home, and this is why. All this sick horrible sex talk over Thanksgiving dinner, I can't take this. It's just Shane this and Shane that. It's sad, but what happened to Shane was not something I did. I know everybody thinks it's my fault, what happened. The truth is Shane destroyed this family. Shane was bad and mean, and he's dead. I'm good and obedient and I'm ignored.

Silence.

All that happened was I was fourteen years old. Somebody put a full can of hairspray in the trash by mistake. It was Shane's job to burn the trash. He was fifteen. He was dumping the kitchen trash into the burn barrel while the bathroom trash was on fire, and the hairspray exploded. It was an accident.

Silence.

Now what I wanted my folks to talk about was me. I'd tell them how Evie and me were shooting a new infomercial. My modeling career was taking off. I wanted to tell them about my new boyfriend, Manus, but no. Whether he's good or bad, alive or dead, Shane still gets all the attention. All I ever get is angry.

"Listen," I say. This just blurts out. "Me," I say, "I'm the last child you people have left alive so you'd better start paying me some attention."

Silence.

"Felching . . ." I lower my voice. I'm calm now. "Felching is when a man fucks you up the butt without a rubber. He shoots his load, and then plants his mouth on your anus and sucks out his own warm sperm, plus whatever lubricant and feces are present. That's felching. It may or may not," I add, "include kissing you to pass the sperm and fecal matter into your mouth."

Silence.

Give me control. Give me calm. Give me restraint.

Flash.

The yams are just the way I like them, sugary sweet but crunchy on top. The stuffing is a little dry. I pass my mother the butter.

My father clears his throat. "Bump," he says, "I think 'fletching' is the word your mother meant." He says, "It means to slice the turkey into very thin strips."

Silence.

I say, Oh. I say, Sorry.

We eat.

Now, Please, Jump to Chapter Five

Chapter 39

Jump way back to one day outside Brumbach's Department Store, where people are stopped to watch somebody's dog lift its leg on the Nativity scene, Evie and me included. Then the dog sits and rolls back on its spine, licks its own lumpy dog-flavored butthole, and Evie elbows me. People applaud and throw money.

Then we're inside Brumbach's, testing lipsticks on the back of our hands, and I say, "Why is it dogs lick themselves?"

"Just because they can . . ." Evie says. "They're not like people."

This is just after we've killed an eight-hour day in modeling school, looking at our skin in mirrors, so I'm like, "Evie, *do not* even kid yourself."

My passing grade in modeling school was just because Evie'd dragged down the curve. She'd wear shades of lipstick you'd expect to see around the base of a penis. She'd wear so much eye shadow you'd think she was a product-testing animal. Just from her hairspray, there's a hole in the ozone over the Taylor Robberts Modeling Academy.

This is way back before my accident when I thought my life was so good.

At Brumbach's Department Store, where we'd kill time after class, the whole ninth floor is furniture. Around the edges are display rooms: bedrooms, dining rooms, living rooms, dens, libraries, nurseries, family rooms, china hutches, home offices, all of them open to the inside of the store. The invisible fourth wall. All of them perfect, clean and carpeted, full of tasteful furniture, and hot with track lighting and too many lamps. There's the hush of white noise from hidden speakers. Alongside the rooms, shoppers pass in the dim linoleum aisles that run between the display rooms and the down-lighted islands that fill the center of the floor, conversation pits and sofa suites grouped on area rugs with coordinated floor lamps and fake plants. Quiet islands of light and color in the darkness teeming with strangers.

"It's just like a sound stage," Evie would say. "The little sets all ready for somebody to shoot the next episode. The studio audience watching you from the dark."

Customers would stroll by and there would be Evie and me sprawled on a pink canopy bed, calling for our horoscopes on her cell phone. We'd be curled on a tweedy sofa sectional, munching popcorn and watching our soaps on a console color television. Evie will pull up her T-shirt to show me another new belly button piercing. She'll pull down the armhole of her blouse and show me the scars from her implants.

"It's too lonely at my real house," Evie would say, "and I hate how I don't feel real enough unless people are watching."

She says, "I don't hang around Brumbach's for privacy."

At home in my apartment I'd have Manus with his magazines. His guy-on-guy porno magazines he had to buy for his job, he'd say. Over breakfast every morning, he'd show me glossy pictures of guys self-sucking. Curled up with their elbows hooked behind their knees and craning their necks to choke on themselves, each guy would be lost in his own little closed circuit. You can bet almost every guy in the world's tried this. Then Manus would tell me, "This is what guys want."

Give me romance.

Flash.

Give me denial.

Each little closed loop of one guy flexible enough or with a dick so big he doesn't need anybody else in the world, Manus would point his toast at these pictures and tell me, "These guys don't need to put up with jobs or relationships." Manus would just chew, staring at each magazine. Forking up his scrambled egg whites, he'd say, "You could live and die this way."

Then I'd go downtown to the Taylor Robberts Modeling Academy to get myself perfected. Dogs will lick their butts. Evie will self-mutilate. All this navel-gazing. At home, Evie had nobody except she had a ton of family money. The first time we rode a city bus to Brumbach's, she offered the driver her credit card and asked for a window seat. She was worried her carry-on was too big.

Me with Manus or her alone, you don't know who of us had it worse at home.

But at Brumbach's, Evie and me, we'd catnap in any of the dozen perfect bedrooms. We'd stuff cotton between our toes and paint our nails in chintz-covered club chairs. Then we'd study our Taylor Robberts modeling textbook at a long polished dining table.

"Here's the same as those fakey reproductions of natural habitats they build at zoos," Evie would say. "You know, those concrete polar ice caps and those rain forests made of welded pipe trees holding sprinklers."

Every afternoon, Evie and me, we'd star in our own personal unnatural habitat. The clerks would sneak off to find sex in the men's room. We'd all soak up attention in our own little matinee life.

All's I remember from Taylor Robberts is to lead with my pelvis when I walk. Keep your shoulders back. To model different-sized products, they'd tell you to draw an invisible sight line from yourself to the item. For toasters, draw a line through the air from your smile to the toaster. For a stove, draw the line from your breasts. For a new car, start the invisible line from your vagina. What it boils down to is professional modeling means getting paid to overreact to stuff like rice cakes and new shoes.

We'd drink diet colas on a big pink bed at Brumbach's. Or sit at a vanity, using contouring powder to change the shape of our faces while the faint outline of people watched us from the darkness a few feet away. Maybe the track lights would flash off somebody's glasses. With our every little move getting attention, every gesture, everything we said, it's easy to pick up on the rush you'd get.

"It's so safe and peaceful here," Evie'd say, smoothing the pink satin comforter and fluffing the pillows. "Nothing very bad could ever happen to you here. Not like at school. Or at home."

Total strangers would stand there with their coats on, watching us. The same's those talk shows on television, it's so easy to be honest with a big enough audience. You can say anything if enough people will listen.

"Evie, honey," I'd say. "There's lots worse models in our class. You just need to not have an edge to your blusher." We'd be looking at ourselves in a vanity mirror, a triple row of nobodies watching us from behind.

"Here, sweetie," I'd say, and give her a little sponge, "blend."

And Evie would start to cry. Your every emotion goes right over the top with a big audience. It's either laughter or tears, with no in-between. Those tigers in zoos, they must just live a big opera all the time.

"It's not just my wanting to be a glamorous fashion model," Evie would say. "It's when I think of my growing up, I'm so sad." Evie would choke back her tears. She'd clutch her little sponge and say, "When I was little, my parents wanted me to be a boy." She'd say, "I just never want to be that miserable again."

Other times, we'd wear high heels and pretend to slap each other hard across the mouth because of some guy we both wanted. Some afternoons we'd confess to each other that we were vampires.

"Yeah," I'd say. "My parents used to abuse me, too."

You had to play to the crowd.

Evie would turn her fingers through her hair. "I'm getting my guiche pierced," she'd say. "It's that little ridge of skin running between your asshole and the bottom of your vagina."

I'd go to flop on the bed, center stage, hugging a pillow and looking up into the black tangle of ducts and sprinkler pipes you had to imagine was a bedroom ceiling.

"It's not like they hit me or made me drink satanic blood or anything," I'd say. "They just liked my brother more because he was mutilated."

And Evie would cross to center stage by the Early American nightstand to upstage me.

"You had a mutilated brother?" she'd say.

Somebody watching us would cough. Maybe the light would glint off a wristwatch.

"Yeah, he was pretty mutilated, but not in a sexy way. Still, there's a happy ending," I'd say. "He's dead now."

And really intense, Evie would say, "Mutilated how? Was he your only brother? Older or younger?"

And I'd throw myself off the bed and shake my hair. "No, it's too painful."

"No, really," Evie would say. "I'm not kidding."

"He was my big brother by a couple years. His face was all exploded in a hairspray accident, and you'd think my folks totally forgot they even had a second child," I'd dab my eyes on the pillow shams and tell the audience. "So I just kept working harder and harder for them to love me."

Evie would be looking at nothing and saying, "Oh, my shit! *Oh, my shit!*" And her acting, her delivery would be so true it would just bury mine.

"Yeah," I'd say. "He didn't have to work at it. It was so easy. Just by being all burned and slashed up with scars, he hogged all the attention."

Evie would go close-up on me and say, "So where's he now, your brother, do you even know?"

"Dead," I'd say, and I'd turn to address the audience. "Dead of AIDS."

And Evie says, "How sure are you?"

And I'd say, "Evie!"

"No, really," she'd say. "I'm asking for a reason."

"You just don't joke about AIDS," I'd say.

And Evie'd say, "This is *so* next-to-impossible."

This is how easy the plot gets pumped out of control. With all these shoppers expecting real drama, of course, I think Evie's just making stuff up.

"Your brother," Evie says, "did you really see him die? For real? Or did you see him dead? In a coffin, you know, with music. Or a death certificate?"

All those people were watching.

"Yeah," I say. "Pretty much." Like I'd want to get caught lying?

Evie's all over me. "So you saw him dead or you didn't?"

All those people watching.

"Dead enough."

Evie says, "Where?"

"This is very painful," I say, and I cross stage right to the living room.

Evie chases after me, saying, "Where?"

All those people watching.

"The hospice," I say.

"What hospice?"

I keep crossing stage right to the next living room, the next dining room, the next bedroom, den, home office, with Evie dogging me and the audience hovering along next to us.

"You know how it is," I say. "If you don't see a gay guy for so long, it's a pretty safe bet."

And Evie says, "So you don't really know that he's dead?"

We're sprinting through the next bedroom, living room, dining room, nursery, and I say, "It's AIDS, Evie. Fade to black."

And then Evie just stops and says, "Why?"

And the audience has started to abandon me in a thousand directions.

Because I really, really, really want my brother to be dead. Because my folks want him dead. Because life is just *easier* if he's dead. Because this way, I'm an only child. Because it's my turn, damn it. My turn.

And the crowd of shoppers has bailed, leaving just us and the security cameras instead of God watching to catch us when we fuck up.

"Why is this such a big deal to you?" I say.

And Evie's already wandering away from me, leaving me alone and saying, "No reason." Lost in her own little closed circuit. Licking her own butthole, Evie says, "It's nothing." Saying, "Forget it."

Now, Please, Jump to Chapter Four

Chapter 40

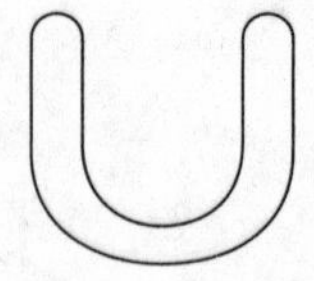ntil I met Brandy, all I wanted was for somebody to ask me what happened to my face.

"Birds ate it," I wanted to tell them.

Birds ate my face.

But nobody wanted to know. Then nobody doesn't include Brandy Alexander.

Just don't think this was a big coincidence. We had to meet, Brandy and me. We had so many things in common. We had close to everything in common. Besides, it happens fast for some people and slow for some, accidents or gravity, but we all end up mutilated. Most women know this feeling of being more and more invisible every day. Brandy was in the hospital for months and months, and so was I, and there's only so many hospitals where you can go for major cosmetic surgery.

Jump back to the nuns. The nuns were the worst about always pushing, the nuns who were nurses. One nun would tell me about some patient on a different floor who was funny and charming. He was a lawyer and could do magic tricks with just his hands and a paper napkin. This day nurse was the kind of nun who wore a white nursing version of her regular nun uniform, and she'd told this lawyer all about me. This was Sister Katherine. She told him I was funny and bright, and she said how sweet it would be if the two of us could meet and fall madly in love.

Those were her words.

Halfway down the bridge of her nose, she'd look at me through wire-framed glasses, their lenses long and squared the way microscope slides look. Little broken veins kept the end of her nose red. Rosacea, she called this. It would be easier to see her living in a gingerbread house than a convent. Married to Santa Claus instead of God. The starched apron she wore over her habit was so glaring white that when I'd first arrived, fresh from my big car accident, I remembered how all the stains from my blood looked black.

They gave me a pen and paper so I could communicate. They wrapped my head in dressings, yards of tight gauze holding wads of cotton in place, metal butterfly sutures gripping all over so I wouldn't unravel. They fingered on a thick layer of antibiotic gel, claustrophobic and toxic under the wads of cotton.

My hair they pulled back, forgotten and hot under the gauze where I couldn't get at it. The invisible woman.

When Sister Katherine mentioned this other patient, I wondered if maybe I'd seen him around, her lawyer, the cute, funny magician.

"I didn't say he was cute," she said.

Sister Katherine said, "He's still a little shy."

On the pad of paper, I wrote:

still?

"Since his little mishap," she said and smiled with her eyebrows arched and all her chins tucked down against her neck. "He wasn't wearing his seat belt."

She said, "His car rolled right over the top of him."

She said, "That's why he'd be so perfect for you."

Early on, while I was still sedated, somebody had taken the mirror out of my bathroom. The nurses seemed to steer me away from polished anything the way they kept the suicides away from knives. The drunks away from drinks. The closest I had to a mirror was the television, and it only showed how I used to look.

If I asked to see the police photos from the accident, the day nurse would tell me, "No." They kept the photos in a file at the nursing station, and it seemed anybody could ask to see them except me. This nurse, she'd say, "The doctor thinks you've suffered enough for the time being."

This same day nurse tried to fix me up with an accountant whose hair and ears were burned off in a propane blunder. She introduced me to a graduate student who'd lost his throat and sinuses to a touch of cancer. A window washer after his three-story tumble headfirst onto concrete.

Those were all her words, *blunder, touch, tumble.* The lawyer's *mishap.* My big *accident.*

Sister Katherine would be there to check my vital signs every six hours. To check my pulse against the sweep second hand on her man's wristwatch, thick and silver. To wrap the blood pressure cuff around my arm. To check my temperature, she'd push some kind of electric gun in my ear.

Sister Katherine was the kind of nun who wears a wedding ring.

And married people always think love is the answer.

Jump back to the day of my big accident, when everybody was so considerate. The people, the folks who let me go ahead of them in the emergency room. What the police insisted. I mean, they gave me this hospital sheet with *Property of La Paloma Memorial Hospital* printed along the edge in indelible blue. First they gave me morphine, intravenously. Then they propped me up on a gurney.

I don't remember much of this, but the day nurse told me about the police photos.

In the pictures, these big eight-by-ten glossies as nice as anything in my portfolio. Black-and-white, the nurse said. But in these eight-by-tens I'm sitting up on a gurney with my back against the emergency room wall. The attending nurse spent ten minutes cutting my dress off with those tiny operating-room manicure scissors. The cutting, I remember. It was my cotton crepe sundress from Espre. I remember that when I ordered this dress from the catalogue I almost ordered two, they're so comfortable, loose with the breeze trying to get inside the armholes and lift the hem up around your waist. Then you'd sweat if there wasn't a breeze, and the cotton crepe stuck on you like eleven herbs and spices, only on you the dress was almost transparent. You'd walk onto a patio, it was a great feeling, a million spotlights picking you out of the crowd, or walk into a restaurant when outside it was ninety degrees, and everyone would turn and look as if you'd just been awarded some major distinguished award for a major lifetime achievement.

That's how it felt. I can remember this kind of attention. It always felt ninety degrees hot.

And I remember my underwear.

Sorry, Mom, sorry, God, but I was wearing just this little patch up front with an elastic string waist and just one string running down the crack and back around to the bottom of the patch up front. Flesh-tone. That one string, the one down the crack, butt floss is what everybody calls that string. I wore the patch underwear because of when the cotton crepe sundress goes almost transparent. You just don't plan on ending up in the emergency room with your dress cut off and detectives taking your picture, propped up on a gurney with a morphine drip in one arm and a Franciscan nun screaming in one ear. "Take your pictures! Take your pictures, now! She's still losing blood!"

No, really, it was funnier than it sounds.

It got funny when there I was sprawled on this gurney, this anatomically correct rag doll with nothing but this little patch on and my face was the way it is now.

The police, they had the nun hold this sheet up over my breasts.

It's so they can take pictures of my face, but the detectives are so embarrassed for me, being sprawled there topless.

Jump to when they refuse to show me the pictures, one of the detectives says that if the bullet had been two inches higher, I'd be dead.

I couldn't see their point.

Two inches lower, and I'd be deep-fried in my spicy cotton crepe sundress, trying to get the insurance guy to waive the deductible and replace my car window. Then I'd be by a swimming pool, wearing sunblock and telling a couple cute guys how I was driving on the freeway in my Stingray when a rock or I don't know what, but my driver's-side window just burst.

And the cute guys would say, "Whoa."

Jump to another detective, the one who'd searched my car for the slug and bone fragments, that stuff, the detective saw how I'd been driving with the window half open. A car window, this guy tells me over the eight-by-ten glossies of me wearing a white sheet, a car window should always be all the way open or shut. He couldn't remember how many motorists he'd seen decapitated by windows in car accidents.

How could I not laugh?

That was his word: Motorists.

The way my mouth was, the only sound left I could do was laugh. I couldn't not laugh.

Jump to after there were the pictures, when people stopped looking at me.

My boyfriend, Manus, came in that evening, after the emergency room, after I'd been wheeled off on my gurney to surgery, after the bleeding had stopped and I was in a private room. Then Manus showed up. Manus Kelley, who was my fiancé until he saw what was left. Manus sat looking at the black-and-white glossies of my new face, shuffling and reshuffling them, turning them upside down and right-side up the way you would one of those mystery pictures where one minute you have a beautiful woman, but when you look again you have a hag.

Manus says, "Oh, God."

Then says, "Oh, sweet, sweet Jesus."

Then says, "Christ."

The first date I ever had with Manus, I was still living with my folks. Manus showed me a badge in his wallet. At home, he had a gun. He was a police detective, and he was really successful in vice. This was a May and December thing. Manus was twenty-five and I was eighteen, but we went out. This is the world we live in. We went sailing one time, and he wore a Speedo, and any smart woman should know that means bisexual at least.

My best friend, Evie Cottrell, she's a model. Evie says that beautiful people should never date each other. Together, they just don't generate enough attention. Evie says there's a whole shift in the beauty standard when they're together. You can feel this, Evie says. When both of you are beautiful, neither of you is beautiful. Together, as a couple, you're less than the sum of your parts.

Nobody really gets noticed, not anymore.

Still, there I was one time, taping this infomercial, one of those long-long commercials you think will end at any moment because after all it's just a commercial, but it's actually thirty minutes long. Me and Evie, we're hired to be walking sex furniture to wear tight evening dresses all afternoon and entice the television audience into buying the Num Num Snack Factory. Manus comes to sit in the studio audience, and after the shoot he goes, "Let's go sailing," and I go, "Sure!"

So we went sailing, and I forgot my sunglasses, so Manus buys me a pair on the dock. My new sunglasses are the exact same as Manus's Vuarnets, except mine are made in Korea not Switzerland and cost two dollars.

Three miles out, I'm walking into deck things. I'm falling down. Manus throws me a rope, and I miss it. Manus throws me a beer and I miss the beer. A headache, I get the kind of headache God would smote you with in the Old Testament. What I don't know is that one of my sunglass lenses is darker than the other, almost opaque. I'm blind in one eye because of this lens, and I have no depth perception.

Back then I don't know this, that my perception is so fucked up. It's the sun, I tell myself, so I just keep wearing the sunglasses and stumbling around blind and in pain.

Jump to the second time Manus visits me in the hospital, he tells the eight-by-ten glossies of me in my sheet, *Property of La Paloma Memorial Hospital*, that I should think about getting back into my life. I should start making plans. You know, he says, take some classes. Finish my degree.

He sits next to my bed and holds the photos between us so I can't see either them or him. On my pad, with my pencil I ask Manus in writing to show me.

"When I was little, we raised Doberman puppies," he says from behind the photos. "And when a puppy is about six months old you get its ears and tail cropped. It's the style for those dogs. You go to a motel where a man travels from state to state cutting the ears and tails off thousands of Doberman puppies or boxers or bull terriers."

On my pad with my pencil, I write:

your point being?

And I wave this in his direction.

"The point is whoever cuts your ears off is the one you'll hate for the rest of your life," he says. "You don't want your regular veterinarian to do the job so you pay a stranger."

Still looking at picture after picture, Manus says, "That's the reason I can't show you these."

Somewhere outside the hospital, in a motel room full of bloody towels with his toolbox of knives and needles, or driving down the highway to his next victim, or kneeling over a dog drugged and cut up in a dirty bathtub, is the man a million dogs must hate.

Sitting next to my bed, Manus says, "You just need to archive your cover-girl dreams."

The fashion photographer inside my head yells:

Give me pity.

Flash.

Give me another chance.

Flash.

That's what I did before the accident. Call me a big liar, but before the accident I told people I was a college student. If you tell folks you're a model, they shut down. Your being a model will mean they're networking with some lower life-form. They start using baby talk. They dumb down. But if you tell folks you're a college student, folks are so impressed. You can be a student in anything and not have to know anything. Just say toxicology or marine biokinesis, and the person you're talking to will change the subject to himself. If this doesn't work, mention the neural synapses of embryonic pigeons.

It used to be I was a real college student. I have about sixteen hundred credits toward an undergraduate degree in personal fitness training. What I hear from my parents is that I could be a doctor by now.

Sorry, Mom.

Sorry, God.

There was a time when Evie and me went out to dance clubs and bars and men would wait outside the ladies' room door to catch us. Guys would say they were casting a television commercial. The guy would give me a business card and ask what agency I was with.

There was a time when my mom came to visit. My mom smokes, and the first afternoon I came home from a shoot, she held out a matchbook and said, "What's the meaning of this?"

She said, "Please tell me you're not as big a slut as your poor dead brother."

In the matchbook was a guy's name I didn't know and a telephone number.

"This isn't the only one I found," Mom said. "What are you running here?"

I don't smoke. I tell her that. These matchbooks pile up because I'm too polite not to take them and I'm too frugal to just throw them away. That's why it takes a whole kitchen drawer to hold them, all these men I can't remember and their telephone numbers.

Jump to no day special in the hospital, just outside the office of the hospital speech therapist. The nurse was leading me around by my elbow for exercise, and as we came around this one corner, just inside the open office doorway, boom, Brandy Alexander was just so there, glorious in a seated Princess Alexander pose, in an iridescent Vivienne Westwood cat suit changing colors with her every move.

Vogue on location.

The fashion photographer inside my head, yelling:

Give me wonder, baby.

Flash.

Give me amazement.

Flash.

The speech therapist said, "Brandy, you can raise the pitch of your voice if you raise your laryngeal cartilage. It's that bump in your throat you feel going up as you sing ascending scales." She said, "If you can keep your voice box raised high in your throat, your voice should stay between a G and a middle C. That's about a hundred and sixty hertz."

Brandy Alexander and the way she looked turned the rest of the world into virtual reality. She changed color from every new angle. She turned green with my one step. Red with my next. She turned silver and gold and then she was dropped behind us, gone.

"Poor, sad, misguided thing," Sister Katherine said, and she spat on the concrete floor. She looked at me craning my neck to see back down the hall, and she asked if I had any family.

I wrote: *yeah, there's my gay brother but he's dead from AIDS.*

And she says, "Well, that's for the best, then, isn't it?"

Jump to the week after Manus's last visit, last meaning final, when Evie drops by the hospital. Evie looks at the glossies and talks to God and Jesus Christ.

"You know," Evie tells me across a stack of *Vogue* and *Glamour* magazines in her lap she brings me, "I talked to the agency and they said that if we redo your portfolio they'll consider taking you back for hand work."

Evie means a hand model, modeling cocktail rings and diamond tennis bracelets and shit.

Like I want to hear this.

I can't talk.

All I can eat is liquids.

Nobody will look at me. I'm invisible.

All I want is somebody to ask me what happened. Then I'll get on with my life.

Evie tells the stack of magazines, "I want you to come live with me at my house when you get out." She unzips her canvas bag on the edge of my bed and goes into it with both hands. Evie says, "It'll be fun. You'll see. I hate living all by my lonesome."

And says, "I've already moved your things into my spare bedroom."

Still in her bag, Evie says, "I'm on my way to a shoot. Any chance you have any agency vouchers you can lend me?"

On my pad with my pencil, I write:

is that my sweater you're wearing?

And I wave the pad in her face.

"Yeah," she says, "but I knew you wouldn't mind."

I write:

but it's a size six.

I write:

and you're a size nine.

"Listen," Evie says. "My call is for two o'clock. Why don't I stop by sometime when you're in a better mood?"

Talking to her watch, she says, "I'm so sorry things had to go this way. It wasn't all of it anybody's fault."

Every day in the hospital goes like this:

Breakfast. Lunch. Dinner. Sister Katherine falls in between.

On television is one network running nothing but infomercials all day and all night, and there we are, Evie and me, together. We got a raft of bucks. For the snack factory thing, we do these big celebrity spokesmodel smiles, the ones where you make your face a big space heater. We're wearing these sequined dresses that when you get them under a spotlight, the dress flashes like a million reporters taking your picture. So glamorous. I'm standing there in this twenty-pound dress, doing this big smile and dropping animal wastes into the Plexiglas funnel on top of the Num Num Snack Factory. This thing just poops out little canapés like crazy, and Evie has to wade out into the studio audience and get folks to eat the canapés.

Folks will eat anything to get on television.

Then, off camera, Manus goes, "Let's go sailing."

And I go, "Sure."

It was so stupid, my not knowing what was happening all along.

Jump to Brandy on a folding chair just inside the office of the speech therapist, shaping her fingernails with the scratch pad from a book of matches. Her long legs could squeeze a motorcycle in half, and the legal minimum of her is shrink-wrapped in leopard-print stretch terry just screaming to get out.

The speech therapist says, "Keep your glottis partially open as you speak. It's the way Marilyn Monroe sang 'Happy Birthday' to President Kennedy. It makes your breath bypass your vocal chords for a more feminine, helpless quality."

The nurse leads me past in my cardboard slippers, my tight bandages and deep funk, and Brandy Alexander looks up at the last possible instant and winks. God should be able to wink that good. Like somebody taking your picture. Give me joy. Give me fun. Give me love.

Flash.

Angels in heaven should blow kisses the way Brandy Alexander does and lights up the rest of my week. Back in my room, I write:

who is she?

"No one you should have any truck with," the nurse says. "You'll have problems enough as it is."

but who is she? I write.

"If you can believe it," the nurse says, "that one is someone different every week."

It's after that Sister Katherine starts matchmaking. To save me from Brandy Alexander, she offers me the lawyer without a nose. She offers a mountain-climbing dentist whose fingers and facial features are eaten down to little hard shining bumps by frostbite. A missionary with dark patches of some tropical fungus just under his skin. A mechanic who leaned over a battery the moment it exploded and the acid left his lips and cheeks gone and his yellow teeth showing in a permanent snarl.

I look at the nun's wedding ring and write:

i guess you got the last really buff guy.

The whole time I was in the hospital, no way could I fall in love. I just couldn't go there yet. Settle for less. I didn't want to process through anything. I didn't want to pick up any pieces. Lower my expectations. Get on with my less-than life. I didn't want to feel better about being still alive. Start compensating. I just wanted my face fixed, if that was possible, which it wasn't.

When it's time to reintroduce me to solid foods, their words again, it's puréed chicken and strained carrots. Baby foods. Everything mashed or pulverized or crushed.

You are what you eat.

The nurse brings me the personal classified ads from a newsletter. Sister Katherine peers down her nose and through her glasses to read: Guys seeking slim, adventurous girls for fun and romance. And, yes, it's true, not one single guy specifically excludes hideous mutilated girls with growing medical bills.

Sister Katherine tells me, "These men you can write to in prison don't need to know how you really look."

It's just too much trouble to try and explain my feelings to her in writing.

Sister Katherine reads me the singles columns while I spoon up my roast beef. She offers arsonists. Burglars. Tax cheats. She says, "You probably don't want to date a rapist, not right off. Nobody's that desperate."

Between the lonely men behind bars for armed robbery and second-degree manslaughter, she stops to ask what's the matter. She takes my hand and talks to the name on my plastic bracelet, such a hand model I am already, cocktail rings, plastic ID bracelets so beautiful even a bride of Christ can't take her eyes off them. She says, "What're you feeling?"

This is hilarious.

She says, "Don't you want to fall in love?"

The photographer in my head says: Give me patience.

Flash.

Give me control.

Flash.

The situation is I have half a face.

Inside my bandages, my face still bleeds tiny little spots of blood onto the wads of cotton. One doctor, the one making rounds every morning who checks my dressing, he says my wound is still weeping. That's his word.

I still can't talk.

I have no career.

I can only eat baby food. Nobody will ever look at me like I've won a big prize ever again.

nothing, I write on my pad.

nothing's wrong.

"You haven't mourned," Sister Katherine says. "You need to have a good cry and then get on with your life. You're being too calm about this."

I write:

don't make me laugh. my face, I write, *the doctor sez my wound will weep.*

Still, at least somebody had noticed. This whole time, I was calm.

I was the picture of calm. I never, never panicked. I saw my blood and snot and teeth splashed all over the dashboard the moment after the accident, but hysteria is impossible without an audience. Panicking by yourself is the same as laughing alone in an empty room. You feel really silly.

The instant the accident happened, I knew I would die if I didn't take the next exit off the freeway, turn right on Northwest Gower, go twelve blocks, and turn into the La Paloma Memorial Hospital emergency room parking lot. I parked. I took my keys and my bag and I walked. The glass doors slid aside before I could see myself reflected in them. The crowd inside, all the people waiting with broken legs and choking babies, they all slid aside, too, when they saw me.

After that, the intravenous morphine. The tiny operating-room manicure scissors cut my dress up. The flesh-tone little patch panties. The police photos.

The detective, the one who searched my car for bone fragments, the guy who'd seen all those people get their heads cut off in half-open car windows, he comes back one day and says there's nothing left to find. Birds, seagulls, maybe magpies, too. They got into the car where it was parked at the hospital, through the broken window. The magpies ate all of what the detective calls the soft-tissue evidence. The bones they probably carried away.

"You know, miss," he says, "to break them on rocks. For the marrow."

On the pad, with the pencil, I write:

ha, ha, ha.

Jump to just before my bandages come off, when a speech therapist says I should get down on my knees and thank God for leaving my tongue in my head, unharmed. We sit in her cinder-block office with half the room filled by her steel desk between us, and the therapist, she teaches me how a ventriloquist makes a dummy talk. You see, the ventriloquist can't let you see his mouth move. He can't really use his lips, so he presses his tongue against the roof of his mouth to make words.

Instead of a window, the therapist has a poster of a kitten covered in spaghetti above the words:

Accentuate the Positive

She says that if you can't make a certain sound without using your lips, substitute a similar sound, the therapist says; for instance, use the sound *eth* instead of the sound *eff*. The context in which you use the sound will make you understandable.

"I'd rather be thishing," the therapist says.

then go thishing, I write.

"No," she says, "repeat."

My throat is always raw and dry even after a million liquids through straws all day. The scar tissue is rippled hard and polished around my unharmed tongue.

The therapist says, "I'd rather be thishing."

I say, "Salghrew jfwoiew fjfowi sdkifj."

"No, not that way," the therapist says. "You're not doing it right."

I say, "Solfjf gjoie ddd oslidjf?"

She says, "No, that's not right, either."

She looks at her watch.

"Digri vrior gmjgi g giel," I say.

"You'll need to practice a lot, but on your own time," she says. "Now, again."

I say, "Jrogier fi fkgoewir mfofeinf fcfd."

She says, "Good! Great! See how easy?"

On my pad with my pencil, I write:

fuck off.

Jump to the day they cut off the bandages.

You don't know what to expect, but every doctor and nurse and intern and orderly, janitor, and cook in the hospital stopped by for a peek from the doorway, and if you caught them they'd bark, Congratulations, the corners of their mouths spread wide apart and trembling in a stiff, watery smile. Bug-eyed. That's my word for it. And I held up the same cardboard sign again and again that told them:

thank you.

And then I ran away. This is after my new cotton crepe sundress arrives from Espre. Sister Katherine stood over me all morning with a curling iron until my hair was this big butter crème frosting hairdo, this big off-the-face hairdo. Then Evie brought some makeup and did my eyes. I put on my spicy new dress and couldn't wait to start sweating. This whole summer, I hadn't seen a mirror, or if I did I never realized the reflection was me. I hadn't seen the police photos. When Evie and Sister Katherine are done, I say, "De foil iowa fog geoff."

And Evie says, "You're welcome."

Sister Katherine says, "But you just ate lunch."

It's clear enough, nobody understands me here.

I say, "Kong wimmer nay pee golly."

And Evie says, "Yeah, these are your shoes, but I'm not hurting them any."

And Sister Katherine says, "No, no mail yet, but we can write to prisoners after you've had your nap, dear."

They left. And. I left, alone. And. How bad could it be, my face?

And sometimes being mutilated can work to your advantage. All those people now with piercings and tattoos and brandings and scarification . . . What I mean is, attention is attention.

Going outside is the first time I feel I've missed something. I mean, a whole summer had just disappeared. All those pool parties and lying around on metal-flake speedboat bows. Catching rays. Finding guys with convertibles. I get that all the picnics and softball games and concerts are just sort of trickled down into a few snapshots that Evie won't have developed until around Thanksgiving.

Going outside, the world is all color after the white-on-white of the hospital. It's going over the rainbow. I walk up to a supermarket, and shopping feels like a game I haven't played since I was a little girl. Here are all my favorite name-brand products, all those colors, French's mustard, Rice-A-Roni, Top Ramen, everything trying to catch your attention.

All that color. A whole shift in the beauty standard so that no one thing really stands out.

The total being less than the sum of its parts.

All that color all in one place.

Except for that name-brand product rainbow, there's nothing else to look at. When I look at people, all I can see is the back of everybody's head. Even if I turn super fast, all I can catch is somebody's ear turning away. And folks are talking to God.

"Oh, God," they say. "Did you see that?"

And, "Was that a mask? Christ, it's a bit early for Halloween."

Everybody is very busy reading the labels on French's mustard and Rice-A-Roni.

So I take a turkey.

I don't know why. I don't have any money, but I take a turkey. I dig the big frozen turkeys around, those big flesh-tone lumps of ice in the freezer bin. I dig around until I find the biggest turkey, and I heft it up baby-style in its yellow plastic netting.

I haul myself up to the front of the store, right through the check stands, and nobody stops me. Nobody's even looking. They're all reading those tabloid newspapers as if there's hidden gold there.

"Sejgfn di ofo utnbg," I say. "Nei wucj iswisn sdnsud."

Nobody looks.

"EVSF UYYB IUH," I say in my best ventriloquist voice.

Nobody even talks. Maybe just the clerks talk. Do you have two pieces of ID? they're asking people writing checks.

"Fgjrn iufnv si vuv," I say. "Xidi cniwuw sis sacnc!"

Then it is, it's right then a boy says, "Look!"

Everybody who's not looking and not talking stops breathing.

The little boy says, "Look, Mom, look over there! That monster's stealing food!"

Everybody gets all shrunken up with embarrassment. All their heads drop down into their shoulders the way they'd look on crutches. They're reading tabloid headlines harder than ever.

MONSTER GIRL STEALS
FESTIVE HOLIDAY BIRD

And there I am, deep-fried in my cotton crepe dress, a twenty-five pound turkey in my arms, the turkey sweating, my dress almost transparent. My nipples are rock-hard against the yellow-netted ice in my arms. Me under my butter crème frosting hairdo. Nobody looking at me as if I've won a big anything.

A hand comes down and slaps the little boy, and the boy starts to wail.

The boy's wailing the way you cry if you've done nothing wrong but you got punished anyway. The sun's setting outside. Inside, everything's dead except this little voice screaming over and over: Why did you hit me? I didn't do anything. Why did you hit me? What did I do?

I took the turkey. I walked as fast as I could back to La Paloma Memorial Hospital. It was almost dark.

The whole time I'm hugging the turkey, I'm telling myself: Turkeys. Seagulls. Magpies.

Birds.

Birds ate my face.

Back in the hospital, coming down the hallway toward me is Sister Katherine leading a man and his IV stand, the man all wrapped in gauze and hung with drain tubes and plastic bags of yellow and red fluids leaking into and out of him.

Birds ate my face.

From closer and closer, Sister Katherine shouts, "Yoo-hoo! I have someone special here you'd just love to meet!"

Birds ate my face.

Between me and them is the speech therapist office, and when I go to duck inside, there's Brandy Alexander for the third time. The queen of everything good and kind is wearing this sleeveless Versace kind of tank dress with this season's overwhelming feel of despair and corrupt resignation. Body-conscious yet humiliated. Buoyant but crippled. The queen supreme is the most beautiful anything I've ever seen, so I just vogue there to watch from the doorway.

"Men," the therapist says, "stress the adjective when they speak." The therapist says, "For instance, a man would say, 'You are so *attractive*, today.'"

Brandy is so attractive you could chop her head off and put it on blue velvet in the window at Tiffany's and somebody would buy it for a million dollars.

"A woman would say, 'You are *so* attractive, today,'" the therapist says. "Now, you, Brandy. You say it. Stress the modifier, not the adjective."

Brandy Alexander looks her Burning Blueberry eyes at me in the doorway and says, "Posing girl, you are *so* god-awful ugly. Did you let an elephant sit on your face or what?"

Brandy's voice, I barely hear what she says. At that instant, I just adore Brandy so much. Everything about her feels as good as being beautiful and looking in a mirror. Brandy is my instant royal family. My only everything to live for.

I go, "Cfoieb svns ois," and I pile the cold, wet turkey into the speech therapist's lap, her sitting pinned under twenty-five pounds of dead meat in her roll-around leather desk chair.

From closer down the hallway, Sister Katherine is yelling, "Yoo-hoo!"

"Mriuvn wsi sjaoi aj," I go, and wheel the therapist and her chair into the hallway. I say, "Jownd winc sm fdo dcncw."

The speech therapist, she's smiling up at me and says, "You don't have to thank me, it's just my job is all."

The nun's arrived with the man and his IV stand, a new man with no skin or crushed features or all his teeth bashed out, a man who'd be perfect for me. My one true love. My deformed or mutilated or diseased Prince Charming. My unhappily ever after. My hideous future. The monstrous rest of my life.

I slam the office door and lock myself inside with Brandy Alexander. There's the speech therapist's notebook on her desk, and I grab it.

save me, I write, and wave it in Brandy's face. I write:

please.

Jump to Brandy Alexander's hands. This always starts with her hands. Brandy Alexander puts a hand out, one of those hairy pig-knuckled hands with the veins of her arm crowded and squeezed to the elbow with bangle bracelets of every color. Just by herself, Brandy Alexander is such a shift in the beauty standard that no one thing stands out. Not even you.

"So, girl," Brandy says. "What all happened to your face?"

Birds.

I write:

birds. birds ate my face.

And I start to laugh.

Brandy doesn't laugh. Brandy says, "What's that supposed to mean?"

And I'm still laughing.

i was driving on the freeway, I write.

And I'm still laughing.

someone shot a 30-caliber bullet from a rifle.

the bullet tore my entire jawbone off my face.

Still laughing.

i came to the hospital, I write.

i did not die.

Laughing.

they couldn't put my jaw back because seagulls had eaten it.

And I stop laughing.

"Girl, your handwriting is terrible," Brandy says. "Now tell me what else."

And I start to cry.

what else, I write, *is i have to eat baby food.*

i can't talk.

i have no career.

i have no home.

my fiancé left me.

nobody will look at me.

all my clothes, my best friend ruined them.

I'm still crying.

"What else?" Brandy says. "Tell me everything."

a boy, I write.

a little boy in the supermarket called me a monster.

Those Burning Blueberry eyes look right at me the way no eyes have all summer. "Your perception is all fucked up," Brandy says. "All you can talk about is trash that's already happened."

She says, "You can't base your life on the past or the present."

Brandy says, "You have to tell me about your future."

Brandy Alexander, she stands up on her gold lamé leg-hold trap shoes. The queen supreme takes a jeweled compact out of her clutch bag and snaps the compact open to look at the mirror inside.

"That therapist," those Plumbago lips say, "the speech therapist can be *so* stupid about these situations."

The big jeweled arm muscles of Brandy sit me down in the seat still hot from her ass, and she holds the compact so I can see inside. Instead of face powder, it's full of white capsules. Where there should be a mirror, there's a close-up photo of Brandy Alexander smiling and looking terrific.

"They're Vicodins, dear," she says. "It's the Marilyn Monroe school of medicine where enough of any drug will cure any disease."

She says, "Dig in. Help yourself."

The thin and eternal goddess that she is, Brandy's picture smiles up at me over a sea of painkillers. This is how I met Brandy Alexander. This is how I found the strength *not* to get on with my former life. This is how I found the courage *not* to pick up the same old pieces.

"Now," those Plumbago lips say, "you are going to tell me your story like you just did. Write it all down. Tell that story over and over. Tell me your sad-assed story all night." That Brandy queen points a long bony finger at me.

"When you understand," Brandy says, "that what you're telling is just a story. It isn't happening anymore. When you realize the story you're telling is just words, when you can just crumble it up and throw your past in the trash can," Brandy says, "then we'll figure out who you're going to be."

Now, Please, Jump to Chapter Two

Chapter 41

Where you're supposed to be is some big West Hills wedding reception in a big manor house with flower arrangements and stuffed mushrooms all over the house. This is called scene setting: where everybody is, who's alive, who's dead. This is Evie Cottrell's big wedding reception moment. Evie is standing halfway down the big staircase in the manor house foyer, naked inside what's left of her wedding dress, still holding her rifle.

Me, I'm standing at the bottom of the stairs but only in a physical way. My mind is, I don't know where.

Nobody's all-the-way dead yet, but let's just say the clock is ticking.

Not that anybody in this big drama is a real alive person, either. You can trace everything about Evie Cottrell's look back to some television commercial for an organic shampoo, except right now Evie's wedding dress is burned down to just the hoopskirt wires orbiting her hips and just the little wire skeletons of all the silk flowers that were in her hair. And Evie's blond hair, her big, teased-up, back-combed rainbow in every shade of blond blown up with hairspray, well, Evie's hair is burned off, too.

The only other character here is Brandy Alexander, who's laid out, shotgunned, at the bottom of the staircase, bleeding to death.

What I tell myself is the gush of red pumping out of Brandy's bullet hole is less like blood than it's some sociopolitical tool. The thing about being cloned from all those shampoo commercials, well, that goes for me and Brandy Alexander, too. Shotgunning anybody in this room would be the moral equivalent of killing a car, a vacuum cleaner, a Barbie doll. Erasing a computer disk. Burning a book. Probably that goes for killing anybody in the world. We're all such products.

Brandy Alexander, the long-stemmed latte queen supreme of the top-drawer party girls, Brandy is gushing her insides out through a bullet hole in her amazing suit jacket. The suit, it's this white Bob Mackie knockoff Brandy bought in Seattle with a tight hobble skirt that squeezes her ass into the perfect big heart shape. You would not believe how much this suit cost. The markup is about a zillion percent. The suit jacket has a little peplum skirt and wide lapels and shoulders. The single-breasted cut is symmetrical except for the hole pumping out blood.

Then Evie starts to sob, standing there halfway up the staircase. Evie, that deadly virus of the moment. This is our cue to all look at poor Evie, poor, sad Evie, hairless and wearing nothing but ashes and circled by the wire cage of her burned-up hoopskirt. Then Evie drops the rifle. With her dirty face in her dirty hands, Evie sits down and starts to boo-hoo, as if crying will solve anything. The rifle, this is a loaded thirty-aught rifle, it clatters down the stairs and skids out into the middle of the foyer floor, spinning on its side, pointing at me, pointing at Brandy, pointing at Evie, crying.

It's not that I'm some detached lab animal just conditioned to ignore violence, but my first instinct is maybe it's not too late to dab club soda on the bloodstain.

Most of my adult life so far has been me standing on seamless paper for a raft of bucks per hour, wearing clothes and shoes, my hair done and some famous fashion photographer telling me how to feel.

Him yelling, Give me lust, baby.

Flash.

Give me malice.

Flash.

Give me detached existentialist ennui.

Flash.

Give me rampant intellectualism as a coping mechanism.

Flash.

Probably it's the shock of seeing my one worst enemy shoot my other worst enemy is what it is. Boom, and it's a win-win situation.

This and, being around Brandy, I've developed a pretty big jones for drama.

It only looks like I'm crying when I put a handkerchief up under my veil to breathe through. To filter the air since you can about not breathe for all the smoke since Evie's big manor house is burning down around us.

Me, kneeling down beside Brandy, I could put my hands anywhere in my gown and find Darvons and Demerols and Darvocet 100s. This is everybody's cue to look at me. My gown is a knockoff print of the Shroud of Turin, most of it brown and white, draped and cut so the shiny red buttons will button through the stigmata. Then I'm wearing yards and yards of black organza veil wrapped around my face and studded with little hand-cut Austrian crystal stars. You can't tell how I look, face-wise, but that's the whole idea. The look is elegant and sacrilegious and makes me feel sacred and immoral.

Haute couture and getting hauter.

Fire inches down the foyer wallpaper. Me, for added set dressing I started the fire. Special effects can go a long way to heighten a mood, and it's not as if this is a real house. What's burning down is a re-creation of a period revival house patterned after a copy of a copy of a copy of a mock-Tudor big manor house. It's a hundred generations removed from anything original, but the truth is, aren't we all?

Just before Evie comes screaming down the stairs and shoots Brandy Alexander, what I did was pour out about a gallon of Chanel No. 5 and put a burning wedding invitation to it, and boom, I'm recycling.

It's funny, but when you think about even the biggest tragic fire, it's just a sustained chemical reaction. The oxidation of Joan of Arc.

Still spinning on the floor, the rifle points at me, points at Brandy.

Another thing is no matter how much you think you love somebody, you'll step back when the pool of their blood edges up too close.

Except for all this high drama, it's a really nice day. This is a warm, sunny day and the front door is open to the porch and the lawn outside. The fire upstairs draws the warm smell of the fresh-cut lawn into the foyer, and you can hear all the wedding guests outside. All the guests, they took the gifts they wanted, the crystal and silver, and went out to wait on the lawn for the firemen and paramedics to make their entrance.

Brandy, she opens one of her huge, ring-beaded hands and she touches the hole pouring her blood all over the marble floor.

Brandy, she says, "Shit. There's no way the Bon Marché will take this suit back."

Evie lifts her face, her face a finger-painting mess of soot and snot and tears, from her hands and screams, "I hate my life being so boring!"

Evie screams down at Brandy Alexander, "Save me a window table in hell!"

Tears rinse clean lines down Evie's cheeks, and she screams, "Girlfriend! You need to be yelling some back at me!"

As if this isn't already drama, drama, drama, Brandy looks up at me kneeling beside her. Brandy's aubergine eyes dilated out to full flower, she says, "Brandy Alexander is going to die now?"

Evie, Brandy, and me, all this is just a power struggle for the spotlight. Just each of us being me, me, me first. The murderer, the victim, the witness, each of us thinks our role is the lead.

Probably that goes for anybody in the world.

It's all *mirror, mirror on the wall* because beauty is power the same way money is power the same way a gun is power.

Anymore, when I see the picture of a twenty-something in the newspaper who was abducted and sodomized and robbed and then killed and here's a front-page picture of her young and smiling, instead of me dwelling on this being a big, sad crime, my gut reaction is, wow, she'd be really hot if she didn't have such a big honker of a nose. My second reaction is I'd better have some good head-and-shoulders shots handy in case I get, you know, abducted and sodomized to death. My third reaction is, well, at least that cuts down on the competition.

If that's not enough, my moisturizer I use is a suspension of inert fetal solids in hydrogenated mineral oil. My point is that, if I'm honest, my life is all about me.

My point is, unless the meter is running and some photographer is yelling: Give me empathy.

Then the flash of the strobe.

Give me sympathy.

Flash.

Give me brutal honesty.

Flash.

"Don't let me die here on this floor," Brandy says, and her big hands clutch at me. "My hair," she says, "my hair will be flat in the back."

My point is I know Brandy is maybe probably going to die, but I just can't get into it.

Evie sobs even louder. On top of this, the fire sirens from way outside are crowning me queen of Migraine Town.

The rifle is still spinning on the floor, but slower and slower.

Brandy says, "This is not how Brandy Alexander wanted her life to go. She's supposed to be famous, first. You know, she's supposed to be on television during Super Bowl halftime, drinking a diet cola naked in slow motion before she died."

The rifle stops spinning and points at nobody.

At Evie sobbing, Brandy screams, "Shut up!"

"*You* shut up," Evie screams back. Behind her, the fire is eating its way down the stairway carpet.

The sirens, you can hear them wandering and screaming all over the West Hills. People will just knock each other down to dial 911 and be the big hero. Nobody looks ready for the big television crew that's due to arrive any minute.

"This is your last chance, honey," Brandy says, and her blood is getting all over the place. She says, "Do you love me?"

It's when folks ask questions like this that you lose the spotlight.

This is how folks trap you into a best-supporting role.

Even bigger than the house being on fire is this huge expectation that I have to say the three most worn-out words you'll find in any script. Just the words make me feel I'm severely fingering myself. They're just words is all. Powerless. Vocabulary. Dialogue.

"Tell me," Brandy says. "Do you? Do you really love me?"

This is the big hammy way Brandy has played her whole life. The Brandy Alexander nonstop continuous live action theater, but less and less live by the moment.

Just for a little stage business, I take Brandy's hand in mine. This is a nice gesture, but then I'm freaked by the whole threat of blood-borne pathogens, and then, boom, the ceiling in the dining room crashes down, and sparks and embers rush out at us from the dining room doorway.

"Even if you can't love me, then tell me my life," Brandy says. "A girl can't die without her life flashing before her eyes."

Pretty much nobody is getting their emotional needs met.

It's then the fire eats down the stairway carpet to Evie's bare ass, and Evie screams to her feet and pounds down the stairs in her burned-up white high heels. Naked and hairless, wearing wire and ashes, Evie Cottrell runs out the front door to a larger audience, her wedding guests, the silver and crystal and the arriving fire trucks. This is the world we live in. Conditions change and we mutate.

So of course this'll be all about Brandy, hosted by me, with guest appearances by Evelyn Cottrell and the deadly AIDS virus. Brandy, Brandy, Brandy. Poor sad Brandy on her back, Brandy touches the hole pouring her life out onto the marble floor and says, "Please. Tell me my life. Tell me how we got here."

So me, I'm here eating smoke just to document this Brandy Alexander moment.

Give me attention.

Flash.

Give me adoration.

Flash.

Give me a break.

Flash.

Now, Please, Jump to Chapter One

Chapter 42

Where you're supposed to be is some big Episcopal church in downtown Newark, New Jersey, with cameramen and actors and stuffed mushrooms all over the church. This is the summer of 2007, and a film based on my fourth book, *Choke*, is being shot on location here. In a side chapel a few steps away, Kelly Macdonald's character is seducing Sam Rockwell's. Plotwise, her goal is to conceive a fetus in order to puree its unborn brain and use that neural tissue to cure the dementia of Anjelica Huston's character. All of that sacrifice is being offered to preserve the memories of one person . . . In real life, Kelly tells me she's been away from home, filming projects in the United States, and hasn't seen her husband in months. This big push is so they can get somewhat ahead, so Kelly can stay at home, she hopes, and have a real baby.

The hospital sequences are being shot in an abandoned asylum, the former Essex County Mental Hospital, a complex of thirty-five buildings covering a hundred acres. A ghost town. "Our own back lot," says the film's director, Clark Gregg. There are buildings to serve as police stations . . . buildings that look like private homes . . . all of them scheduled to be demolished in another month. The landscaping is overgrown, with white-tailed deer wandering the waist-high grass. Rabbits graze in this Arcadian setting, and, at dusk, fireflies hover as winking lights. Left behind are a century of hospital beds and dirty sheets, and the shabby jigsaw puzzles are beyond number.

In Hollywood jargon, everyone has warned Clark that *Choke* was "very E.D." By this, they don't mean "erectile dysfunction." A comedy about food and death and sex? They mean that the film's success will be very "execution dependent." By *execution*, they mean *how it's told*, not *how it's killed*.

Jump to midnight in this mental hospital. Anjelica Huston walks toward me down a long hospital corridor, her cheeks smeared with a mask of chocolate pudding, her eyes locked on mine. "You," she says, pointing at her face, "you did this to me!" We stand and talk while the crew sets up another shot. She tells me a strange, funny story about her father, John Huston, speaking to her a few days *after* his death. I won't spoil it or steal it by retelling that story here. Kelly Macdonald talks about learning a Texas accent a few weeks ago for a film called *No Country for Old Men*. Before that she was working on a project in Chicago. Sam Rockwell talks about his next film, to be shot in England, about a man who lives alone on the moon.

A maze of underground tunnels connect the basements of the different hospital buildings, concrete utility tunnels, branched and dripping, lined with steam pipes. Between setups, crew members wander by flashlight through these, sending back camera-phone snapshots of butchered dogs sacrificed on subterranean altars by Satanists no longer in evidence. After a few days of shooting, everyone has a spooky story about being touched or pinched by invisible hands. This was a high-security loony bin. Meaning, if you walk through the wrong door it will lock behind you, trapping you in a deserted ward or wing with no exit. Steel bars block the windows. The walls are red brick, and your only hope is that someone might hear you screaming among the soiled mattresses and bedpans. A caterer circulates constantly, handing everyone hot fudge sundaes.

Here in this madhouse, it's getting harder and harder to tell apart reality and make-believe. This essay I'm constantly writing and revising in my mind, I call it "A Catered Nightmare." I write it, but it keeps crumbling under the weight of too many quirky details. A better writer, a smarter writer, would be able to find the Unified Field Theory that would tie together all of these facts. For example, someone brilliant, like Joy Williams. David Foster Wallace could nail the big lesson that's being demonstrated, but all I can do is watch and take notes. I'm sitting on the shaggy asylum lawn eating a hamburger with my editor, Gerry Howard, while fireflies twinkle around us. The catering company is passing smoked salmon en croute garnished with sprigs of fennel. An assistant director steps up to ask if we'll move our picnic to another spot because we're in Sam Rockwell's eye line during a very emotional speech. Before Sam, Heath Ledger was cast as the male lead. Before Ledger, Ryan Gosling had been cast.

Jump to New York City, to a sex shop in the West Village where I'm buying their entire stock of latex anal stimulation beads. Every movie shoot needs a wrap gift, and Clark Gregg's original thought was to give everyone custom-made chrome Ben Wa balls, highly polished and engraved with the film's title and the dates of principal photography, but that gesture would've cost half the production budget. Instead, I've gone with Gregg's assistant to every sex toy shop in Manhattan. Two men buying every string of butt beads in every store . . . in New York that doesn't raise an eyebrow. In the West Village shop, a middle-aged female clerk warns us, "The ones with the white cotton string are sold strictly as a novelty. You use those one time, and you'll never get that string white again." After that, we go to the Chelsea Kmart to buy a child's car seat. Our car filled with sex toys and a baby seat, we go to collect Jennifer Grey, Clark Gregg's wife, at her father, Joel Grey's home. We're at Starbucks and Jennifer Grey spills her vanilla latte, and I'm honestly thrilled to help clean up the mess and fetch her another. She's *that* lovely and charming, but she doesn't look like Jennifer Grey. The more of this I recount, the more I feel as if I'm on an analyst's couch recounting the absurdities and coded symbols of a dream.

William T. Vollmann would be able to decipher the hidden patterns. David Foster Wallace could decode the deeper profound message. But it's all I can do to kneel down on the Starbucks floor and sop up vanilla latte with a paper napkin. Starstruck, I ask Sam to autograph my butt beads and he inscribes them, *O that I were a glove upon that hand, that I might touch that cheek!* Sam's character in the film suffocates himself, hoping someone will come to his rescue. I'm so stupid that I thought he made up what he wrote.

A wandering makeup artist leaves a voice mail on my phone saying, "I'm locked behind the door of a room down a hallway in the basement of a building . . ." She says, "Don't ask me where. I don't know where. Just come get me out!" A passing caterer offers me mushroom pâte baked in shells of herb-infused puff pastry.

Jump to the interior of a commercial jetliner cabin. This is a rented film set assembled in the gymnasium of the abandoned mental hospital. The cabin is filled with extras, everyone wearing headsets and directed to look engrossed in a nonexistent film supposedly being shown outside the frame of the shot. A thunderstorm shakes the building, and air traffic into Newark has been rerouted to roar low and directly overhead. Surrounding the bright oasis of set lights, the gymnasium is dark and crowded with a milling party of entertainers and investors. This celebrity audience watches the "audience" of extras who stare intently into space. The caterers pass hors d'oeuvres. Sam Rockwell wears a red satin dressing gown, more like a prizefighter's robe, over a black mini-Speedo type of bikini, which he wears to look nude in the next scene. Dave Matthews jokes about this stripper wear. "I always thought you stuffed it, man," he says, loud against the noise of thunder and jets, "but that's all *you* in that banana hammock."

Jump to the Sundance Film Festival, to some crowded nightclub surrounded by snowdrifts where the film's producers are negotiating a deal with 20th Century Fox. Otherwise the shuttle buses circling through Park City are filled with people weeping openly because distributors are buying little else. The next day every phone in every Sundance theater starts to vibrate, so many that it's the equivalent of a cell phone earthquake. The day's screenings are effectively ruined because Heath Ledger's body has just been found.

Jump to Switzerland, where *Choke* is showing at the Locarno International Film Festival, projected on a screen larger than a billboard, before an audience of seven thousand people in the medieval town square. In the past few weeks my mother has been diagnosed with lung cancer, and I'm commuting between this real-life tragedy and the media events to launch a movie about a woman dying in a hospital bed. My schedule goes like this: hospital, Switzerland, hospital, London, hospital, New York, hospital, Los Angeles. It was a coincidence in 1999 when the film of *Fight Club* was released and my father was shot and killed. Now *Choke* is being released and my mother is dying in a hospital. It's my sister who points this out, and suggests I've brought a curse on our family. She's joking, but she's not. I do all of my crying in airplane toilets. Twice, flight attendants knock at the door, loudly asking me to return to my seat because they've heard the noise and assume I'm having wild sex.

During the press junket at the Beverly Hills Hilton I catch up with Anjelica Huston, who's splitting her schedule between gala star-studded media events and—sadly, yes—her husband's hospital bed. I keep trusting that these pieces will fall into some perfect order. If Amy Hempel were writing this, the pacing would be spot-on, with each moment juxtaposed perfectly. This account would be something beyond me parroting her style. Amy, Amy could offer some redemption. In this world of chaos, I keep hoping to wake up one morning . . . enlightened.

In the Swiss Alps I had no cell phone coverage, and the voice mails from my mother have accumulated: updates about her chemotherapy, her blood work, her garden. Each one ends with *I love you* instead of *Good-bye*. Instead of pressing seven to erase them, I press nine to save them for another ninety days. I can't listen to them all before I just start pressing nine.

The next morning, room service delivers a lavish breakfast to my sumptuous penthouse suite at the Hilton, and there folded on the table next to my egg white omelet and my whole-wheat toast, no butter, and my coffee, black, no sugar, is the Sunday *Los Angeles Times*, and on the front page is an obituary for David Foster Wallace. Next to that are a knife . . . a fork . . . and a bud vase holding a yellow rose. Two days earlier, a few miles east of here, while I was pretending to journalists that *Choke* is a romantic comedy—

because who ever heard of selling a *romantic tragedy*?—David Foster Wallace hung himself. It's not until he's dead, and I'm reading his obituary, that I see we have the same birthday. We were both born on February 21, 1962. Please don't ask me if this means something. Please don't ask me if *anything* makes sense.

Anjelica Huston's husband dies.

Flash.

My mother dies. I erase the message from the trapped makeup artist and wonder if anyone ever helped her escape. Otherwise, I keep pressing nine, trying to buy the sound of my mother's voice, her words, another three months, then another three months. Then, yet another three months.

Flash.

Every story is an experiment in collecting, organizing, and presenting details. An inventory of facts. Yes, all of this effort is being expended to preserve the memories of one person . . . I mean, I keep quilting together these moments I've loved, but as per usual I've failed. The heaped-up truths, they're already starting to teeter sideways. Coincidence fatigue sets in. Pathos overload occurs, and after five pages the details shudder and topple into dust. A better architect could keep his lines plumb and distribute the stresses, but me, I can only start over:

Where you're supposed to be is at home folding the clean laundry . . .

Where you're supposed to be is feeding the dog . . .

The caterers are passing Thai salad rolls with peanut dipping sauce. The caterers are passing blackened tilapia topped with a sweet corn salsa. If you ask me why I keep trying, all I can say is: So far, so good.

I'm still pressing nine. I'm always pressing nine.

Where I'm at is a big Episcopal church in downtown Newark, New Jersey, sitting in the dark while I try to write down everything. But isn't that always the impossible impulse? Don't we always try to rescue the doomed bits and pieces of life, in the hope that a mere story can become Noah's Ark and deliver all the living things of the past to a bright and glorious immortality?

Now, Please, Jump to Chapter Thirteen